John Gilmary Shea, Félix Martin

The Life of Father Isaac Jogues

Missionary Priest of the Society of Jesus

John Gilmary Shea, Félix Martin

The Life of Father Isaac Jogues
Missionary Priest of the Society of Jesus

ISBN/EAN: 9783337416584

Printed in Europe, USA, Canada, Australia, Japan

Cover: Foto ©Raphael Reischuk / pixelio.de

More available books at **www.hansebooks.com**

FATHER ISAAC JOGUES,

Missionary Priest of the Society of Jesus,

Slain by the Mohawk Iroquois, in the present State of New York, Oct. 18, 1646.

BY THE

REV. FELIX MARTIN, S. J.

WITH

FATHER JOGUES' ACCOUNT OF THE CAPTIVITY AND DEATH OF HIS COMPANION, RENÉ GOUPIL, SLAIN SEPT. 29, 1642.

Translated from the French by

JOHN GILMARY SHEA.

With a Map of the Mohawk Country, by Gen. John S. Clark.

NEW YORK, CINCINNATI, AND ST. LOUIS:

BENZIGER BROTHERS,

PRINTERS TO THE HOLY APOSTOLIC SEE.

1885.

TRANSLATOR'S PREFACE.

FILLED from my youth with the deepest veneration for Father Isaac Jogues, whose amiable character and heroic death attracted even those who could not appreciate fully his virtues as a Christian and a priest, I had read in manuscript the life written by Father Felix Martin, my guide and constant encourager in my historic studies. To its publication I earnestly looked forward, hoping to be able to translate it into English. In the long delay I contributed what I could to make the illustrious missionary known. When the Life by Father Martin finally appeared, my work on the translation was soon begun ; but a respected friend, the Rev. Joseph M. Finotti, told me that his translation was far advanced, and begged me to yield it to him. To this I consented, but though he completed his task, he found no one ready to publish it, and after his death the manuscript fell into my hands. To encourage the work of Rev. Father Loyzance in erecting the Chapel of Our Lady of Martyrs at Auriesville, where Father Jogues and René Goupil were put to death, I offered this manuscript, which Messrs. Benziger Brothers agreed to publish. On revising it for the press, however, I found that the translation made during the long illness of Rev. Mr. Finotti had never been carefully compared, and that some parts were missing, so that I could more easily make a new translation than revise the work of my late friend. Hence the present version is mainly my own.

To General John S. Clark of Auburn, all who feel any devotion to the pioneer priest of New York are indebted for establishing, by his long examination in records, maps, and the successive sites of Indian towns, the exact locality where Father Jogues suffered; and to his personal kindness this volume is indebted for the map.

All profit arising from this volume will be devoted to the erection of the Chapel of Our Lady of Martyrs.

CONTENTS.

INTRODUCTION.

AT the first glance it might seem a matter of surprise to see the life of a modest servant of God published more than two centuries after his death. The name of Father Jogues, however, is not unknown in history. Father Charlevoix, the annalist of New France, recounted his labors, and especially his sufferings, in pages full of deep emotion. He had only to condense and group together the long and numerous details scattered through the precious collection of " Relations of the Missions of New France," for the years 1646 and 1647.*

* The Jesuit Relations, as they are called, comprise 41 small octavo volumes, prepared generally by the Superior of the Mission. One was published each year, and the last appeared in 1672. These Relations are the most important, and often the only, material for Canadian history at that remote period. Some of these volumes became so rare that they could not be found even in the great libraries in Europe. With a patriotic feeling worthy of all praise, the Canadian Government in 1848 encouraged their reprint in three large octavo volumes. Protestant writers beyond suspicion (Bancroft, Sparks, Parkman) have paid a noble tribute to the value of this collection. " With regard to the condition and character of the primitive inhabitants of North America, it is impossible to exaggerate their value as an authority. I should add, that the closest examination has left me no doubt that these missionaries wrote in perfect good faith, and that the *Relations* hold a high place as authentic and trustworthy historical documents" (Parkman, " The Jesuits in North America," Preface).

This had already been done in biographical collections,* published in Latin, German, Italian, Spanish; but the size of these works and the languages in which they are written make them acceptable only to a privileged class of readers.

Towards the close of the last century, the Abbé J. B. Forest, animated with just patriotism, impelled, too, by a feeling of piety and fraternal love, undertook to be the historian of Father Jogues. Like him a native of Orleans, and a Jesuit till the suppression of the Society, he was better able than any other to seek information at the proper sources. His work fulfilled the desire of the family of the servant of God and the wishes of his native city, by making known one of its glorious sons. This Life was completed just as the French Revolution burst forth in all its fury. The publication of such a work was out of the question. Religion was persecuted, and virtue itself was about to be proscribed. To the shame of humanity, it found in the midst of France less liberty and respect than Father Jogues himself experienced at the hands of the bloodthirsty Iroquois.

We have taken up his task by endeavoring to complete it. The author had not at his disposal the precious documents still preserved in Canada, or in the archives of the Gesù at Rome. Two of these manuscripts, drawn up in the lifetime and soon after the death of Father Jogues, deserve particular mention. One is the autograph journal of the Superior of the Missionaries in New France, which notes day by day everything that bore on their labors, and sometimes

---

* Alegambe, S. J., "Mortes Illustres et Gesta, . . . Soc. J."—Al. de Andrade, S.J., "Varonis Illustres de la Compañia de Jesus."—M. Tanner, S.J., "Societas Jesu, usque ad sanguinis et vitæ profusionem militans" (also in German).—G. Patrigrani, S.J., "Menologia di pie Memorie d'alcuni Religiosi de la C. de G."—Jos. Cassani, "Glorias del Segundo Siglo de la Compañia de Jesus."

events simply of colonial interest.* The other is still more important. It is a quarto manuscript, entitled "Mémoire Touchant la Mort et les Vertus des PP. Isaac Jogues, Anne de Nouë, Jean de Brébeuf," etc. The first 150 pages are devoted to Father Jogues. To invest this monument with a character of special authority, and render it available for use in case of necessity in a canonical process, each account, and in some cases each separate document, is confirmed by the signature of the Superior of the Mission and his attestation under oath.

The geography and history of that period seemed to us to require some details to enlighten readers who might be unfamiliar with the country.

Before entering on our narrative, we borrow from Mr. Parkman, a Protestant writer, the sketch which he gives of the Canadian missionaries, and which applies so well to our hero. His testimony has all the greater value because, amid his eulogistic words, he omits no opportunity to give currency to false, unjust, and even calumnious ideas in regard to the Society, and he cannot avoid self-contradiction in spite of this frank declaration : "No religious order has ever united in itself so much to be admired and so much to be detested. Unmixed praise has been poured on its Canadian members. It is not for me to eulogize them, but to portray them as they were" ("Jesuits in North America," p. 13).

Thus he portrays them: "All the weapons of Satan's malice were prepared against the bold invader who should assail him in this, the heart of his ancient domain. Far from shrinking, the priest's zeal rose to tenfold ardor; . . . he stood prompt to battle with all the hosts of Hell. A life sequestered from social intercourse and remote from every prize which ambition

---

* This precious manuscript, now at the University Laval, Quebec, was printed a few years since in that city.

holds worth the pursuit, or a lonely death, under forms, perhaps, the most appalling—these were the missionaries' alternatives. Their maligners may taunt them, if they will, with credulity, superstition, or a blind enthusiasm; but slander itself cannot accuse them of hypocrisy or ambition" (p. 43).

" A fervor more intense, a self-abnegation more complete, a self-devotion more constant and enduring, will scarcely find its record on the page of human history" (p. 83).

"In all the copious records of this dark period, not a line gives occasion to suspect that one of this loyal band flinched or hesitated " (p. 125).

This Life is better fitted to interest the pious than the learned. Yet it may serve as an indirect and irrefragable reply to the odious and calumnious insinuations made against the Jesuits of Canada by the Jansenist Arnauld and his imitators—insults revived in our day by writers without religion or principle, who seem to pique themselves when insulting religion and her ministers on outdoing their predecessors.*

I make it a duty to mention here the active and kindly part taken in the work by the Viscount de Lastic Saint Jal.

In conformity with the decree of Urban VIII., we declare that everything related in this life, and every praise or honorable title given to those of whom it treats, have no authority but human testimony, without any wish to anticipate in any manner the judgment of the Church.

---

* As an example, see Michelet, *Revue des deux Mondes*, 15 Jan., 1863, on the " epicurean" life of the Jesuits in Canada.

LIFE OF FATHER ISAAC JOGUES,

OF THE SOCIETY OF JESUS.

CHAPTER I.

Birth of Isaac Jogues—His Education—First Mass—The Canada Mission.

FATHER JOGUES was the first apostle of the Iroquois, and the first missionary victim to their cruelty. His short apostleship of six years has no striking features; but his two captivities in the hands of the fiercest Indians of Canada, the horrible tortures he endured, and his tragical death present a magnificent picture of the sublime virtues of Religion and the Apostleship. Such a character reveals the most excellent heavenly gifts in a soul, and proves that it had been long prepared for the combat.

Isaac Jogues was born at Orleans, January 10, 1607, of a worthy family. Deprived of his father at an early age, he found in his mother, Frances de Saint Mesmin, a woman after the heart of God, who understood the holy mission which the Almighty had confided to her in the education of her children. At his baptism in the Church of St. Hilary he received the name of Isaac, as though God had thus chosen to presage the sacrifice which his pious mother was one day to make, and that which he himself was to offer to the Lord. His happy disposition responded admirably to the care bestowed on his infancy, and every day saw rare dispositions for virtue develop in the boy. He loved to listen to the narrative of the passion of our Lord and the sufferings of the Saints. They excited deep emotion in his heart, and more than once affected him to tears. While still young he was moved by occasional impulses of great fervor. This was manifested in prayer, and in his eagerness to profit by occasions of suffering for God's sake. Instead of murmuring at those who reproved or punished him for any fault, he would express his gratitude as if for a great service done him.

In 1617, at the moment when Isaac Jogues reached the age for beginning his studies, the Fathers of the Society of Jesus opened a college at Orleans.* He immediately entered, and ere long rapid progress gave him a pre-eminence over his fellow-scholars which he never lost. His success was acquired by constant application, guided by a solid judgment, a happy memory, and great penetration.

Nothing tends more to develop the intellect than the best disposition of the heart. Isaac's, so well trained by his excellent mother from early childhood, profited in the highest degree by the advantages afforded in the course of life followed in the new academy, where all

---

* Long opposition had retarded the foundation of this college. The first letters-patent were issued by Henry IV., January 16, 1609, but the authority of Marshal de la Châtre, governor of the city, could not overcome these obstacles. The matter was not taken up again till 1617, the Queen Regent issuing new letters-patent on the 19th of March; on the 12th of May the Governor and municipal officers installed the Jesuits in a house on the Rue Sainte Anne, but the college was not opened for scholars till October 18, in another building on the Rue de la Vieille Monnaie, but it was only temporarily. An eminent benefactor, Raoul Gazille, Prior Commendatory of Saint Sanson, introduced them on the 9th of March, 1619, into his priory, where he had erected the necessary buildings for a college.

were animated by piety. His virtue, like his learning, grew with his years ; his assiduity and fervor in prayer, pious reading, serious conversation, tender devotion to the Blessed Virgin, frequent participation in the sacraments, all developed in him a religious feeling and habit. Isaac became a perfect model of a virtuous scholar, and the often critical tests of this college life never made him swerve from the line which he had traced for himself. Works of charity and zeal—an ordinary characteristic of souls predestined for the service of God—already claimed his leisure hours, and he was never happier than when he had been able to lead others to virtue.

At an early age Isaac sought light from heaven as to his vocation: it was the frequent subject of his prayers, and he prepared himself in advance to fulfil the divine will as soon as it became known to him. The light of grace did not fail him; he soon understood that he was called to the religious and apostolic life. His eyes turned toward the Society of Jesus, which seemed to embody all the aspirations of his heart from both points of view. He solicited admission, and as soon as he received a favorable reply he longed to put his project into effect at once, although he had only just finished his course of rhetoric; but he was impelled by the thought that one who resolves to dedicate his life to God's service can never do it too soon.

Filled, however, with respectful deference for his mother, he would take no step without her consent; he imparted his design to her. This valiant woman knew her duty too well to give ear only to the voice of affection, which is so easily blinded, and so easily influenced by self-love. Above all, she weighed the interest of God and the happiness of her son. Having convinced herself that his vocation was real, she left him absolutely free to follow it, and like Abraham, did not falter in her sacrifice.

Isaac was seventeen years old when he entered the novitiate of the Society of Jesus at Rouen, on the 24th of October, 1624. To guide his steps in the career which he had embraced, and be initiated into the interior life, which forms the spiritual man, and prepares the apostle, he found there a master deeply versed in the practice and knowledge of the things of God. Father Louis Lalemant,* a religious of eminent virtue, was endowed with extraordinary talent for imbuing others with the spirit of self-denial and zeal which animated him. Notwithstanding his earnest solicitation, he had not been permitted to bear the gospel to savage nations, and atoned for the loss by selecting and forming good missionaries to accomplish that eminently Catholic work—men who had all his predilection for it.

He had been struck by young Jogues' aptitude and disposition. Nor was he long in discerning in the young man a soul full of uprightness, energy, and ardor, a heart capable of the greatest sacrifices, and a virtue to stand every test. These were the qualities characteristic of a good missionary. Accordingly, when the mission of New France was opened to the Jesuits in 1625 for the second time, Father Lalemant loved to repeat to his disciple these prophetic words: "Brother, you will not die anywhere but in Canada."

The young religious thought indeed of devoting himself to the preaching of the gospel in remote countries, but his aspirations did not incline him towards that American province, then little known: he longed to go to the burning sands of Ethiopia, where the success of the faith called for many laborers. He even manifested this pious desire to his superiors, and begged them to inscribe his name in advance on the list of those who were to have the happiness of being summoned to extend the kingdom of Jesus Christ in that region.

---

* Three members of this family are still famous in the history of the Canada missions—Charles, his brother Jerome, and their nephew Gabriel, who was put to death by the Iroquois in 1649.

His youth allowed time for his projects to mature, and gave him full leisure for an excellent preparation. He was about to enter on the career of study and teaching through which the younger members of the Society of Jesus must usually pass before they are elevated to the priesthood. After his novitiate he was sent to La Flèche to study a three-years' course of philosophy. This college was at that time in a very prosperous condition, through the munificence of Henry IV. It had three hundred boarders and nearly two thousand day-scholars.

The young Jesuit scholastics formed a little body by themselves, and were engaged only in their studies. That species of retreat combining religious recollection with the pursuit of science was most providential for Brother Jogues. Several of his fellow-students were destined to share at a future day his stern labors in Canada. They were: René Ménard, Charles Dumarché, James Delaplace, Claude Quentin, and Nicholas Adam. There too were at this period Brothers Julian Maunoir and Vincent Hubi, already eminent for virtue, who were in later days to shed a brilliant lustre by their labors and their sanctity.

Brother Jogues' residence at La Flèche had familiarized him with the Canada Mission,—the only one of his order in French America,—and this doubtless at a later day caused the change in his destination. Father Masse,* after ten years' residence at La Flèche, had left it the year before, to return to New France, from which he had been expelled by the English in 1611. During his stay in Europe he had sighed incessantly for that remote mission, which he styled his *Rachel*. His accounts of Canada, preserved traditionally in the house, kept

---

* Father Enemond Masse was a member of the Acadian Mission in 1611, and of that of Quebec in 1625. After being expelled by the English, he returned to Canada in 1633, and died in 1646. A pious monument was raised to his memory, in 1870, over his grave at Sillery, near Quebec.

alive an emulation for the conversion of souls and the propagation of the gospel in heathen lands.

At this time the Society of Jesus was passing through one of the most brilliant phases of its history. Nothing was lacking for its prosperity on the various stages where its zeal was displayed—not even the trial of the most envenomed and bloodiest persecution. In Catholic countries hatred in the hearts of unbelievers invented the grossest calumnies against it, while Protestantism in England and Holland and idolatry in Japan endeavored to overwhelm its flourishing missions in blood. Then the converts and their apostles renewed the finest examples of Christian heroism, which has been set in the primitive ages of the Church, and the glory of religion expanded as at its cradle, just as hell reawakened in the executioner, the same instincts of rage and cruelty that marked the persecutions of old. These desperate struggles stimulated courage, and the most perilous missions were the most coveted.

The death of Father Spinola,* burnt in Japan in 1622, whose life presents so many touching circumstances, had singularly impressed Father Jogues. It inspired him from that moment with a keen desire for martyrdom, God apparently thus preparing him for the tortures which he himself was one day to undergo. He often fixed

---

* A touching scene occurred at the death of Father Spinola. From his funeral pyre he perceived the mother of a child that he had baptized four years before. This remembrance touched his heart. "Where is my little Ignatius?" he exclaimed. The mother then raised towards him the child, who, like all the others, was arrayed in its finest clothes for the sacrifice. "Here he is, Father," she exclaimed; "he is rejoiced to die with you for God's sake." Then addressing her son, she continued in a lively sentiment of faith: "See the one who made thee a child of God!—ask his blessing for thyself and thy mother." Ignatius fell on his knees, his hands clasped, and the confessor blessed the martyr-child. A cry of pity rose from every mouth. To arrest it, the executioners hastened to complete their work. Father Spinola was enrolled among the Beatified in 1867.

his eye on a small picture, which represented the generous confessor attached to the stake, amid the fagots, his eyes raised to heaven; he seemed to hear him, when at the very moment of his torture he intoned in a triumphant voice the Psalm *Laudate pueri Dominum*, which his thirty companions continued with the same enthusiasm till their voices were extinguished forever.

Brother Isaac henceforward carried that picture of the servant of God on his breast and prayed to the holy religious to obtain grace to imitate him in his labors, and to die like him for his God; but he had not yet overcome all the obstacles, and, full of submission to the divine will, he contented himself for the time being with a more modest field of battle, though rich in merits and fruitful in sacrifices. In 1629 the Superiors sent him to the College of Rouen to teach the sixth class, and there continue his course of instruction till he had presided over the class of *belles-lettres*.

Providence seemed to guide Brother Isaac to this house in order to bring him into intercourse with three of the chief Canada missionaries, whom the English had just expelled after a most iniquitous aggression on that colony. Father Charles Lalemant,* first Superior of Quebec, Father Brébeuf,† and Father Masse, already mentioned, returned to France in 1629 with the firm hope and ardent desire of resuming their work at a future day. As there was nothing to indicate when the moment would come, each received a position in the College

---

* Father Charles Lalemant made eight voyages across the Atlantic. He was the first Superior at Quebec. Having returned to France for good in 1838, he became Rector of Clermont College, Superior of the professed house and vice-provincial. He died in 1674, at the age of eighty-seven. The esteem he enjoyed led to his selection as one of those proposed for the Bishopric to be erected in Canada.

† Father Brébeuf is the most popular missionary in Canada, on account of his virtues, his hardships and labors, and especially the heroism of his last sacrifice. He underwent most frightful tortures at the hands of the Iroquois in 1649.

of Rouen.   They waited for three years; then, through
the efforts of Champlain and the energetic administration of Richelieu, Canada was at last restored to France,
the generous laborers in the vineyard of the Lord were
successively restored to their beloved mission.

Brother Jogues was thus enabled to acquaint himself,
not only with the obstacles which the faith encountered
in that distant country, but also with the rigors of its
arctic climate, and the manifold hardships of that young
mission, already regarded as one of the most laborious
undertaken by the Society.   The difficulties and sufferings, far from damping his courage, only excited his
ardor; but as yet he could dream only of gratifying it
in the remote future.

To show himself more worthy of it, Brother Isaac gave
himself up wholly to his duties as professor and to the de-
velopment of the youth confided to his care.   While stor-
ing their minds with human learning, he sought especially
to train them in the science of the saints.   He would fain
have inspired them all with his horror of sin and his love
for virtue.   His active zeal suggested a thousand de-
vices to attain this end.   He stimulated especially a love
of prayer, the frequentation of the Sacraments, and a
tender devotion to the Blessed Virgin.   His piety towards the august Queen of Heaven induced him on a
solemn occasion to select her as the theme of a literary
exercise which had been assigned to him.   At the end of
the collegiate year it was usual for one of the professors
to read in public at the distribution of prizes some
composition, the choice of which was left to himself.
Brother Jogues, then professor of the class of Humanity,
was selected for this exercise, and he delivered a short
Latin poem based on a fact related by Evagrius.*

---

* It was an ancient custom at Constantinople, when some particles
were left of the Sacred Body of our Lord at the Mass, to give them to
the little school-children.   The child of a Jewish glass-blower, min-
gling among his classmates, received it.   On his return home his fa-

This piece, devoted entirely to the glory of the Blessed Virgin and of the Blessed Sacrament, was recited by Brother Jogues, with an eloquence born of faith and enthusiasm. Unfortunately, the work of the young scholastic has not come down to us; we only know that it won the praise of the numerous audience. He was then twenty-five years of age.

The hour for his theological studies had come at last. He was sent to Clermont College,* Paris, to pursue them. Yet this did not absorb all his time; he at the same time filled the position of prefect over the students. This important trust was at that time confided to theological students in the great colleges of Paris, Bourges, and La Flèche.

Father Buteux, one of the Canadian missionaries who knew Father Jogues most thoroughly, and who has left

---

ther asked him the cause of his delay. He told where he had been, and that he had eaten with the other children. The Jew, enraged at these words, threw his son into the raging furnace, where the glass was melted. His mother, looking for her little child and not finding him, roamed through the city, uttering piteous cries and offering fervent prayers to God. Three days after, while standing near the door of her husband's glass-house, she called her son by name aloud in a transport of her grief. The child recognizing his mother's voice, instantly replied from the interior of the furnace. The mother tore the door open and saw her son standing in the midst of the burning coals, utterly unharmed. She questioned him to learn how he could be there safe and sound. "A woman robed in purple," he replied, "came to see me and gave me water to put out the fire around me; and she brought me something to eat whenever I was hungry." The fact having been laid before the Emperor Justinian, he ordered the mother and child to be baptized, in accordance with the desire they expressed; and the father, who obstinately refused to become a Christian, was crucified for his crime at the entrance of the Fig-tree suburb (Cat. III., part 1, ch. 4).

* This college owes its name to William Duprat, Bishop of Clermont, who founded it in the reign of Henry II. On the occasion of a solemn visit made to it in 1682 by Louis XIV., it received the name of Louis-le-Grand.

us extended details of his life, says of him, when treating of this period of his studies: "It was at this moment that I first saw him, and I sought to know him. I always discerned in him rare prudence, and a punctual observance of the rule. This was all the more striking in the college where he lived, because amid such surroundings it is apt to become less strict. I had an equal admiration and respect for his humility. He displayed it especially then, by his earnest entreaties to his Superiors to be allowed to withdraw from the study of theology, under the pretext of want of ability, and to be sent to New France."

Isaac announced to his mother his change of residence and employment. "After having been a master," he wrote on the 10th of October, 1633, "here I am a scholar again. This position is all the more agreeable to me, because it confines me to the study of a holy and sacred science, which is to render me better fitted than ever to work for God's glory, by disposing me to be promoted to holy orders in a few years. This is the grace to which I aspire. May it be granted to me, and then give greater efficacy to the prayers which I offer the Almighty for our whole household !"

When they saw that he returned to Paris, the family felt great pleasure, hoping to be more easily favored with his presence. The marriage of his brother Philip even seemed a favorable pretext for obtaining a visit from him to Orleans, and his mother resolved to show him that it was her desire ; but Isaac modestly excused himself, alleging his studies and the charge over the students confided to him.

It would seem that his reasons were not well received, and that they drew upon him reproaches, which he felt keenly. He obeyed an obligation to the law of duty in thus renouncing the impulses of nature. The sacrifice which he had made to God required him to forego the lawful family celebrations, and he replied to his mother with a firmness tempered by sincere love: "I never even thought of laying the matter before my Superiors. The pressing obligations of my position do not permit me to leave the house a single day. Moreover, my presence at that ceremony was not necessary. The prayers one can offer for the happy result of such alliance, and that as well at a distance, as on the spot, are all the affectionate marks that I can give you of the interest I take in your welfare. I beg my brothers and sisters to accept the assurance I give them, that my prayers are often offered for their welfare. This I shall do even more efficaciously, I hope, the coming year, in which I shall be able to enjoy the happiness of being promoted to the priesthood, unworthy as I am of such a favor."

This letter is dated April 25, 1635, and early in the next year the fervent religious was ordained priest. At the same time God disposed another favor in his behalf, which he always regarded as crowning it. The Superiors then announced to him that his aspirations for the missions were about to be gratified; he was selected for that of Canada.

An unforeseen circumstance and the increasing wants of that remote field had caused missionaries to be sent earlier than was originally designed. A large fleet was then equipping for Canada, and it was important not to lose the opportunity it afforded of greater safety—always rare in those days. This decision gratified the great desire of Father Jogues; he willingly abandoned his theological studies, although he had made only two years of the course, and at once prepared to receive holy orders.

On hearing of her son's ordination, the mother of Isaac felt a holy emotion. For one of her faith such an event was the happiness and glory of her life. In her legitimate maternal ambition she solicited the favor of receiving the first priestly blessing of the dearest of her children. The Superiors willingly consented, as it was the most favorable means to dispose this Christian and sensitive heart for the painful trial of a speedy separation—much more painful than that previously accomplished.

On the 1st of February, 1636, Father Jogues announced to his mother the impatiently desired tidings that he would soon reach Orleans, and he begged her "to solicit prayers for him in all quarters, that God might give him the graces necessary to discharge so holy a ministry."

On the 5th of the month, after a short apparition in his family, he secluded himself in the college to devote his time to the exercises of a retreat, and to prepare speedily to ascend the altar. The 10th, the first Sunday of Lent, was fixed for this great occasion. In presence of all his kindred, of his religious brethren, and his many friends, the newly ordained priest offered the august Victim for the first time. His pious mother, affected to tears, had the happiness of receiving holy communion from the hands of her son, and of at last seeing her heart's fondest wish accomplished.

Meanwhile her dear Isaac, as she delighted to call him, was to ask of her the very next day a sacrifice more painful than all she had hitherto made. He was to break to her the announcement of his speedy departure for his mission, and to bid her what seemed to be a last farewell. Though most delicately conveyed, the unexpected tidings produced on her maternal heart an impression that nothing could efface; her tears flowed copiously; but amid the struggles and fears of nature she heard the teachings of faith, and her feelings of Christian resignation finally triumphed. The word of the young apostle was already mighty; this was its first victory.

The fleet for Canada set sail early in April, and before embarking, Father Jogues was to make a retreat to take the place of the third year of novitiate, which it would no longer be possible for him to enjoy after he was once on the mission. The Society of Jesus requires that her sons, after the absorbing labor of teaching and study, should withdraw to spend a whole year in solitude and meditation, in order to revive in their souls the fervor and practice of solid virtue.

Having fulfilled all the duties of filial piety, Father Jogues proceeded to the novitiate at Rouen, there to pass the brief term left him, but he derived from it the greatest possible benefit. There are hearts endowed with such happy dispositions, that they possess the secret of turning everything to advantage. Their progress in the way of virtue is so rapid that it cannot be measured by the length of their course.

Soon after the first of April, Father Jogues was to proceed to Dieppe, where the fleet was preparing to weigh anchor. Before leaving Rouen he wrote a few words to comfort his mother. This letter is lost, but this good son would not embark without again addressing her, to give that afflicted heart a new token of his filial piety, and some of those words of faith which revive the courage. He addressed to her the following letter, the autograph of which is preserved with religious respect in the family of the servant of God, and which we copy literally :

"MOST HONORED MOTHER : It would be in violation of the first point of duty of a good son towards a good mother if, when ready to embark at sea, I did not bid you a last farewell. I wrote to you last month from Rouen, by Mr. Tanzeau, who took charge of my letters, that I sailed from Dieppe, from which we expected to clear about Holy Week; but contrary winds, and the weather, which has been unfavorable, have detained us until now, without permitting us to sail. I hope that God will give us a good and happy voyage, both because a number of vessels are going together, and because especially a great many persons most pleasing to God are praying for us. Endeavor also, if you please, to contribute something by your prayers to the safety of our voyage, and chiefly by a generous resignation of your will to that of God, conforming your desires to those of the divine goodness, which can be only most holy and honorable to us, since they spring from the heart of a Father full of love for our welfare.

"I hope, as I said on another occasion, that if you take this little affliction in a proper spirit, it will be most pleasing to God, for whose sake it would become you to give not one son only, but all the others, nay, life itself, if it were necessary. Men for a little gain cross the seas, enduring, at least, as much as we; and shall we not, for God's love, do what men do for earthly interests?

"Good-by, dear mother. I thank you for all the affection which you have ever shown me, and above all at our last meeting. May God unite us in His Holy Paradise, if we do not see each other again on earth!

"Present my most humble recommendations to my brothers and sisters, to whose prayers, as to yours, I commend myself in heart and love.

"Your most humble son and obedient servant in our Lord, ISAAC JOGUES.

"DIEPPE, April 6, 1636.

"P. S. We sail to-morrow, please God—that is to say, the second Sunday after Easter, or Monday morning at latest. Our vessels are already out in the harbor. My affectionate excuses if I do not write to Mr. Houdelin."

This language, full of love, resignation, energy, denotes a heart prepared for combat, and already trained to sacrifices of every kind. His virtue will throw still greater lustre over the arena where God has in store for him trials worthy of his courage.

CHAPTER II.

Canada—The Huron Mission—The Missionaries Fall Sick— Their Recovery.

THE colony of Canada then dated back but a few years, and might be considered as yet in the cradle; and yet the country had been discovered more than a century before.

Francis I., jealous of the Spanish and Portuguese conquests in America, longed to see the French standard floating over some portion of the New World. The Florentine Verrazani, to whom he entrusted the mission, accomplished it at the cost of his life, with no other reward than of having reached and bestowed on the unknown country the name of New France.

Ten years after, Francis I. renewed the attempt, and the illustrious Jacques Cartier of St. Malo planted the cross on the same soil, and took possession of it in the name of his King. He, moreover, pushed his discovery up the river St. Lawrence, thus named by him, and opened intercourse with the natives. In spite of four successive voyages, and some attempts at colonizing, he did not succeed in forming any durable settlement. The severity of the winters was not the least of the obstacles he had to encounter. The death of that intrepid navigator, and the misfortunes which overwhelmed France arrested for a time all further operations.

More fortunate, or rather better served by circumstances and by men, Henry IV. was at last enabled to carry into effect some of his predecessor's designs. In 1604 he began a settlement in Acadia, and four years later he dispatched Champlain to lay the foundation of Quebec.

An iniquitous invasion by the English destroyed all these undertakings in 1628. They seized the rising colony and sent the missionaries back to Europe.

Canada was restored to France in 1632, and Champlain, who is justly regarded as the father of that colony, was commissioned to raise it up again from its ruins. With heroism in war, devotion to his religion and his country, Champlain combined perseverance that nothing could discourage, a magnanimity that nothing could depress.

Feeling deeply the spiritual wants of that land, he had sent some Recollect missionaries to it in 1615; and ten years later those religious called upon the Jesuits to share their labors.

The Mission of Canada was to receive a powerful reinforcement in 1636. Five Jesuit Fathers and one lay-brother sailed with the new Governor, Montmagny, appointed to succeed Champlain, who had died the previous year. These missionaries were Peter Chastelain, Charles Garnier,* Nicholas Adam, Paul Ragueneau,† Isaac Jogues, and Brother Cauvet. The fleet, composed of eight vessels, under command of Duplessis-Bochard, weighed anchor on the 8th of April, and after a favorable voyage of two months entered the Gulf of St. Lawrence. The vessel on which Father Jogues was, anchored for a short time at the island of St. Louis de Miscou, in the entrance of Chaleur Bay, where the mission of St. Charles had been established for two years, and not till the 2d of July did he arrive at Quebec.

---

* Father Charles Garnier was born in Paris. He was a priest of many and rare virtues. He spent only thirteen years in Canada, and always among the Hurons. He was killed by the Iroquois while hastening to minister to his neophytes, whom the savages were slaughtering. He had just attained his forty-fourth year.

† Father Paul Ragueneau lived in Canada twenty-six years, Superior of the Missions there for twenty years. He died in Paris, A.D., 1680, at the age of threescore and three.

It was not then a very important post; yet a few houses began to cluster together on the crest of the promontory, protected by the guns of the fort thrown up by Champlain. Near by stood the modest residence of the missionaries, and the chapel of Notre Dame de Recouvrance, the first sanctuary of the Upper Town and a pious monument of the devotion of the first colonists towards the Mother of God. The principal residence of the Fathers was at Our Lady of the Angels,* more than a mile away.

Father Jogues gave his mother an account of his voyage, at the moment when he was to take a canoe to proceed to the Huron country:

"DEAR MOTHER: At last it has pleased our Lord to allow me to alight on the shores of New France, the goal of my long aspirations. We sailed from Dieppe, April 8th, eight vessels together, and we arrived here eight weeks after our departure. I landed at an island called Miscou, where two of our Fathers serve the French, who have begun a settlement there, and attempt the conversion of the Indians found there. After spending a fortnight, I embarked in another vessel that conveyed me to Tadoussac, where large vessels lie to, while barks and lighter vessels run up the St. Lawrence as far as Quebec, a French settlement which is growing every day. I landed on the 2d of July, the feast of the Visitation of Our Lady.

---

* Our Lady of the Angels, on the banks of the river Lairet, near Quebec, recalls more ancient memories than the residence of the Jesuit Fathers. There Jacques Cartier, the great explorer of Canada, reared a little fort in 1534 to winter with his hardy sailors. Before leaving its banks, where his company was decimated by scurvy, and where he was forced to abandon one of his ships, he planted a huge cross with the arms of France and the inscription, "*Franciscus primus, Dei gratia rex, regnat.*" To it he made a pilgrimage in the snow, pronouncing a vow to Our Lady of Roc-amadour.

"My health has been so good, thank God, at sea and on land that it has been a matter of wonder to all, it being very unusual for any one to make such a long voyage without suffering a little from sea-sickness or nausea. The vestments and chapel service have been a great comfort to me, as I have offered the holy sacrifice of Mass every day the weather was favorable—a happiness I should have been deprived of, had not our family provided me with them. It was a great consolation to me, and one which our Fathers did not enjoy the preceding years. Officers and crew have profited by it ; as but for that the eighty persons on board could not have been present at the Holy Sacrifice for two months, whilst, owing to the faculties I enjoyed, they all confessed and received communion at Whitsunday, Ascension, and Corpus Christi. God will reward you and Madam Houdelin for the good you have enabled me to do.

"You shall have letters of mine every year, and I shall expect yours. It will ever be a consolation for me to hear from you and from our family, as I have no hope of seeing you in our lifetime. May God in His goodness unite us both in his Holy abode to praise Him for all eternity ! For this we must work in all earnestness as long as we live. Let us so husband the time granted unto us that we may do in life what we will wish to have done at our death. And oh ! what a comfort on that day for a soul that departs in the satisfaction afforded by conscience, that we have served God with as little imperfection as we could, and that we have endeavored in all things and all places to do what was most agreeable to His Divine Majesty. I believe that such were the thoughts and the motives which have urged us to beg with so much importunity to be sent to these countries, where, there being so much to suffer, we can also give such sincere proof of our love for God.

"Were I able to give you good advice, or were you to need it, I would advise you to place yourself in the hands of some holy director, to whom you should intrust the guidance of your soul, and who would engage you in a more assiduous practice of the Sacraments. Devotion, which gives you pleasure, should more than ever engross your utmost attention. Your advanced age and the rest you now enjoy will render you the more adapted for it.

"I write this to you at a distance of more than a thousand leagues, and perhaps I shall be sent this year to a nation called the Hurons, who live at a distance of more than three hundred leagues. They give tokens of great dispositions for embracing the Faith. It matters not where we are, provided we rest in the arms of Providence and in His holy favor. This is the prayer offered every day at the altar for you and our family by him, who is, etc.

"THREE RIVERS,* August 20, 1636.

"P. S. I have just received orders to get ready to start for the mission among the Hurons in two or three days."

On the occasion of the first Mass he offered in Canada he thus feelingly wrote to his mother : "I do not know what it is to enter Paradise ; but this I know, that it is difficult to experience in this world a joy more excessive and more overflowing than that I felt on my setting foot in New France, and celebrating my first Mass here on the day of the Visitation. I assure you it was indeed a day of the visitation of the goodness of God and Our Lady. I felt as if it were a Christmas day for me, and that I was to be born again to a new life, and a life in God."

How these letters are dictated by the best of sons—one who never lost sight of his duties toward a loving mother, and blending in admirable union his love for his family

---

* Three Rivers, on the St. Lawrence between Montreal and Quebec, derives its name from the river which near it discharges its waters into the St. Lawrence by three mouths. It was founded by Champlain in 1634.

and his love of God!—sentiments equalled only by an apostle's zeal for the salvation of souls.

When Father Jogues arrived in Canada there were on the Mission eighteen priests and six lay-brothers. They lived in six stations, scattered over a line of more than one thousand miles, from Cape Breton to the shores of Lake Huron. There were two at Cape Breton, two at Miscou, two at Quebec, five at Our Lady of Angels, two at Three Rivers, and five among the Hurons.

The new accessions from France were especially intended for the Huron Mission. It was on it that the French relied most for their success in opening the immense countries of the West to religion and commerce. Thus a twofold interest was felt in drawing that nation closer to friendship and civilization through the propagation of the Gospel. It occupied a small territory on the eastern shore of the lake called after them, and which Champlain had at first named *Mer douce* (Fresh Sea). The position of the tribe was very favorable to their mode of life, devoted to trade, hunting, fishing, and to agriculture to some extent. Divided into twenty villages, the Hurons formed in 1635 a population of from thirty to thirty-five thousand souls. The Faith had struck some roots already ; but its growth was slow, and it was attained only by the hardest labor, dangers, and privations of every kind.

The departure of Father Jogues for the country of the Hurons was hastened by a fortuitous circumstance. While he tarried at Three Rivers, awaiting an opportunity to start, there arrived a convoy of young natives, whom Father de Brébeuf had succeeded in banding together, and whom he sent to Quebec to receive instruction there so as to become subsequently the main-stay and propagators of the faith in their country. Fathers Daniel *

---

* Father Anthony Daniel, a native of Dieppe, went to Canada in 1632, and spent fifteen years on the Huron Mission, where he died gloriously at the hands of the Iroquois, in 1648.

and Davost accompanied these youths. Father Jogues had the happiness to witness their landing, and to experience some of the details of that apostolic life he was so anxious to share.

Father Daniel's canoe led the rest. "At the sight," writes Father Le Jeune, "our heart was deeply moved. The good Father's countenance was beaming with joy and cheerfulness, but it was gaunt. He was barefooted, with a paddle in his hand, his cassock in shreds, the breviary hanging from his neck, and a worn-out shirt on his back." But charity has a balm for all sufferings : a most affectionate reception awaited the missionary and his neophytes, and of course there was a feast in readiness for the Indians who had escorted them. Almost all belonged to the village of Ossossané, the most attached to the French, who had surnamed it *La Rochelle*, its location bearing some resemblance to the city of that name in France.

After a few days' rest the Indians were ready to return. Then a scene occurred which Father Jogues considered as providential, and which decided his departure. In the midst of a farewell feast some of the Indians made the Jesuits a touching reproach, which showed their attachment and esteem. They had not been asked to take back with them any of the missionaries, perhaps from the fact that Fathers Garnier and Chastelain had left for the Huron country scarcely one month before. "What! do the French love us less, and none of them will come with us now?" said one of the chiefs. "Will they not replace those whom we have brought back, and shall we return without a black-gown?"

Father Le Jeune, Superior of the Canada Mission,*

* Father Paul Le Jeune abjured Protestantism in his youth, and became one of the founders of the Canada Mission. He was Superior for nearly fifteen years, and wrote most of its history. Having returned to France in 1649 to become procurator of the Mission, he died there in 1664, at the age of seventy-two. His merit led to his

could not withstand the appeal, and to his extreme delight Father Jogues was appointed to accompany the
Hurons in their homeward journey. On the morrow he
started, taking his seat in a frail birch-canoe. It is not
without misgivings that a white man steps for the first
time aboard one of those light craft, to brave the
rapid currents and the vast lakes of Canada. The slight
framework is formed of slender poles, fastened at the
extremities between two stringpieces somewhat stronger,
which serve for rim. These are covered with bark of
the birch, of the thickness of a silver dollar. Threads of
the root of the cedar, an incorruptible tree, fasten together the pieces of bark. Seams and holes are calked
with rosin. These canoes vary in size. The smallest
will carry only three men. The largest will bear as
many as twenty-four, with more than 3000 pounds of
freight. They are propelled by paddles, and from their
lightness are capable of great speed. Once in their
place the travellers were not allowed to shift their position, as any movement tends to capsize the little craft.
Father Jogues well knew the difficulties of such navigation from Father de Brébeuf's experience transmitted to
his brethren: "However smooth the passage may appear,
there is enough to appall a heart not thoroughly morti-
fied. The skill of the Indians does not shorten the
journey, smooth the rocks, or avert the dangers. No
matter with whom you may be, you must make up
your mind to be at least three or four weeks on the
way, with no companions but men whom you have never
seen before, in a bark-canoe, in a most inconvenient
position, forbidden to move right or left, to be fifty
times a day in danger of capsizing or dashing against the
rocks. You are scorched by the sun in the day-time, and
the mosquitoes devour you by night. Sometimes you

nomination, with those of Fathers Charles Lalemant and Paul Ragueneau, for the episcopal see of Quebec (Archives of the Gésu, Rome).

have to ascend five or six falls in one day, and at night all your refreshment is a little corn simply boiled in water, and your bed the ground or a rough and bristling rock; generally the sky is your canopy, with an unbroken stillness for your lullaby." *

Father Jogues himself gives his mother an account of part of this painful voyage in a letter dated June 1, 1637. It will enable us to appreciate this heart full of gratitude to God and zeal for His glory.

"DEAR MOTHER: As only one opportunity is afforded every year of writing to you, I cannot let it pass without acquitting myself of my duty towards so good a mother. I feel sure that you will be happy to acknowledge the special providence with which Divine Goodness has led me, since He has accorded me the grace of landing in this Huron country. I wrote to you last year in the month of August, when on the point of starting on my journey. I left Three Rivers the 24th of August—St. Bartholomew's Day. I was put in a birch-canoe that could carry five or six persons at the utmost. It would not be easy to give you in detail all the discomforts of this mode of travel; but the love of God, who calls us to these missions, and our desire to do something towards the conversion of these poor barbarians, render it all so sweet, that we would not exchange our hardships for all the pleasures of earth. The traveller's food is a little Indian corn, crushed between two stones, and boiled in water innocent of all seasoning. We lay ourselves to sleep on the ground, or on the sharp rocks bordering this great river, by the light of the moon. You must sit in the canoe in a very uncomfortable position. You cannot stretch out your legs, for the place is narrow and crowded. You dare not move lest you capsize. I was forced to observe a strict silence, for I could not understand our Indians nor could they understand me.

---

* Relation, 1637.

"Another surplus of pain and labor. We meet in this journey some sixty to eighty water-falls, which descend so furiously and so far that canoes going too near are carried over and perish. As we were paddling against the stream we were not exposed to this danger; but then we had often to land and march over rocks and through tangled woods about one league to make a detour, carrying on our backs all the luggage and even the canoes.* For my own part I carried not only my own little baggage, but I also aided and relieved our Indians as much as I could; and in the journeys caused by the falls I have mentioned I was compelled to carry on my shoulders a child ten or eleven years old, who belonged to our caravan, and who had fallen sick."

But let us interrupt the letter to add some details, which Father Jogues' modesty led him to treat too briefly. That child had been placed under his charge from the start. Sick after the seventh day, he became a source of indescribable hardship to the missionary; but charity does not stop at any sacrifice. The young Indian grew so feeble that he could not walk, nor even get out of the canoe. After consenting two or three times to help Father Jogues, his uncouth guides refused to aid the priest any more. Thus the care of the sick boy fell wholly upon him, and he had to carry him on his back whenever they landed; from his inexperience, and the asperities of the ground, this became a labor of great peril to both. More than once he endeavored to make the guides understand his fears, but to no avail; until, from dread lest some mishap should compromise them, they agreed to carry the invalid on condition that the missionary took charge of part of their baggage, consisting of kettles, iron axes, and other heavy objects. The pleasure of seeing his young charge protected from danger gave the missionary renewed strength, and he did

---

* This is called making a portage.

not spare himself. As for the sick boy, he grew better as they approached the Nipissings, and good nourishment enabled him to end his journey in good health.

"But by great exertion," continues Father Jogues, "instead of the twenty-five or thirty days ordinarily required for this voyage, it took me but nineteen days to reach the spot where five of our Fathers resided, some of whom have been in this country five or six years. The two last-comers, Fathers Charles Garnier and Peter Chastelain, had arrived only one month before me.

"Thus has Providence vouchsafed to keep me full of strength and health to this day. He grants me grace to be far more contented amid the privations inseparable from our position than if I were enjoying all the comforts of the world. God makes Himself felt with far greater sweetness. He guards us amongst the savages with so much love, He gives such abundant consolations in the little trials we have to endure, that we do not even think of regretting what we have renounced for His sake. Nothing can equal the satisfaction enjoyed in our hearts while we impart the knowledge of the true God to these heathen. About two hundred and forty have received baptism this year: among them I have baptized some who surely are now in heaven, as they were children one or two years old.

"Can we think the life of man better employed than in this good work? What do I say? Would not all the labors of a thousand men be well rewarded in the conversion of a single soul gained to Jesus Christ? I have always felt a great love for this kind of life, and for a profession so excellent, and so akin to that of the Apostles. Had I to work for this happiness alone, I would exert myself to my utmost to obtain a favor, for which I would fain give a thousand lives.

"Should you receive these lines, I entreat you, by the bonds of the love of Jesus Christ, to give thanks to the Lord for this extraordinary favor He has bestowed upon me—a favor so earnestly wished and craved by many servants of God endowed with qualities far above what I possess."

On the 11th of September, 1636, Father Jogues reached the village of Ihonatiria, called St. Joseph, where the missionaries had their residence. They all hastened to the river-side to welcome the traveller. The arrival of a new brother, who had come to share their labors and their hopes, brought great joy to their humble cabins. Father Jogues then recalled to mind the feeling and affectionate invitation which Father de Brébeuf had tendered to the future missionaries of the Hurons, and he experienced its effects in himself. Here are the words : "When you arrive among the Hurons," he wrote, "you shall indeed meet with hearts overflowing with charity. We will receive you with open arms, as an angel from heaven. We shall all have every inclination to render you services, but it will be almost beyond all possibility to do so. We shall receive you in a cabin so poor that I despair of finding one in France wretched enough for me to say, 'See how you will be lodged!' Fatigued and harassed as you may be, we can offer you only a poor mat, and at utmost some skins for your bedding ; and moreover, you will arrive in a season when annoying little creatures, called *touhac* here,—in good French, *puces*,*—will, night after night, prevent your closing an eye, for in these regions they are far more importunate than in France. The five or six winter months are besieged with uninterrupted vexations, excessive cold, smoke, and the importunity of the Indians. Our cabin is built merely of bark, but so well knit together that we have no need of going into the open air to know the state of the weather. The smoke is often so dense, so pungent, and so perverse, that for five or six days at a time, unless you are well inured to it, it is all you can do to make out a few words in the breviary."

---

* Fleas in English.

Father Ragueneau, the historian of that time, gives these touching details of the welcome Father Jogues met with : "I made all the preparations for his reception ; but oh, what a feast !—a handful of little dried fish, with a sprinkling of flour. I sent for a few ears of corn, which we roasted for him after the fashion of the country. But it is true that at heart, and to hear him, he never enjoyed better cheer. The happiness felt at these meetings seems to reflect in some sort the joy of the blessed on their entrance into heaven, so full of sweetness is it !" *

This painful voyage, which served as a noviceship to his apostolic life, was only the prelude to more serious trials. The joy he experienced in having attained what he had so ardently desired prevented his feeling at once the effects of his hardships; but on the 17th of September he fell ill. What at first seemed a light sickness in a few days showed alarming symptoms, and soon carried him to the brink of the grave. With nothing but a mat for his bed, like his brethren, and some decoction of roots to assuage the burning fever, his courage was supported by the charity of his fellow-missionaries, his patience, and humble resignation to the will of God. Soon after, the same disease attacked Fathers Garnier and Chastelain, and two domestics. The missionaries' hut was transformed into a hospital. Fathers de Brébeuf, Peter Pijart, and Le Mercier alone escaped the disease. †

The last of these Fathers, who had charge of the sick, gives the following affecting account of those days of trial and anguish : " We then were almost without domestics. Francis Petit-Pré, the only one in health, was away day and night hunting. This was, under God, our only resource for food. On the first days, as we had no game, we had scarcely anything for our patients but

---

* Relation, 1637.

† Father Le Mercier was twice Superior-General in Canada. After his recall to France in 1673, he was sent to Cayenne as Visitor, and died at Martinique in 1692.

a tea of wild purslane and sour grapes. These were our first broths. True, we had a hen, but she did not lay an egg every day; and what was one egg among so many sick persons? It was amusing to see us who remained well watch for the laying of that egg; then a consultation was to decide on the patient to whom it should be given, as most in need of it, and our patients debated who should refuse it.

"On the 24th of September Father Jogues grew so much worse that we all thought he must be bled. We had not been able to stay a bleeding at the nose so copious that he could not take any food except with great difficulty. . . . . But where find a surgeon? We were all so well skilled in this art that the sick man did not know who would perform the operation, and every man of us only waited the blessing of the Superior to take up the lancet and strike the blow. However, he resolved to do it himself, as he had once before bled an Indian successfully. It pleased God that this second operation should also prove successful, and that what was deficient in art should be abundantly supplied by charity. . . .

"God lavished His benedictions on us during this little domestic affliction. Sick and well, none ever were in better spirits. The sick were as willing to live as to die, and their patience, piety, and devotion lightened the care we paid them day and night. As for the Fathers, they enjoyed a blessing scarcely ever granted in France—they received every morning the Holy Sacrament of the altar. From this treasure they drew so much holy resolution and so many good sentiments, that they loved their position dearly, and preferred their poverty to all the ease they might enjoy in France." *

This malady, which had visited the good Fathers before the contagion invaded the Huron villages, was pro-

***

* Relation de la Nouvelle France, 1636.

vidential in every respect. It taught them to rely, above
all, on God's help rather than human remedies ; then it
rendered them better able to do service to the Indians,
when, in their turn, they caught the disease. Their remedies, already tested, gave them more confidence, and their
words gained in weight from this visible protection of the
Master of Life. Had not the disease broken out among
them first, these ignorant and credulous people would
certainly have accused them as the cause of all their
misfortunes, and would have wreaked on them an unjust revenge. Thus good does often come from evil,
and what seems as undeserved punishment is a benefit
at the hands of Providence.

CHAPTER III.

Recovery of the Missionaries—The Huron Language—The Epidemics—Celestial Favors.

FATHER JOGUES, in the full strength of manhood and with an excellent constitution, conquered his disease. God reserved him for a more glorious end. About the middle of October he felt so far recovered as to be able to resume his work. The other patients had a slow convalescence, and all sighed for the time when they could again labor in the vineyard. However, one task adapted to the state of their convalescence was the study of the Huron language—the first indispensable preparation for the Mission.

The cabin had served as an hospital : it now became a school-room ; and Father Jogues with the rest took his place among the pupils of Father de Brébeuf, who was proficient enough to be a teacher to others. But a knowledge of that language was one of the hardest difficulties of the Mission. Two missionaries, who had in France given the best proofs of extraordinary talents, never mastered this language so as to be able to use it in the propagation of the Gospel—its mechanism, constituent elements, and syntax are so very peculiar ; for instance many of our letters are wanting in their alphabet, such as B, F, L, M, P, Q, X, Y. On the other hand, the Hurons give the letters H and K a guttural articulation, which is common to several other Indian languages, but unknown to the French, and which was expressed by Khi. Many of their words seemed formed only of vowels.

Father de Brébeuf remarks, that "undoubtedly this absence of *labials* is the reason why all Indians open their lips so ungracefully."

There are no limits to their compound words, such is the wealth of the language. Nouns and adjectives are conjugated, and verbs undergo infinite modifications.

Before the French arrived, these tribes had no words to express *religion, virtue,* and *science,* and most metaphysical ideas were unknown to them; accordingly, the missionaries were long puzzled to find terms to express our mysteries and explain them. They were often compelled to employ a long string of words to express one.

Father Jogues applied himself earnestly to this uncongenial labor, and God blessed his exertions. He was soon able to be of service. To spare his strength, Father de Brébeuf would not at first permit him to undertake long and painful excursions. He appointed him to superintend the house, and the work of their domestics, as well as the cultivation of the little field adjoining the cabin. The Fathers had already turned to account a few grains of wheat they had received from Europe mingled with other provisions. Carefully grown, these had multiplied, and the husbandmen looked forward to a little harvest, which, in time of need, would supply altar breads. This really came to pass. In 1637 they gathered half a bushel of grain; and moreover, they succeeded in making a small keg of wine from the wild grapes which abounded in those virgin forests.

To satisfy the Indians that the missionaries meant to become identified with them, they adopted much of their way of living as regards food and lodging. Father Jogues adapted himself to all this with the greatest ease. It seemed as if he had lived many years among them. In spite of all the drawbacks of their position they lived up to the forms of a community life.

Two of the laborers in this Mission have left interesting details of the lives of the Huron missionaries, a faithful portrait of their private life, with all its sacrifices, privations, and constraints. Father Chaumonot* writes : " Our dwellings are built of bark, like the Indians', without any interior partition, except for a chapel. For the want of tables and furniture, we eat on the floor and drink out of cups made of bark. All our kitchen and refectory ware consists of a large bark platter filled with *sagamité*, which I can compare to nothing but the paste used for papering walls. We are not much troubled with thirst, for we never use salt, and our food is almost always liquid. Our bed consists of bark, on which we spread a blanket. As for sheets, we have none, even for the sick ; but the greatest inconvenience is the smoke, which, for want of a chimney, fills up the whole cabin and ruins all that we wish to preserve. In certain winds it is unendurable, for it makes the eyes ache dreadfully. In winter nights we have no other light than that of the fire, by which we read our breviary, study the language, and do all that is needed. By day, the opening at the top of the cabin serves as a chimney and a window."

Then Father Francis Duperron,† in a letter of April 27, 1639, gives us their distribution of time for each hour in the day : " At four the bell rings for us to rise, then medi-

---

*Father Chaumonot left in Canada a glorious memory for zeal and virtue. After mission work among the Hurons and Iroquois he was for more than forty years in charge of the fugitive Hurons who had taken refuge near Quebec. He left a most interesting autobiography. He died at Quebec in 1693, at the age of eighty-two, after celebrating the golden jubilee of his priesthood, of his religious life, and of his mission labors.

† Father Francis Duperron arrived in Canada in 1638, labored among the Hurons for twelve years, and returned to Europe after the destruction of that Mission. Though he was in Canada five years afterwards, he was soon recalled. A touching letter is preserved at Rome, which he addressed to the General of the Order, soliciting permission to return to his Mission. He obtained it in 1665 ; but it was only to die there the same year. His brother Joseph Imbert, was also a missionary in Canada for seventeen years. He returned to France in 1658.

tation, after which we celebrate Mass in turn until eight ; silence is kept in the meanwhile, each one being engaged in his spiritual reading, or the recitation of the Little Hours. At eight o'clock we open the door for the Indians, who have access to the cabin until four in the afternoon. Some of the Fathers go their rounds among the cabins. At two o'clock the bell gives the sign for the Examination of Conscience, which is followed by dinner, during which a chapter of the Bible is read, while at supper we read the *Philagie de Jésus*, by Father du Barry. We say grace in Huron, for the sake of the Indians who are present.

"At four o'clock we dismiss the Hurons who are not Christians, and we recite together Matins and Lauds. Then we hold a consultation of three quarters of an hour on the progress or obstacles of the Mission. Then we take up the study of the language until half-past six, when we have supper. At eight o'clock the Litany and Examination of Conscience." *

As soon as Father Jogues had fully recovered he took his share in the apostolic labors of his brethren. He accompanied those most familiar with the language in their excursions ; he rehearsed the catechism with the little ones, he taught them how to pray, and administered baptism to the dying.

Meanwhile the spiritual needs became ever more pressing. A disease began to spread among the Indians. Limited at first to the village where the Fathers resided, it spread to the neighboring towns, and threatened the whole country. The main effort of the Fathers was to find out those who were sick, in order to assist, and, if possible prepare them for baptism. They organized regular visits to the villages, and established a kind of medical service, which became the best means to gain entrance into the cabins.

---

* Manuscript in the Richelieu Library.

The destitution in which the missionaries lived was extreme; their medicines, reduced to the minimum, scarcely deserved the name. A small package of senna was divided into doses for more than fifty persons. The smallest quantity had to serve as remedies, and God gave them sometimes such virtue, that the Indians never doubted their efficacy. The remedy frequently consisted of two or three prunes, five or six raisins, a pinch of sugar in water, a little slice of citron or orange, etc.

The blind confidence of these simple souls in whatever was given them often gave rise to amusing scenes. Once a chief came to ask the Fathers for something to relieve his sister, who was suffering with a violent headache. He pointed to some salve, which he had seen applied to an abscess and had proved efficacious. In vain did the Fathers endeavor to make him understand that it was a different case altogether. He would have his own way. The box of salves was opened, and he insisted that it was just what he required. As he saw salves of different colors, he begged for the white and red and green, and formed one plaster of them, which he laid on the centre of his sister's forehead. His triumph was complete when the next day the patient was relieved.

But the epidemic made immense ravages. The village where the missionaries lived suffered the most, and the misfortune was looked upon as a punishment from God, for in this very spot had His graces met with the greatest neglect and even opposition. The town was so sadly decimated, that shortly after it was abandoned and the inhabitants dispersed among the neighboring villages.

"Although we were every day and all day near the dying," wrote Father Jogues to his mother, May 7, 1638, "in order to gain them to Jesus Christ, and in spite of the pestilential air we breathed near them and around them, not one of us fell sick. After this we should prove ourselves truly ungrateful did we not thank the Lord for so visible a protection on His part, and did we not henceforward put all our trust in His paternal goodness."

The missionaries had not, indeed, awaited this extremity to draw upon themselves celestial favor. In union with his fellow-missionaries and all the French who were in the Huron country, Father de Brébeuf, then Superior of the Mission, had made a solemn vow to obtain protection against the scourge. The priests promised to offer three Masses in honor of Our Lord, of Our Lady, and of St. Joseph, the patron of the country. Those who were not priests were to offer three communions and four rosaries for the same intention.

Although their success with the sick did not correspond to their wishes and efforts, the missionaries did not labor in vain. They acquired a better insight into the Indian character, and heaven seemed ever to gain some elect souls. Thus, in a letter to his brother Samuel, a Capuchin, Father Jogues says: "During the epidemic the Fathers baptized more than one thousand two hundred persons. Even in the village where they were the most exposed to the perversity of the people, there were always some anxious to follow the instructions of our Fathers; about one hundred have been regenerated in the waters of baptism, amongst them twenty-two little children." Whole villages even, as at Ouenrio and Ossossané, begged the intervention of the Fathers to avert the scourge.

Father de Brébeuf selected for his companion Father Jogues when he started for the latter village to meet the wishes of the inhabitants. Father Jogues witnessed all that the zeal of that great servant of God inspired him to adopt at this time which could prove advantageous to the faith. He saw the grand ceremonial followed by those people when they discuss affairs of importance; and Father de Brébeuf took great pains to conform with their rules most scrupulously in order to win their minds more completely to his cause. Thus Father Jogues attended one of the great councils of sachems and war chiefs,

Already the chief movers in the affair had mounted the tops of the cabins, and had repeatedly raised the cry of convocation, and at the appointed hour a large and anxious assembly met. They desired to know what the Black Robe had to say, and all eyes were riveted on his person.

Father de Brébeuf first addressed a prayer to the Great Spirit, and then distributed some pieces of to- bacco, for Indians would regard themselves unfit for any deliberation unless their calumet was lighted. Then he threw into the midst of the assembly a moose-skin, two hatchets, and eighty wampum beads. Any proposition made to Indians must always be affirmed by presents. At this point Father de Brébeuf, with all the freedom which these steps gave him, solemnly told them that Faith alone could remedy all their evils. He earnestly urged them to abandon all their superstitious observ- ances, and to implore God's mercy with perfect confi- dence. " As a warrant of your good-will, and of the sin- cerity of your dispositions, solemnly pledge yourselves,'' said he, " to raise at once a chapel to the Great Spirit in your village." The assembly ended, as usual, with a ban- quet. The Indians all seemed to have been gained over; but their natural inconstancy, and some unforeseen cir- cumstances which occurred, retarded the execution of the pious project. The Fathers had hastened back to Ihonatiria, where a new storm had been raised against the missionaries.

Some Indians who had been at Manhattan Island re- ported that they had been warned by the whites living there (the Dutch) of the danger they ran. " Be on your guard," they said, " against these Catholic missionaries, and above all, the Jesuits—woe to the country into which they effect an entrance ; it will be at once made desolate and utterly ruined: they dare show themselves in Eu- rope no more, and wherever they are caught they are put to death."

Their gross and credulous minds, always easily impressed when their interests are concerned, were soon induced to believe these calumnies, which were magnified by the hatred and fanaticism of some very bad men among them. They at once gave out that the Black Gowns were the authors of the plague, and had in their cabins the sources of all evils. According to some, it was the pictures hung up in the chapel; whilst others avowed that it was the tabernacle on the altar, within which was kept the body of a child killed in the woods and preserved with great care. Everything used by the missionaries, and their most trifling actions, received an unfavorable interpretation. Every little act of devotion, even the sign of the cross, was regarded as a spell cast on them or the cloak of some evil design. A missionary's walk up and down, his recital of his breviary, even the weathercock perched on a pole near the cabin, all to their eyes portended mischief and mystery. The boldest among them would come to the Fathers, entreating them earnestly, even with threats, to stop the scourge or give up their incantations; nor would they listen to any explanation.

The hand of God evidently restrained those wicked men; for the Fathers, altogether defenceless amidst a people who made so light of human life, remained perfectly tranquil. No one dare touch them. This was beautifully expressed by Father Jogues in a letter to his mother: "God was far more powerful to protect those who for His glory had thrown themselves into the arms of His Providence, than men were wicked to hurt them."

It is especially in days of trial and sickness that heathen Indians resort to all sorts of superstitions. Their simplicity leads them to adopt readily whatever they imagine to be a means of relief. Their belief in dreams is unlimited, and never did an Indian refuse anything required for the fulfilment of a dream. They study their **dreams** carefully to find a remedy for their diseases; and when they think they have discovered it, the remedy must be employed at any cost. The medicine-men, always very numerous among them, were the ordinary and interested interpreters of their dreams. Moreover, they had recourse to numberless acts of superstition, which they palmed off as efficacious remedies. Now they would blow on the sick with all their might to drive off the evil spirits; then they would throw into the fire small pieces of tobacco as a sacrifice to the spirits, who were adjured to protect the cabin. They could be seen searching everywhere for the spell which they supposed to be the source of the evil; and when recovery seemed certain, they had tact enough to pretend they had just found it. They almost always had recourse to dances, which Indians like, and which enter largely into their superstition. Sometimes these dances were disgustingly lascivious—generally only grotesque. The dancers assumed the forms of hunchbacks or cripples, and hid behind wooden masks of the most ridiculous and varied forms. Afterwards the masks were attached to manikins placed on the roofs of the cabin, for the purpose of frightening away sickness, and the spirits that are the cause of death In the midst of such coarse vagaries of idolatry, in the presence of a stubborn resistance to the faith, against every kind of calumny aimed at their work and baptism. in continual danger of death, the missionaries had no other comfort than to mourn at the foot of the altar, and pray to God for that unfortunate people. Yet their fervent hearts, burning with zeal for the glory of God, suffered far more from all these impediments placed in the way of the Gospel, than from all the privations entailed by their residence among savages.

To feelings of this kind Father Jogues gave vent in writing to his mother, at a time when the missionaries were denied admittance to any of the great towns. "It had become impossible for us to enter." he wrote, "and we had to endure the harrowing pain of seeing more than a hundred unfortunate people dying before our eyes who in vain entreated our assistance."

This life, crucified in every aspect, might justly be regarded as a protracted martyrdom. Father Jerome Lalemant, after having endured its tortures in person, did not hesitate to state, in the Relation of 1639 : "I had my doubts at first whether we could hope for the conversion of this people without shedding blood. I must acknowledge that since I am here and witness what occurs every day,—I mean the struggles, the general attacks and assaults of every kind, which the evangelical laborers encounter every day, and at the same time their patience, their courage, their unflinching pursuit of their aims,—I begin to doubt whether any other martyrdom is requisite for the end for which we labor ; and I have not the least doubt that many would be found who would rather feel at once the keen edge of a hatchet on their head, than endure for years a life such as we have to live here every day."

Yet the divine Consoler, who dwelt in the midst of His servants, and communed with them every day, upheld their courage. He often rewarded all this long-suffering with some of the unspeakable consolations which are truly a foretaste of the holy joys of heaven.

About this time Father Jogues was deemed worthy of one of these heavenly favors, and although it came to him only in a dream, there were such circumstances attached to it, and its effects had been so beneficial, that his confessor requested him to record it in writing. We are indebted to Father Ragueneau for an extract from it in 1652, which we translate from the Latin :

"On Tuesday, May 4, 1637, the eve of the Ascension of our Lord Jesus Christ, while, after dinner, I was studying the Huron language with Father Chastelain, I felt overcome by sleep, and I begged him to allow me a moment of rest. He advised me to visit the chapel, and rest awhile before the Blessed Sacrament, remarking that he

was in the habit of doing so, and always to the benefit of
his piety, and that in such sleep he had occasionally
enjoyed celestial happiness.

"I arose, but thinking that I could not without irrever-
ence sleep in the awful and adorable presence of my
sovereign Lord, I went to the adjoining woods, much
confused to know that others, even in their sleep, were
more united with God than I in the very act of prayer.

"I had scarcely lain down, when I fell asleep and
dreamed I was singing vespers with the other Fathers
and the domestics. On one side stood Father Peter
Pijart, * close by the door, and I was a little farther
on. I do not know who were on the other side, or in
what order.

"Father Pijart began the first verse of the psalm *Verba
mea auribus percipe, Domine* [Give ear, O Lord ! to my
words] (I do not exactly know the number of it) (Ps. v.).
As he could not continue it alone, we ended it with him.

"When the verse was ended, I seemed to be no longer
in our cabin, but in a place I knew not, when all at once
I heard verses sung (I forget which) which had reference to the happiness of the Saints, and the delights they
enjoy in the kingdom of heaven. The chanting was so
beautiful, and the melody of voices and instruments so
harmonious, that I have no recollection of ever having
heard the like, and it even seems to me that the most
perfect concerts are nothing compared to it. To compare such harmony with that of earth would be insulting.

"Meanwhile this most admirable concert of the angels excited in my heart a love of God so great, so ardent, so burning, that, unable to bear such an overflow-

---

* Father Peter Pijart, after fifteen years on the Canada Mission,
returned to France in 1650. His elder brother, Claude, came over two
years after him, and died at Quebec in 1683, aged eighty-three, in
high repute for virtue.

ing of sweetness, my poor heart seemed to melt and di-
late under this inexplicable wealth of divine love. I experienced this feeling especially as they sang the verse I
so well remember, *Introibimus in tabernaculum ejus, adora-
bimus in loco ubi steterunt pedes ejus* [We will go into His
tabernacle, we will adore in the place where His feet
stood (Ps. cxxxi. 7)].

"While yet half asleep, I began at once to think that
it all was in accord with the words Father Chastelain had
spoken to me.

"I awoke soon after, and all disappeared, but there
lingered in my soul so great a consolation that its remembrance filled me with inexpressible delights. The
fruit I have derived is, it seems to me, that I feel more
drawn, for the love of our Lord, to pant after the celestial country and eternal joys. Happy moment ! oh, how
short ! I do not think it lasted longer than it takes to
recite a Hail Mary. If, O Lord! thou dealest with us
thus in our exile, what wilt Thou give unto us in our
home ?" [St. Augustine.]

CHAPTER IV.

**New Residences—Saint Mary—Mission among the Tionontate
Nation—Voyage to Sault Sainte Marie.**

THE dispersion of the village of Ihonatiria was necessarily followed by the departure of the missionaries.   They settled in two great villages, to which
they had already made regular visits, and where they had
a number of fervent converts.

Ossossané, called Conception by the Fathers, was already considered a residence, as a chapel, with a cabin
for the missionaries, had been established there for more
than a year.   Father Jogues had visited it several times,
and in 1639, writing to his brother Samuel, he says:
" Our poor Indians treat us as true friends.   We have in
Ossossané a cabin thirteen fathoms in length.   A chapel
has been built entirely of boards, which attracts the eyes
and the admiration of all the inhabitants.   Besides the
conversations we hold every day in each cabin, we have
a public catechism class every Sunday in our own, when
many of the sachems of the nation attend, headed by a
family of Christians of seven or eight persons.   Thus
does God still the tempest and bring peace ' at His
will.' "

The other village, which was especially to replace
Ihonatiria, was Teanaustayae, called also St. Joseph.   It
was one of the largest in the country.   Here the Faith
had warm followers as well as fierce enemies, who were
the earnest promoters of all the calumnies invented
against the Gospel and its apostles.   To gain a complete triumph over the systematic opposition which some
miscreants kept up against admitting the missionaries,

Father de Brébeuf, after making sure of the presence of devoted friends, boldly appeared before the assembly of the sachems, pleaded his own cause, and gained it.

The first mass was celebrated in this town on the 25th of June, 1638, in the cabin of the brave Stephen Totiri, whom we shall meet again, sharing the captivity and tortures of Father Jogues. This Father was one of the first residents at the post. He happily began his ministry by the baptism of an Iroquois prisoner, who was running the horrible gauntlet of torture ; and in the first year he regenerated in baptism forty-eight children and seventy-two adults.

However, the foundation of these two residences satisfied neither the hopes of the missionaries nor the needs of the country. Hence, in 1639, they resolved not to remain separated, but to select a central site, apart from any Huron town and completely independent. This they would make their centre of action, from which they could proceed in any direction as they were required. This course enabled them to consult quietly as to the best means to forward the welfare of the Mission, and afforded a place of rest to those whose courage exceeded their strength, and for all when they wished to reanimate their souls by the holy exercises of a retreat. They made choice of a solitary spot in the northeastern part of the Huron peninsula. It lay in the tribe of the Attaronchronons, almost in the very centre of the land, and on the banks of a small river (the Wye), which near it empties into the great lake. It is a point from which there was easy communication with all parts of the country. This plan was strongly approved in Europe, and Cardinal Richelieu, not content with mere words of commendation, promised a large sum to build a fort on the spot, and maintain a small garrison. The fathers, in their isolated position, needed this defence against the frequent and sudden inroads of the Iroquois.

The new establishment was called *The Residence of St.*

Mary, and work was commenced at once. A vast inclosure of palisades formed a first rectangular defence; part of the inclosed ground was to serve for tillage and part for a cemetery. At the four corners a cross was erected to show that it was dedicated to the Lord. Within the palisade was the fort inclosing the house of the French and the chapel. Not far from these were two large cabins—one to serve as a hospital for sick Indians, the other a hospice for travellers. It soon became a place of great resort for the Indians, especially for the Christians. "The exterior splendor of our ceremonies," writes Father Ragueneau; "the beauty of our chapel, which, though poverty itself, is regarded in this country as one of the wonders of the world; the masses, sermons, vespers, processions, and benedictions, all performed with a pomp unknown to the Indians—gives them some idea of the majesty of God, whilst they are made to understand that He is honored all over the world with a worship a thousand times more solemn."

The catechumens came here to be finally instructed, and the good Christians to advance in the practice of their religion; the sick to obtain relief in body and comfort in soul; some even to beg but one thing—the privilege of dying near their fathers, and resting in peace in blessed ground.

Father Jogues took an active part in the foundation of the Residence of St. Mary, and from the very first he was appointed to superintend the work of putting up the palisade, which gave him charge over the domestics and some fifteen laborers. They were the only French then among the Hurons. The Governors of Canada would not allow any to settle except under the supervision of the missionaries, in order to prevent the great disorders which had in early times given great scandal, still brought up against religion.

Father Jogues found in them simple and docile hearts, exemplary for their virtue and devotedness. There were some among them who formed a special class in Canada, and rendered the greatest services to the mission. They were called *donnés*,* for they gave themselves by contract and for life to the service of the Mission, without pay. The Mission enjoyed the benefit of their work, and were bound to provide for all their wants as long as they lived. They took the place of lay-brothers, whom it was impossible to secure in number large enough for the wants of the Mission; and not being bound by vows, these *donnés* formed, as it were, an intermediate class between the religious and servants. At the time we write there were only six of them, but in 1649 there were as many as twenty-three. The care of temporal affairs did not absorb Father Jogues' time so exclusively that he could not aid the three Fathers attached to the post in the labors of the ministry. He took care of the numbers of Indians who visited them, and made frequent excursions to four little villages in the neighborhood, which had been left to the care of the Fathers of Saint Mary.

A difficult mission was intrusted to his care in 1640. He was detailed with Father Charles Garnier to attempt the establishing of a mission in a neighboring nation which had not yet been visited by the missionaries. After being for a long time hostile to the Hurons, it had just concluded a close alliance with them. Similar in habits and language, it shared the same apprehensions of danger from the Iroquois. This seemed the favorable time to speak to them of the Faith.

---

* This new class and title, instituted by the members of the Society of Jesus, and for their service excited criticism and complaint, which were carried to Rome. Some regarded it as an innovation, and the introduction of a kind of third order like that existing in several religious orders, but not in use in the Society. Father Jerome Lalemant drew up in 1643 a memoir to justify this course and remove the fears. He received the approbation of his Superiors (Archives of the Gesù, Rome).

It was the nation of the Tionontates, called Petun or Tobacco Indians by the French, on account of their large trade in that plant, of which they seemed to have almost a monopoly. They lived about thirty miles southwest of the Hurons, in what are now called the Blue Mountains. As there were no open roads or means of transportation, travel in winter could be made only on foot and with snow-shoes.* In that season, too, the streams could not obstruct travel, nor was there much danger from the Iroquois. But whether from fear of the enemy or misgivings of the undertaking, the guides of the missionaries played false at the moment of starting. There was no other resource left but to trust to vague information, which rendered their route anything but certain. But heroic souls enjoy the loss of all human means, in order to trust more generously to Divine providence. And thus did these men of God act. They started under the guidance of God and of His holy angels. Before they had accomplished half the distance they lost their way, and were forced to stop and pass the night in the woods. They had learned from the Indians to clear the snow from the spot where they intended to make their beds of spruce-branches, and to raise around them a little breastwork as a shelter against the wind. Then they lighted an immense fire to keep the frost off, and lay down to sleep.

The next morning they started again at haphazard, their whole provisions consisting of a piece of bread; but at last, at eight o'clock at night, footsore and exhausted, they reached the first hamlet of the Tionontate nation. Well acquainted with the ready hospitality of the Indians, with whom the stranger is always welcome, they boldly entered the first cabin they reached to spend the night.

---

* Snow-shoes are fastened firmly under the feet, and keep a person from sinking in the snow. The French call them *raquettes* from their resemblance to the *racket* used in some games of ball.

They knew it not; but Providence was guiding them by its hand for the salvation of a poor soul. The news of the arrival of the black-gown was soon known. In a few moments a young man arrived in haste, who wished the missionaries for a woman lying sick in his cabin. She was a poor creature at the point of death, and she had but one desire—to be admitted to the prayer of the French. The Fathers, hastening to the spot, found a predestined soul filled with all the ineffable blessings of grace. She had the happiness of receiving baptism and breathed her last in peace.

But hell was alarmed at the coming triumphs of the Faith: it let loose its agents, and the calumnies spread among the Hurons found their way, with a tenfold increase of terror, through all the villages. The two Fathers inspired such terror that often women and children fled at their approach. A chief with whom they lodged was a prey to the greatest apprehensions. He told them his fears, and no explanations could allay them. Their slightest actions, even their kneeling at prayer, seemed to him some act of sorcery. He resorted to every means to make them depart, as he could not violate the laws of hospitality by driving them out. Above all, he feared lest in a moment of exasperation some Indians might come and put the strangers to death in his cabin; for among the Indians any one has a right to kill a sorcerer, but no one wishes his own cabin defiled by blood.

Persecution attained such a height that the missionaries could scarcely remain two days at a time in one village. Sometimes they would hear their hosts start up at night and order them out of the house at once; others would shout to them from outside that they must leave before daybreak, and without stopping in the village, or else they would tomahawk them.

The two Fathers had spent two months in these incessant perils without having the least chance of making any stable mission: they resolved to return; yet their labor had not been fruitless. They had surveyed the ground and prepared the way. The next year, Father Charles Garnier returned and formed a flourishing church, known as the Mission of the Apostles. In 1649 he bedewed it with his blood.

By this time Father Jogues was looked upon as an experienced missionary, and was again detailed for important duties.

In 1641, some Indians of Algonquin origin, called Ottawas,* descended from the shores of Lake Superior to visit the Algonquin tribes dwelling near the Hurons, and to witness their great Feast of the Dead. This was a solemn occasion with these wild tribes, and its celebration occurred only every ten or twelve years. Some of the missionaries who resided among the Hurons had attended these Algonquin tribes, and reckoned among them a good number of converts. These Fathers were at hand, during this great gathering, in order to open intercourse with the visiting tribes, and thus open new paths for the Gospel.

Impressed with what they had heard of the prayer of the French, and what they saw with their own eyes, the Ottawas readily accepted the advances of the missionaries, who willingly agreed to visit them in the fall, at Sault Sainte-Marie,† when those nomadic tribes assembled to catch white-fish.

Father Jogues, now well versed in the Huron language,

---

* The Ottawas were a tribe living on the upper lakes, and closely connected with the Chippewas, called Sauteux by the French, from their residing at Sault Sainte-Marie; but the word Ottawa was loosely applied to all the Western Algonquins, and the Ottawa River received its name from the fact that it was the route to the Ottawa country.— Ed.

† The Hurons called this rapid Skiae, and the first French explorers named it Sault de Gaston. It took the name of Sault Sainte-Marie, which it still retains, from a Mission founded there about 1669.

was associated with Father Charles Raymbault,* who had mastered the Algonquin, and they took their departure for Sault Sainte-Marie on the 17th of September, 1641. Able to speak these two mother-tongues, they could converse with any Indians they might encounter. They had before them a journey of 250 miles, to be made in their birch-canoe over the great Lake Huron, coasting the northern shores, through the forest of islets which border it. Upwards of two thousand Indians were awaiting them, and gave them a flattering reception. The Fathers reciprocated as usual with presents and feasts. The chief of the Chippewas desired something more: he raised his voice in the name of his tribe, and made the strongest appeal, in order to retain the missionaries among them. Said he: "Stay with us: we will embrace you like brothers; we will learn from you the prayer of the French, and we will be obedient to your words" (Rel. 1641).

---

* Father Raymbault had been in Canada from 1637, but his delicate constitution could not endure the hard Mission life. After this excursion he returned to Quebec, utterly exhausted, and aware that the end of the struggle had arrived. He died there October 22, 1642, aged forty-one. "The self-denying man," says Bancroft, "who had glowed with the hope of bearing the Gospel across the continent, through all the American Barbary, even to the ocean that divides America from China, ceased to live; and the body of this first apostle of Christianity to the tribes of Michigan was buried in 'the particular sepulchre' which the justice of that age had 'erected expressly to honor the memory of the illustrious Champlain. Thus the climate made one martyr." He was the first Jesuit who died in Canada. A touching incident is told of the close of his life: He had long desired to gain to the Faith an Algonquin chief who had shown great kindness to the missionaries. He did not gain him till the last moment, so that he may be said to have died triumphant. "Mangouch," he said to him in a failing voice, "you see that I am surely going to die. At this time I would not deceive you. Believe me when I assure you that there is below a fire which will burn for eternity those who refuse to believe." This truth, which the Indian had frequently heard without heeding, now struck him like a thunderbolt, when it came from the lips of a dying man. He became a fervent Christian.

It was not possible to yield at once to this earnest appeal. The small number of missionaries, and the ever-increasing wants of the Huron Mission forbade them to divide their forces. They had advanced so far only like the bold explorers of new lands, to examine the soil, to know the inhabitants, and prepare a way to the conquests of Faith, when the proper time should arrive; but the road was open, and the first seed planted.

The missionaries did not depart from this hospitable land without leaving behind a token of their presence—a mark, as it were, that they had taken possession in the name of the Gospel. They raised a tall cross on the banks of the river, to show the limits reached by the preaching of its apostles. They made it face the immense Valley of the Mississippi, to which their attention had been called in a vague manner, but which they were told was inhabited by numerous tribes of nations still unknown.

The end had been attained. Furnished with valuable information, the two envoys of the Faith returned to their Huron Mission before winter. There was plenty of labor in that field, but it attained success only at the cost of many trials and sacrifices.

Father Jogues resumed his peaceful and humble duties at the Residence of St. Mary; but the call to stern combats was about to be sounded. He was to meet the most formidable, the most ferocious enemy, both of the Hurons and of the Christian Faith—the Iroquois.*

---

* According to Charlevoix, the name Iroquois was given to this people by the French. It comes from the word *Hiro* or *Hero—I have said it*, with which, like the old Romans, they ended their speeches, and *Koué*, a guttural cry, more or less prolonged, which they then uttered to uphold their words. The learned George Horn sought a more remote origin, but less probable. In his work *De Origine Americanorum* he makes the people and the name descend from the Ircans of Herodotus.

CHAPTER V.

The Iroquois—Father Jogues goes down to Quebec—His Captivity.

ALTHOUGH not the most numerous,* yet the Iroquois were the most terrible of all tribes then known to the French in Canada. They did not thirst after wealth, for the passion of riches does not enter the heart of the savage, but they would admit no rival in their ascendancy over the rest. Successful in all their undertakings for fifty years past, they were drunk with pride. Their name inspired terror far and near. All their neighbors had learned at bitter cost to dread their warlike valor, which was equalled only by its own cruelty. Their arrogance, as well as their superiority over adjoining tribes, was increased by the fact that the Hollanders of Manhattan had begun just then to supply them with fire-arms.

The Iroquois formed a kind of federal republic, composed of five cantons or nations, called by the French from their own names, Agniers, Oneiouts, Onontagués, Goiogoens, and Tsonnontouans, though the English colonists styled them the Mohawks, Oneidas, Onondagas, Cayugas, Senecas, and collectively the Five Nations. They were commanded, like all Indian tribes, by chiefs or captains, and public affairs were administered by the great councils of the Sachems. Each canton had its own separate political existence, and was independent in the administration of its internal affairs. In a common cause they united and supported each other.

---

* According to the Relation of 1660, the Iroquois cantons then had a population of 25,000, the warriors being one tenth that number.

The geographical position favored their warlike instincts, their hunts, and external relations. Ranged along the southern shores of the Lake Ontario, and on the Mohawk River, from the Niagara to the Hudson, they had easy access on the west to the great lakes, and even to the Mississippi, and on the east they could easily, in their light canoes, reach the Atlantic.

The Agniers (Mohawks), nearest to the Dutch post of Rensselaerswyck (the Albany of our day), where we shall soon meet Father Jogues, carried on a brisk traffic with the Europeans, exchanging their rich peltries, the great object of mercantile cupidity, for arms employed in war or hunting. But intercourse with the Dutch was most fatal to the Indians, as it fostered their intense avidity for spirituous liquors, and imbued them with feelings of hatred against the Catholic faith and its apostles. For some years the Mohawks had waged a relentless war on the Indian tribes which were allied to the French, and especially the Hurons and the Algonquins, who traded the most with the colony in Canada. The Mohawks descended by Lake Champlain and the river Richelieu, long known by their name, and were ready to attack and plunder the flotillas of canoes, as they made their way to or from the French posts.

At this time the French had only little cities, or rather posts, in those distant regions—Quebec and Three Rivers. The palisades which inclosed them were guarded only by a few soldiers. Had the Iroquois known their weakness, and attacked with more skill, the colony could not have resisted long. At first they seemed only to covet the blood of the Indians and their goods; but the presence of the French, whose dominion they feared, and whose religion they hated as repugnant to their savage instincts, goaded them to a war for the destruction of both the native tribes and the new-comers. They constantly beset the Ottawa River. Their warriors, in bands of twenty, fifty, or one hundred, were posted along a line of more than two hundred and fifty miles, and in most advantageous positions, so as to command all the passes. A party escaping one band was sure to fall into the hands of another. Well aware of the influence of the French over their allies, the Iroquois were anxious to capture a *pale-face,* and above all a black-gown. Father Jogues became their victim.

The information we have as to the terrible sufferings of his captivity and of accompanying events is drawn from the recitals of Christian captives who succeeded in making their escape, and from two long letters in which the pious missionary relates the main incidents to his Superiors. One of these, full of charm and candor, is written in terse and elegant Latin; it is a precious record of his trials, all the more entitled to credit from the fact of its coming from the pen of a man who always avoided publicity, and whose modesty only obedience could overcome. Piety and humility are his plea for describing these sad days in Latin: "I could more easily employ the very words of our sacred books,"* he writes with great simplicity; "they formed my greatest consolation in my extreme trials, and at the same time this letter will be less easily read."

His brethren, to whom he loved to unbosom his heart in conversation, succeeded in obtaining from him many details which he had buried in profound silence, and of whose merit he seemed unconscious. In what we shall relate it is Father Jogues, who to a great extent is the narrator.

While returning from the Chippewas, Father Jogues had, in his intercourse with God, apparently been favored with some revelation of what was to befall him. While prostrate before the Blessed Sacrament, and earnestly beseeching our Lord to allow him to drink of the chalice of His sufferings in order to labor more efficaciously for

---

* The references to the Bible are added by us; Father Jogues cited only from memory.

the glory of His holy name, he heard as it were a voice replying to the aspirations of his heart, *Thy prayer is heard* (Acts x. 31); thou shalt have what thou hast asked (4 Kings ii. 10); *take courage and be strong* (Jos. i. 6). These words sank in his heart with an impression akin to the certainty of faith. He never forgot them: amidst his tortures they bore him up. He never doubted but they had been uttered by Him who knows the future, and who alone can make man invincible in struggles which exceed our natural strength.

Father Jerome Lalemant,* then Superior of the Huron Mission, unaware of what had passed between God and His servant, had chosen him for a very perilous undertaking,—a journey to Quebec,—on business connected with the Mission. While proposing to Father Jogues to accept it, he left him free to decline the dangerous undertaking.

At that time it was a most dangerous expedition, for the great river swarmed with Iroquois warriors, who seemed frantic with rage. To accept the task assigned was risking almost certainly loss of liberty, and even of life.

The year before the French had rejected peace, because the terms offered by the Iroquois were, as will be seen, impossible. In February, 1641, two young men, Francis Marguerie and Thomas Godefroy, were surprised by the Iroquois while hunting. The track of their snow-shoes enabled the enemy to surprise and carry them off to their country. They were at first objects of curiosity. Some Iroquois who had been prisoners among the French took them under their protection, and one of them, in recognition of former favors received from Marguerie, declared boldly that the captives should not be

---

* Father Jerome Lalemant was twice Superior-General in Canada. "He is the holiest man I ever knew," wrote the Ven. Mother Mary of the Incarnation. He died at Quebec in 1673, aged eighty.

put to death; he even offered presents for their ransom. The matter was debated in a council, and it was resolved to employ the aid of the two Frenchmen in securing a treaty of peace. Five hundred warriors set out on this errand; but some of them took post along the great river St. Lawrence to plunder the Hurons and Algonquins, whilst the rest, to the number of three hundred and fifty, arrived at Three Rivers in the beginning of June. Early one morning a man was seen approaching alone in a canoe, hoisting a white flag in token of peace. It was Marguerie. He announced in the name of the Iroquois, that he came to treat of peace with the French, but not with the Indians. Privately he informed our people that it was the plan of the Iroquois to conquer our allies, to exterminate them, and thus to become masters of the whole country.

The Governor of Quebec, on being informed of the fact, went up to Three Rivers; and meanwhile the French-man returned to the Iroquois with another Frenchman, who took a large supply of food. Father Ragueneau, also Superior of the Mission, visited their camp and was well received; but they did not disguise their hostile feel-ings towards the other Indians, and even during these preliminaries some Algonquins were surprised and mur-dered by Iroquois runners.

Governor de Montmagny arrived at last, and was re-ceived with a salvo of musketry. Father Ragueneau and Mr. Nicolet* were appointed to discuss the condi-tions of peace.

A council was held in the camp of the Iroquois, on the 10th of June, with great solemnity. Onagan, one of the chiefs, made an able speech, offered presents, and set the two Frenchmen free. The Governor consented to a

---

* Nicolet, at first merely an Indian interpreter, deserves, for the ser-vices he rendered, an honorable place in Canadian history. He ar-rived in 1618, and was drowned in 1642. He is the first Frenchman who reached the Mississippi, about 1639.

peace provided his Indian allies were included. Seeing that they could not attain their end, the Iroquois dissembled, and while deferring their answer, they insulted the French, and even fired on their boat. The Governor then ordered a general discharge of his artillery; but the Indians had sought cover, and the following night they decamped.

This was the signal of a more bitter war than ever.

During this short armistice Father de Brébeuf had left the Hurons in very bad health, and had escaped the Iroquois, who lay in wait for him. Father Jogues was not so fortunate. He knew that the negotiations were broken off, and that hatred had revived in the hearts of the Iroquois; but he had been made ready for the sacrifice long ere this. "They only proposed this voyage to me," he said. "I received no command; I offered to go the more willingly, as its necessity would have thrown some better missionary than myself into the dangers we foresaw." Thus was the victim prepared for the sacrifice in charity and humility. In his wonted deference to the will of his Superior he took this proposal as an order from heaven, and he prepared to fulfil it by a retreat of eight days and a general confession.

On the 2d of June, 1642, four canoes were moored at the little harbor of St Mary. They were freighted with precious peltry, to be used by the Indians for bartering in the colony. Twenty warriors, most of them Christians, formed this party, which required tried courage and energetic souls. Three Frenchmen, with Father Jogues and Father Raymbault, whose shattered health needed a change of climate, completed the caravan.

At a given signal, the paddles, plied with skill, sent the canoes with the intrepid travellers over the smooth waters, amid the benedictions of the Fathers, and the God-speeds of kindred and friends from the shore. It took thirty-five days to reach Three Rivers. This passage of more than six hundred miles was seldom accomplished without alarm, hardships, and dangers. But no enemy appeared. The only drawback they met was the wreck of two canoes while shooting a rapid, and the loss of part of their baggage.

During this long passage Father Jogues did not allow his zeal to rest. He divided his time between the care of his sick companion, and practices of piety, regularly observed by the whole party. Prayers were said aloud morning and evening, and he improved their precarious situation to inspire them with fear lest they should die in a state of mortal sin. Then he employed his time in keeping up the fervor of the Christian converts by pious discourses, and completed the instruction of the catechumens, so that they should be prepared to receive baptism in case of danger. Without tarrying long at Three Rivers, the pious party soon passed on to Quebec, the end of their journey. They were received with every manifestation of joy, and with fervent thanks to God. The Fathers in Quebec eagerly listened to the accounts of the labors and sufferings of their brethren, and rejoiced at the opportunity of being able to send them some help. Great was the edification with which the colony of Quebec impressed the Indians. The convents of the Ursulines and Hospital Nuns * seemed to attract their attention. They never tired in visiting them ; all seemed wonderful in their eyes.

Their surprise increased when they were told of all that these holy virgins had sacrificed—their family ties, the comforts of their native land, every convenience in

---

* These two precious houses, the supports of faith in Canada and one of its glories, have continued uninterruptedly from 1639 to our time, developing their mission of charity and zeal with the necessities around them. The Duchess of Aiguillon, Richelieu's niece, founded the Hôtel-Dieu or Hospital at Quebec, at the same time that Madame de la Peltrie, a rich young widow of Alençon, established the Ursulines there, with the celebrated Ven. Mother Mary of the Incarnation as their Superior.

life—in order to come to encourage and teach them, impelled only by the love of God and love of their neighbors.

The Mission of Sillery, founded for the Algonquins by the Commander of that name, two miles and a half from the city, was then at the height of its fervor. The Hurons were impressed as deeply as they had been by the communities at Quebec. There they beheld the wonders wrought by prayer in hearts not long ago idolatrous, and abandoned to vice and superstition. The change filled them with esteem and love for the Faith.

The Indians soon transacted their business. The rich furs were readily exchanged for hatchets, iron pots, glass beads, knives, awls, blankets, fire-arms, powder and shot. The barter was mutually advantageous, and was easily effected.

Father Jogues meanwhile had received packages and provisions to the amount of about two thousand dollars, all to be appropriated to the Huron Mission.* There were vestments, altar-plate, articles to decorate the churches, and some books—a precious treasure for a country destitute of everything. He was also intrusted with letters for the missionaries.

After nineteen days spent in Quebec, and when all arrangements had been made, the fervent missionary was anxious to retrace his steps. He desired to rejoin his brethren, and afford them some relief in their life of privation. He re-embarked with the same courage and trust in God that had inspired him at the outset. His party had received an increase. Some Hurons who had remained at Quebec from the previous year resolved to profit by this opportunity of returning to their country. The presence of the servant of God seemed to inspire them with confidence. Two Frenchmen, René Goupil

---

* The Mission then comprised fourteen Jesuit Fathers, some lay-brothers, and other Frenchmen in charge of their temporal affairs, in all thirty-three persons (Relation, 1641–42).

and William Couture, men of great virtue and tried devotedness, took passage also for the Hurons. Both were *donnés* of the Mission, and merited what Father Jerome Lalemant said of them in the Relation of 1643 : " These two young men were above all praise in their way, and were fitted for this country." A young Huron woman, Teresa Oïouhaton, from the town of Ossossané, who for two years had been under the care of the Ursulines, and had admirably profited by their training, joined the party to return home with her uncle, Joseph Theondechoren. Only by the authority of . Father Jogues could she be prevailed on to leave the Sisters, to whom she clung with the tenderest affection. Her love of virtue made her shrink from the sight of scandals. But the missionaries based great hopes on her example and influence for the Faith. God had other designs in her regard. Notwithstanding her youth, her virtue was to shine amid the dangers and trials of captivity.

This pious party formed a fleet of twelve canoes, carrying forty persons. History has preserved the names of some of those gallant companions of Father Jogues —men who will play a glorious part in the sad scenes we are soon to describe. Among them were Joseph Theondechoren, Charles Tsondatsaa, Stephen Totiri and another Stephen, Theodore, Paul Ononhoraton, and above all, Eustace Ahasistari, as well as his nephew.* Father Jogues left Quebec with his numerous companions at the end of July. It was an event for the little city : its pious inhabitants were too much interested in the progress of the Faith not to crowd around them, help them aboard, and give them a hearty God-speed, with a thousand benedictions.

The convoy halted a short time at Three Rivers, where Governor de Montmagny† then was, carrying out a

---

* See Appendix.

† The Hurons and Iroquois called him Onnontio (great or beautiful mountain), and the name became the official one of his successors, to whom this term was always given.

measure regarded as a highly important defence against the Iroquois. By order of the Cardinal Prime Minister, he was about to erect a fort at the mouth of the river by which these savages made their inroads on the colony. He named it Fort Richelieu.* Foreseeing the danger to which the missionary and his Hurons were exposed, the Governor insisted upon detailing some soldiers for their escort, but either from a feeling of pride or false security the Huron chiefs obstinately refused the offer. An Indian never believes in danger until he faces it. Yet they took many precautions, and above all, they earnestly prayed to Heaven to be taken under its protection. At Three Rivers they celebrated the feast of St. Ignatius, and all received Holy Communion. The next day, just before embarking, the Hurons held a council, as is usual with the Indians in critical affairs, in order to encourage each other. It showed the influence which Faith had acquired over their hearts. One of the chiefs said : " Is there any amongst us who would renounce his belief in God were he to be burned by our enemies ? We are Christians to be happy in heaven, not on this earth !" They all applauded the words, and professed to be of the same sentiment.

Ahasistari spoke last, and he did it as a Christian hero : " Brothers, should I fall into the hands of the Iroquois, I cannot hope for life ; but before I die I shall ask them, ' What have the Europeans brought into their country ?— hatchets, blankets, pots, guns. And I will say to them, They love you not : they hide from you the most costly of all ware, which the French give us without barter. They have made us acquainted with a God who has created all things, an eternal fire destined for those who offend Him, and a place of happiness everlasting for those

---

* Now Sorel, or William Henry. This Fort Richelieu must not be confounded with another of the same name erected by Champlain in 1634 on Isle Ste. Croix, thirty-seven miles above Quebec, but which was not long maintained.

who serve Him, when our souls and our bodies, which will one day arise again, shall be in glory.' And I will say again, 'Behold my great happiness. Wreak now all your cruelties on my body; by your torments you will separate my soul from it, but you cannot tear this hope from my heart.'" Then turning to Charles Tsondatsaa : "My brother, if it be God's will that I fall captive to the enemy, and you escape, return to my country, bring my relations together, and tell them, for the love of me, and much more of themselves, to embrace the Prayer. Prayer alone can strengthen and give comfort. If they follow the part of Faith, we shall one day be united. God, the Master of life, is all my hope ; and wherever I may be I shall live and die for Him."

Such language carries us back to the time when the Christians of the primitive Church encouraged each other to martyrdom. How beautiful to witness in savage hearts, yet infants in the Faith, the same resignation, the same fervor, and the same earnestness !

On the second day of August our travellers entered their canoes and began their journey under happy auspices. All seemed to favor their undertaking. The first day they made thirty miles,* and in the evening they landed on the bank facing the islands in Lake St. Peter,† to camp for the night. They started betimes the next day, hugging the shore, to avoid the current. Whilst some at the head of the flotilla were on shore towing their canoe, they were brought to a halt, a little more than a mile after starting, by the discovery of a fresh Indian trail on the sand. 'They are Iroquois," cried some. "No ; Algonquins," others replied. The brave Ahasistari, whose experience and virtue inspired respect, put

---

* Charlevoix ("History of New France"), misled by a note of Mother Mary of the Incarnation, incorrectly makes the capture of Father Jogues occur fifteen or sixteen leagues from Quebec.

† A wide part of the river a little above Three Rivers.

an end to the discussion by exclaiming, "Friend or
foe, what does it matter? If we trust to this trail, they
are only a few ; what need we fear?" In his brave im-
petuosity he forgot that they were in a hostile country,
and that all was to be feared from men whose cunning
was only equalled by their fury.

In fact, near by a band of seventy Iroquois lay in ambush, led by a Huron traitor adopted among the Mohawks : a vile apostate * who used his knowledge of the
route usually followed by his countrymen to lie in wait
for them at a secure spot and surprise them as they
passed. Hidden among the reeds and rushes, they
awaited their prey. As soon as they saw it in reach they
rose, and with fearful yells poured in a volley of musketry. Only one Huron was wounded—in the hand ;
but many canoes were riddled, and their occupants took
refuge in the nearest woods, carrying along a number of
the Hurons before they had time to take in the situation and organize their defence. Disorder in an army
is almost always the forerunner of defeat, and if able
commanders can at times control its results, with Indians it is impossible.

Eustace, on beholding the enemy, fell on his knees,
and cried, "O God! in Thee alone I trust." For his
part, Father Jogues, forgetful of all but his priestly
duty, thought of the salvation of souls: he offered a
short prayer with those who were preparing to repel the
attack, and who indeed fought gallantly. His first care
was for Bernard Atieronhonte, the steersman of his canoe,
and the only one in it who had not yet been baptized,
although for some time a catechumen. He had himself
solicited this favor before confronting the risks of battle,

---

* Known as Mathurin's man, because, before his capture by the
Iroquois and adoption of their hatred of the French, he had guided to
Quebec a young man named Mathurin, who had rendered the Huron
missionaries great services, and who, returning to France, became a
Capuchin.

and he received it with joy and calmness, while the bul-
lets were whizzing around and the welkin rang with the
war-cry. It was the last act of the priest in his freedom, and it was rewarded with God's benedictions; for
Bernard, after he had made his escape from the Iroquois,
always remained a faithful Christian. He related with
deep emotion the heroic charity of the good missionary
at that critical moment: "I thank God that I entered
the Church by such a way, and I shall never forget that
beautiful day. The self-devotion of my Father was
enough to confirm me in my faith. Who could, then,
withstand belief? Indeed, these men who come to teach
us must be very certain of the truth they preach, and
look to God alone for the only reward they seek, for
Ondesonk* forgot himself altogether in the moment of
the greatest danger, to think only of me. Instead of
seeking safety for himself, he baptized me; he loved me
more than himself. Death here below had no terrors
for him, but he was alarmed for my eternal death."

Meanwhile a dozen Hurons stood their ground and
continued the struggle. Whilst gallantly fighting, they
saw some forty Iroquois, who lay in ambush on the
other side of the river, crossing to re-enforce their comrades. The odds became too great: they fled in haste,
leaving behind a few who still fought bravely on. At
their head was René Goupil, a young man of admirable
intrepidity and of still greater virtue. He soon found
himself almost alone, facing the whole host of enemies.
With some Hurons who fought beside him, he was at last
surrounded and taken.

Father Jogues had gained the shore, and, concealed
behind bushes and reeds near the battle-ground, watched
the fight, resigned to whatever its result might be.
The Iroquois passed by him several times in their pursuit of the fugitives, but had not seen him. Had he re-

---

* Father Jogues' Huron name.

mained there he would have escaped captivity; but let us hear him express the feelings of his heart when he beheld the complete defeat of the Hurons and the capture of the last of the warriors: "The thought of flight never entered my mind; besides, I was barefooted.* How could I fly? Could I abandon that good Frenchman, the Hurons already captive, and those that would eventually be also taken, some of them not yet baptized?" He wavered not, and looking upon it as providential that a chance was offered him to devote himself to the service of God and the salvation of the poor Huron prisoners, he resolved to brave all the tortures of the Iroquois rather than abandon his neophytes to the fires of hell. The good shepherd gave his life for his sheep.

He accordingly arose, and calling to one of the guard placed over the prisoners, he cried: "Know that I am their fellow-traveller, and it is proper that I should share their captivity. You can take hold of me; with all my heart I wish to partake their destiny." The Iroquois, fearing an ambush, dared not approach him. He could not credit such noble devotedness and such a proof of friendship; but assured by the manner of the servant of God, and seeing no one near him, he came forward. "He took me by the arms," writes Father Jogues, "and placed me with those whom the world calls unfortunate. I embraced René most affectionately, and said to him, 'O my brother, God's intention in our regard is mysterious; but He is the Lord: let Him do what is good in His sight (1 Kings iii. 18). As it hath pleased the Lord, so it is done; blessed be the name of the Lord forever." (Job i. 21.)

The youth threw himself on his knees, made his confession, and offered his life to God. Profiting by the last moments of freedom, the missionary gave his final in-

---

* Indians require all to enter the canoes barefooted, so as to bring in no earth or sand.

struction to the catechumens, and baptized them. This occupation and administering other sacraments did not cease, as from time to time other fugitives were brought to the camp. How consoled the poor souls felt to find their Father again! Captivity, tortures, and death ceased to be a terror.

The loss of a convoy which carried the supplies for the Huron Mission for a whole year was irreparable. The missionaries there were deprived of what was most indispensable for the very necessaries of life. "But God gives us comfort," writes one of these apostolic laborers, "for it aids our spiritual progress, which is the only allurement to bring us here. Faith makes notable progress among our Hurons. Had this fleet of Huron Christians and catechumens arrived safely, as we expected, the conversion of the country seemed almost certain. It is one of the secrets to be revealed only in eternity. But would you believe that we never roused better courage, both for temporals and spirituals, than since the capture of Father Jogues and our Hurons? I see these tribes more disposed than ever for a complete conversion."

CHAPTER VI.

Sufferings and Resignation of the Missionary—Execution of Three Hurons—A Christian and Generous Death.

THE chief Eustace left the field the last of all, and, cutting his way through the heart of the enemy, plunged into the woods. But, finding that the missionary did not follow him, he reproached himself for his flight, and could not bear to be separated from him. Recalling to mind the pledge of never quitting his side, he preferred to give himself up to his executioners rather than break his word. He turned back to seek him, but found him only by sharing his bonds. He unconsciously only followed the example of his guide and pattern. "O my Father!" he cried, falling into his arms; "I swore to thee that I would live and die at thy side; here we are together again!" The missionary pressed him to his heart, and bathed him in his tears. "I do not know what reply I made to that touching greeting: I was so affected, and my soul so oppressed with grief," wrote Father Jogues.

William Couture, another Frenchman, had also stood the first shock gallantly. But, carried on by the Hurons who sought safety in flight, he dashed with them into the adjoining forest. Young and fleet of foot, he was soon out of gunshot and in a safe spot. Then his heart was torn with remorse. He could not forgive himself for having abandoned his beloved Father and left him to the rage of the savages. He halted, hesitating whether to return or keep on his flight. His better nature prevailed, and he resolved to strike a blow to save his brethren or share their fate.   As he turned back he came upon five Iroquois.

One of them aimed at him, but the gun flashed in the pan.   William fired, and laid his antagonist dead on the spot.   He was a chief. The other four rushed upon him like furies from hell, tore off his clothing, beat him with clubs, tore out his nails, and chewed his fingers with their teeth; then they drove a sword through the hand that had fired the fatal shot.   The brave young man bore it all with admirable patience.   He even bore his last wound with joy, thinking of our Saviour's wounds, as he afterwards avowed to Father Jogues. "Would to God," exclaims the missionary, "that he had escaped, and not come to swell our wretched number!   In such cases it is no comfort to have companions in your misery, especially those you love as yourself. But such are the men who, though seculars, and with no motive of earthly interest, devote themselves to the service of God and of the Society of Jesus in the Huron Mission."

Meanwhile the Mohawks bound their prisoner, and, proud of having a Frenchman in their hands, placed him with the other prisoners.

"The moment I saw him," continues Father Jogues, "bound and stripped of all clothing, I could not contain myself, and, leaving my guards, I made my way through the warriors who surrounded him, and throwing my arms around his neck, I cried: 'Ah! courage, my dear William; courage, my dear brother!   I love you now more than ever, for God in His goodness has made you worthy to suffer for His holy name.   Let not these first sufferings and torments shake your constancy. Terrible will be the tortures, but they will not last long, and a glory without end will soon follow.'   Couture was deeply moved at these words, broken by sobs, and replied, 'My Father, fear not: the goodness of God has granted me too many graces.   I deserve it not, and far less than all do I deserve the firmness and courage I feel in my heart. I trust He who gave it to me will not withdraw it'" (MSS. of Father Buteux).

These manifestations of fraternal love were a matter of wonder to the Indians, and at first a feeling of mercy even sprang up in their hearts; but then, unable to credit feelings so unlike their own, they imagined that the missionary was congratulating the young man on his exploit in killing one of their chiefs. They accordingly rushed upon the man of God, stripped him of all his clothes, except his shirt, and discharged upon him a volley of blows with fists, sticks, and war-clubs. Father Jogues fell to the ground insensible. He was just coming to, when two young braves, who had not been there to take part in the first onslaught, sprang at him like two wild beasts, tore out his nails with their teeth, and crunched the two forefingers until they had completely crushed the bones of the last joint.

Good René Goupil was treated with the same cruelty. Thus the Indians retaliated on the French for having rejected their terms of peace the year before; yet these acts of ferocity were but preliminaries of what was to follow. As soon as all the warriors who had been in pursuit of the fugitives had reassembled, the whole band hastened to recross the river with their captives, to the mouth of the Iroquois.* There they felt more secure, and halted to divide the spoils. It was a large booty. Besides what each Frenchman carried as his own, there were twenty packages of church articles, vestments, books, and other things for the missionaries. Valuable as this treasure was for the Mission, it was almost worthless to the Indians; but these articles had the great attraction of novelty, and they were proud of having taken them from the French. As they displayed article

---

* Now called the Richelieu or Sorel, the outlet of Lake Champlain into the St. Lawrence.

after article, they gave vent to their joy in shouts, and their attention seemed riveted in their treasures. Their distribution gave some respite to the prisoners, and Father Jogues improved it to console and encourage them, while affording the succors of religion. There were twenty-three of them.

Before leaving this shore, the Iroquois, after their wont, cut on the bark of trees a record of this their important exploit. By the aid of rude hieroglyphical marks they recorded their victory, and the number and quality of their captives. It was easy to distinguish Father Jogues from the rest. The Christians, who shortly after discovered this sad record, wished to perpetuate and hallow its remembrance. They raised a cross on the spot. It was proper that the sign of redemption should mark the way of the heroes of Faith.

After the booty had been divided the enemy made ready to enter their canoes with their prisoners, and return to their country. At the very moment of entering the canoes, Ondouterraon, an old man of fourscore, whom the missionary had just baptized, cried aloud, " At my age one does not care to visit foreign countries, and one cannot adapt himself to new ways of life. If you wish to put me to death, why not do so now?" No sooner said than done: a blow from a tomahawk at once laid him low.

The Iroquois started at last, and after ascending the river which bears their name, entered Lake Champlain,*

---

* Named after the illustrious Champlain, who discovered it in 1609, and defeated the Iroquois on its banks. Its Indian names were *Pata-wabouque*—alternation of water and land, alluding to the great many islands and points; and *Canadieri guarunte*, the lips or door of the country. It was indeed the path from the valley of the Hudson to that of the St. Lawrence. It was sometimes called Lake Corlaer, from Arendt van Corlaer, commandant at Schenectady, who in 1650 saved a Canadian war-party from the fury of the Iroquois. He was drowned in the lake while on his way to visit the Governor of Canada. Lake

to cross it from end to end. The voyage proved the occasion of increased torture to the prisoners. They often spent days without food, and nights without sleep. Hunger, heat, festering wounds swarming with vermin and uncovered, the sting of clouds of mosquitoes, rendered their situation terribly painful. At times, whilst bound at the bottom of the canoes or tethered to pickets, unable to snatch a moment of rest, their savage keepers, especially young braves, would steal up and amuse themselves by irritating and exasperating the wounds of the fingers or the most sensitive parts of the person, digging their long and sharp nails into them or pricking them with awls. They delighted especially to torment the servant of God by plucking out his beard and hair. But his interior tortures were even more acute than those he suffered in body. "My heart suffered even more," wrote Father Jogues, " when I beheld that band of Christians, among whom I saw five old converts, the mainstay of the rising church of the Hurons. More than once I acknowledge I could not withhold my tears. I was afflicted at their lot, and that of my other companions, and I was full of forebodings for the future. In fact, I foresaw that the Iroquois were raising a barrier to the progress of Faith among a great number of other tribes, unless there came a very special interposition of Divine Providence." Yet Father Jogues' only consolation amid so many afflictions was to see the heroic resolve of his companions, and to be able to comfort them by his charitable counsels. They needed them indeed for they were only at the beginning of their trials.

On the eighth day of their march, they met two Iroquois runners, who brought the news that, at one day's distance, two hundred Iroquois out on the war-path, were

---

Champlain from St. John's to Whitehall is about sixty-five miles long and about ten wide. Many spots on its banks are famous for operations in the Old French War and the Revolution.

encamped on an island. The victorious party made all haste to reach them, and the captives knew at once what was in store for them. It is worth noticing that it is an instinct with the savages that they must nerve themselves for war by acts of cruelty, and that ill-treatment of prisoners is an omen of success. Facts will afford a melancholy proof of the power of this fanatical idea.

When the Indians descried the captives they raised yells of joy, and began to thank the Sun, who is their god of war, for his delivering their foes into the hands of their countrymen, and they discharged a volley from their fire-arms. A platform was soon set up on a neighboring hill, and each man cut in the woods a club or thorny branch, according to his fancy, in order to receive the prisoners in a proper manner.

Before landing, and entering the double file of executioners lining the way from the shore to the platform, the victims were stripped of all their clothes. The missionary was the last to land, that, being alone and walking slowly, he might offer a surer mark for their blows.

We will let Father Jogues himself describe this horrible scene: " They showered blows on us so that I fell under their number and cruelty, on the rocky path leading to the hill. I thought that I must surely die under this frightful torture. Either from weakness or cowardice, I could not rise. God alone, for whose love and glory it is sweet and glorious to suffer thus, knows how long and how savagely they beat me. A cruel compassion prompted them to stop, that I might be taken to their country alive. They carried me to the platform half dead, and streaming with blood. The moment they saw me revive a little, they made me come down, and overwhelmed me with insults and imprecations, and again showered blows on my head, back, and all over my body. I would never end were I to tell all we Frenchmen had to endure. They burned one of my fingers, and crushed another with their teeth. Those that had been crushed before were now so violently twisted that they have remained horribly deformed, even since they healed. My companions shared the same treatment.

"But God showed us that He had us in His care, and that He wished not to discourage but to try us. In fact, one of the Indians, who seemed not to be sated with cruelty and blood, came up to me when I could hardly stand on my feet, and taking hold of my nose with one hand prepared to cut it off with a large knife he held in the other. What could I do? Satisfied that I would soon be burned at a slow fire, I waited the blow without flinching, only in my heart offering a prayer to Heaven; but a secret force held him back, and he let go. In less than fifteen minutes he returned, as if ashamed of his weakness and cowardice, and again prepared to carry out his design. Again an invisible power repelled him, and he slunk away. Had he proceeded in his attempt I should have been put to death immediately. Indians never let a prisoner so mutilated live long " (MSS., 1652).

When relating this episode of his tortures to Father Buteux, the man of God added, that far from alarming him, the savage appeared to him rather an instrument of justice and mercy of God, and from his heart he exclaimed, "Lord, take my nose, and my head also!"

The Huron who suffered most was the brave and fervent Eustace. His executioners cut off his two thumbs, and through the wound of his left hand they drove a sharp stick up to the elbow. He endured it all like a true Christian hero; but Father Jogues, who had been unmoved by his own tortures, wept at the sight of the sufferings of his child. The intrepid convert saw the tears, and addressing his torturers, said, "Do not think that these are tears of weakness. No: it is no lack of courage that makes them flow, but his love and affection for me. You saw him shed no tears for his own sufferings." The missionary, deeply affected, replied, "Indeed your sufferings I feel more than I did mine; and, in spite of my wounds, my body suffers even less than my heart. Courage, my poor brother: forget not that there is another life ; God sees all, and He will reward us one day for what we have suffered for His sake." "I know it well, and I shall hold steadfast until death," answered Eustace; and truly the disciple, worthy of his Master, was a prodigy of patience, resignation, and intrepidity.

The Indians spent only one night on the island. They resumed their journey the next day—one party towards the St. Lawrence, and others for the Iroquois towns. The latter met other bands of warriors proceeding to attack the French, and the unfortunate prisoners on every occasion paid the tribute of their blood. The melancholy and bloody convoy continued until they reached Point Ticonderoga, called by the French Carillon, and well known for a glorious victory of Montcalm. It was a stopping-place never passed by the Indians. Here they landed to gather flints, which abound on the shores, and to perform one of their superstitious rites, by throwing bits of tobacco into the waters in order to propitiate a nation of invisible people who dwell there, and prepare the flints for the benefit of travellers, who are expected to repay them in tobacco. Should the offer be niggardly their anger is roused: they excite the waves and cause shipwrecks. A superstitious belief so like the traditions of ancient Paganism, must have originated in the fact that in consequence of the strong winds prevailing at that place wrecks frequently occur. Father Jogues could only lament such blind credulity. He did not know their language well enough to disabuse them; but he fervently prayed that the light of faith might come to scatter such dense darkness.

One day more enabled the Iroquois to reach the southern point of Lake George. It was the 10th of August. There remained still four days' march on land to reach the first Iroquois town. The great heat and the pitiable condition of the prisoners made the passage extremely painful, as they were forced to carry the heaviest part of the baggage. Heedless of the Father's weakness and weariness, Father Jogues' keeper put part of his burthen on his bleeding and mangled shoulders. Yet with sentiments of admirable charity and humanity he remarks : "However, they spared me somewhat, either because of my feebleness or because I did not seem to mind it much —so great was my pride even in captivity and in the presence of death !"

The hardship of this march was rendered even more intense by the want of all food ; their provisions being exhausted, they lived on berries gathered in the woods.

On the second day the captives hoped for some relief. Fires were lighted where they encamped, and the pots were made ready. They thought a hunter had brought in some game that was to be cooked. Vain hope ! To quiet their hunger the Indians swallowed large draughts of lukewarm water. They lay down supperless, and next morning they resumed their march fasting. Hunger made the Indians push on rapidly; but the French, exhausted by their sufferings, slackened their steps in spite of themselves. Towards night, Father Jogues, lagging behind at some distance alone with René Goupil, advised him to hide in the forest and escape from the savages. "But you, my Father—what will become of you?" said the pious young man. "For my part," replied the missionary, "I cannot do it: I will rather suffer everything than leave so near death those whom I can at least console and nourish with the blood of Christ in the sacraments of the Church." "Then allow me to die with you, my Father," replied pious René; "for I cannot desert you." A young brave, noticing their slow progress, waited, and reproving them as sluggards, ordered them to take off their trousers; and thus they had to continue their march in their shirts and drawers.

The convoy soon reached a small river called Oiogué,

which means Beautiful River, and had to cross it. The current was not very rapid, but the water was deep; the Indians plunged into it at once, and forced Father Jogues along, without caring whether he could swim; luckily he could, or he would certainly have drowned (MSS., Father Buteux).

Before following Father Jogues to the towns of the Agniers (called Maquaas by the Dutch and Mohawks by the English), let us say something of their geographical position, and of their towns. It was the first Iroquois canton. On the north the French were their neighbors, and the Dutch on the south. Their villages were situated on the right bank of the river Mohawk. They had three main towns, and sometimes a fourth; but changes of name and position have led to much confusion in history.

The first town on the east was over thirty miles from Rensselaerswyck (now Albany). It was called *Osserion, Ossernenon,* or *Oneougioure,* and lastly *Holy Trinity*—the name given it by Father Jogues. Later it became *Cahniaga, Gandawagué, Caughnawaga,* or simply *Aniè,* and lastly in 1674 *Saint Peter's.* It was inclosed within two palisades, and contained about twenty-four large cabins, which gives about six hundred inhabitants. The second town, *Anndagaro* or *Gandagaron,* was about six miles farther up. The third, the largest of all, *Tionnontoguen* or *Tionnontego,* was about eleven miles farther west. This town was eventually called *St. Mary's.**

At last, after thirteen days'† march, on the eve of the

---

* Not to confuse the reader, we have here substituted the results of the careful exploration made of these town sites by Gen. John S. Clark. Ossernenon is near the present station of Auriesville, in Montgomery County; Tionnontoguen on a hill just south of Spraker's Basin, about sixteen miles west of Ossernenon; Andagaron, between them, and, like them, on the south side of the river.

† Father Bressani in his "Breve Relatione," and Father Alegambe in his "Mortes Illustres," say eighteen days, and Charlevoix four

Assumption of Our Lady, at three o'clock in the afternoon, our travellers reached the bank of the second river, three quarters of a mile from the village called Ossernenon.

Their usual signals, given from a distance by blowing into large conch-shells pierced at the end, had been heard, and the people in a mass swarmed to the shores to receive the prisoners. Every man, woman, and child rushed down, armed with sticks or iron rods. "I had always thought," remarks the missionary, "that this day of so much rejoicing in heaven would prove unto us a day of suffering, and I was therefore thankful to my Saviour Jesus, for the joys of heaven are purchased only by partaking of His sufferings." The captives were welcomed by a shower of blows. But as the Indians hate a bald-head above all, Father Jogues' drew upon himself the largest amount of cruel treatment: his flesh was hacked or torn with nails to the very bone.

An old Huron, who had formerly been taken prisoner, but set free, seeing them, cried out, "Frenchmen, you are lost; there is no hope for you. Prepare to die; the stakes are ready; you will be burned." A natural feeling of compassion for his countrymen prompted him to reveal to them and their allies the fate in store for them. But even some Iroquois seemed moved to pity their lot on beholding them reeking with blood. Hardened as he was, the savage owner of the missionary approached, and wiping the blood from his face, said, "Brother, what a wretched state you are in!" Whether true or feigned, this trait of compassion was accepted by the martyr as a gift from heaven.

Meanwhile the Indians had crossed the river, but before climbing the hill on which the village stood, they halted a moment to thank the Sun for their prosper-

---

weeks ; but Father Jogues' narrative corrects the error, which does not appear in the Relation of 1646–47, or in the precious Manuscript of 1652.

ous expedition and rich booty. Then the lugubrious triumphal march was marshalled.

At the head of the line strode Couture, for he was the most guilty, having slain a distinguished chief. After him followed the Hurons, at equal distances from each other—Goupil in the centre. Father Jogues closed the line.

Some of the Iroquois were stationed at intervals to check the speed of the prisoners, and afford the executioners, who lined the path, every opportunity to deal their blows effectually. Then one of the chieftains addressed the young braves, and told them how they should give a hearty welcome to the prisoners. It was one of the ironically cruel expressions in vogue for the savage reception of captives.

"On beholding these preliminaries, so forcibly reminding us of the Passion," says Father Jogues, "we recalled the words of St. Augustine, 'Whoso shrinks from the number of the scourged, forfeits his right to be numbered among the children'—*Qui eximit se a numero flagellatorum, eximit se a numero filiorum.* We therefore offered ourselves with our whole heart to the fatherly care of God, as victims immolated to His good pleasure and to His loving displeasure for the salvation of these tribes." At a given signal, the procession started on this "narrow path of heaven," as the saintly missioner calls it. At the same time all arms were raised and swung in the air, and a shower of blows descended on the victims. Father Jogues seemed to behold his Saviour scourged at the Pillar, and with David exclaimed, "The wicked have wrought upon my back : they have lengthened their iniquity" (Ps. cxxviii. 3).

Good René, horribly mangled and covered with blood, fell exhausted—not a spot of white was visible in his countenance except his eyes. He had no strength to ascend the platform, and was dragged up to it. "In this condition," adds Father Jogues, "he was all the more beautiful in our eyes, because he resembled him of whom it is written, "We have thought him as it were a leper, and as one struck by God;". . . . "there is no beauty in him, nor comeliness" (Isaias liii. 4, 2).

But there was something more in store for the heroic Father to endure. An iron ball, weighing more than two pounds, fastened to a sling, was hurled at him, and struck him in the middle of the back. He fell on the spot as though dead; but soon recovering his breath and summoning all his strength, he rose bravely and reached the platform.

When the prisoners had all reached this horrible stage, which was to be so glorious for them, they were allowed a' moment's respite; but it was not long before one of the chiefs in a loud voice called upon the young braves to caress the Frenchmen; for "they are traitors," he continued: "they have broken their promises; they have slaughtered our Iroquois." At this, an Indian armed with a stout club ascended the platform, and deliberately dealt three blows on the back of the Frenchmen, but perceiving that the missionary had yet three nails left, he tore them out with his teeth. Then the savages, armed with knives, fell upon the captives to cut off their fingers, or slices of their flesh. As their cruelty is gauged by the importance of the victim, they treated the missionary as a chief by subjecting him to greater tortures than the rest. The respect paid him by his companions won him this distinction. Soon after an aged man, a famous magician of the land, and a bitter enemy of the French, ascended the platform, followed by Jane, an Algonquin Christian woman, captured two months before. He ordered her to cut off Father Jogues' left thumb; "for," he added, "I hate him the most." Three times did the wretched woman recoil with horror; at last, under threat of losing her life, she obeyed. With trembling hand, sick at heart, she cut or rather sawed off the thumb at its root and threw it down. The man of

God did not utter a sigh. "I picked up the amputated member," says he, "and I presented it to Thee, living and true God, in remembrance of the sacrifices which for the last seven years I had offered on the altars of thy Church, and as an atonement for the want of love and reverence of which I had been guilty in touching thy Holy Body." But Couture, perceiving this, warned the missionary that if the Iroquois observed him, they might force him to eat the bloody thumb, he hastily threw it far away.

"I bless the Lord," adds Father Jogues, "that he vouchsafed to leave me the right thumb, that by this letter I may beseech my Reverend Fathers and my Brothers to offer their holy sacrifices, their prayers, their good works, and their devotions in God's holy Church, to which we have by two new titles become dear, for she always prays for the afflicted and for prisoners."

René Goupil endured the same torture. They cut off the thumb of his right hand at the first joint with an oyster-shell; and during this cruel operation he was heard repeating aloud the sacred names of Jesus, Mary, and Joseph.

Blood flowed copiously from the wounds, and death would soon have resulted; but an Indian perceived it, and either from pity or from a desire of prolonging the parade with the life of the victims, he ascended the platform, stanched the wounds, and tearing some shreds of Father Jogues' shirt, he bandaged the priest's and Goupil's thumbs. This simple dressing sufficed, and God permitted it to answer for better treatment. While the missionary was receiving this care, a woman came and deprived him of the shoes and the wretched stockings that had thus far been left to him.

As night approached, the captives were ordered down from the platform and led to a cabin for the night. The Indians, before they betook themselves to rest, gave their victims some roasted ears of corn, and some water colored with meal. It was very little after such a long fast and such terrible treatment; but there was enough to keep them alive, and afford their butchers the cruel hope of a renewal of their torments.

But the night, far from being to the captives an occasion of rest, was only the beginning of new tortures. They spent it stretched on the ground, hands and feet secured to four stakes driven in the earth. In this posture they could not move, and yet they were at once assailed by swarms of insects, and the vermin which the filthy habits of the Indians attract to their cabins to multiply there. A more painful torment was that to which they were subjected by the Indian children, who were allowed to approach the prisoners and begin on them their apprenticeship in cruelty. They evinced their proficiency only too well. They amused themselves by driving awls into the tenderest parts of the body, by opening the wounds so as to make the blood flow, or by throwing burning coals and hot cinders on the bodies of the martyrs, all the while enjoying the useless efforts of their victims to shake them off.

Proud of their victory, the victorious war-party took pride in exhibiting their trophies in the other Mohawk towns.

They first led their prisoners to the neighboring village called Andagaron, some five or six miles off. On the way the man of God had to undergo a new humiliation. He thus relates it:

"My jailer, undoubtedly afraid that he might lose the chance of securing my shirt, took it from me at once. He made me start on my march in this exposed state, with nothing on me but a pair of wretched old drawers. When I beheld myself in this state, I felt bold enough to say to him, 'Why do you strip me so, brother, when you have already got all the rest of my property?' The Indian took pity on me, and gave me a piece of coarse canvas in which my bundles had been done up. There was enough of it to cover my shoulders and a part of my back; but my festering wounds could not stand this rough, coarse texture. The sun was so hot that during the march, my skin was baked as if in an oven, and peeled off from my neck and arms."

The captives received the same welcome at this village as in the former, and though it is contrary to custom to make prisoners run the gauntlet more than twice, they were not spared, and a refinement of cruelty was added. As the crowd was smaller, the executioners could take better aim. They struck particularly the shin-bones, covering the legs with bruises, and causing acute pain. The prisoners remained two days and two nights in this village: by day on the pillory, exposed to every sort of insult and ill-treatment; at night in a cabin, at the mercy of the children.

Let us hear Father Jogues relate, with beautiful candor, the feelings that then possessed his soul, and which depict him so clearly to us as an apostle and a martyr: "My soul was then in the deepest anguish. I saw our enemies come up on the platform, cut off the fingers of my companions, tie cords around their wrists, and all so unmercifully that they fainted away. I suffered in their sufferings, and the yearnings of my affection were those of a most affectionate father witnessing the sufferings of his own children; for, with the exception of a few old Christians, I had begotten them all to Christ in baptism. However intense my suffering, God granted me strength to console the French and the Hurons who suffered with me. On the way, as well as on the platform, I exhorted them together and individually to bear with resignation and confidence these torments, which have a great reward (Heb. x. 35); to remember that through many tribulations we must enter into the kingdom of God (Acts xiv. 21). I warned them that the days foretold by our Saviour had arrived in their behalf: 'Ye shall lament and weep, but the world shall rejoice. . . . But your sorrow shall be turned into joy' (John xvi. 20). And then again I added: 'A woman, when she is in labor, hath sorrow, because her hour is come; but when she has brought forth the child, she remembereth no more the anguish for joy that a man is born into the world' (John xvi. 21). Believe, then, my children, that after a few days of suffering you shall enjoy everlasting happiness. And surely it was to me a source of great and legitimate consolation to see them so well prepared, especially the old Christians—Joseph, Eustace, and the two others. Theodore had escaped the day we reached the first town; but as a ball had shattered his shoulder in the fight, he died while endeavoring to reach the French settlements."

The captives were then led to Tionnontoguen, the third Mohawk village, about sixteen miles from Ossernenon. They were there welcomed as in the other villages, but with less cruelty. On ascending the platform where they were to be exhibited, Father Jogues was deeply grieved to find four other Huron prisoners already prepared for execution. These unhappy men were doomed to death, but they were pagans; the servant of God, touched at their condition, endeavored at least to aid them spiritually. He approached them, and succeeded in gaining their confidence by the interest he took in their fate. They saw him forget his own sufferings to think of theirs! On the threshold of eternity, they did not refuse to hearken to words of hope. When the missionary saw them disposed to receive the word of salvation, he gave a summary instruction on the principal articles of our faith, and with the aid of a few drops of water which the rain had left on the leaves of corn given them for food, he baptized them. The other two, condemned as they were to perish in the fourth village, were afterwards regenerated in the waters of baptism, while crossing a stream on the way.

Such were the consolations of faith which God bestowed on the apostolic heart of His servant and which supported his courage. He needed it for this new scene of sorrow. The temperature had changed; heavy rains had been succeeded by piercing cold winds, which made the naked captives suffer intensely, and increased the pain of their wounds.

Good William Couture had not yet lost any of his fingers. An Indian undertook to repair the omission. With the fragment of a shell, sharpened into a knife, he sawed off one half of his right forefinger, and as he could not cut the hard, tough sinew, he dragged it out with such violence that the arm swelled prodigiously up to the elbow.

The tortures inflicted by the younger Indians at night were extremely cruel. "Our executioners," adds Father Jogues with humility, "first commanded us to sing, as is usual with captives. We undertook to sing the song of the Lord in a strange land (Ps. cxxxvi. 4). Could we sing anything else? After the chant began the torments. . . . . They suspended me by my arms, with bark ropes, from two posts raised in the centre of the cabin. I thought they were going to burn me, for such is the posture usually given to those who are condemned to the stake.

"To convince me that if I had suffered so far with some courage and patience I owed it not to my own virtue, but to Him 'that giveth strength to the weary' (Isa. xl. 29), the Almighty, as it were, left me then to myself in this new torment. I groaned for 'gladly will I glory in my infirmities, that the power of ·Christ may dwell in me' (2 Cor. xii. 9), and the excess of my sufferings made me implore my tormentors to loosen the cords a little. But God justly permitted that the more I entreated the closer and tighter the bonds were drawn. After I had suffered for a quarter of an hour they cut the ropes; had they not done so I should have died. I thank Thee, O my Lord Jesus! for having taught me by this little trial how much Thou must have suffered on the

the cross, when Thy most holy body was so long hanging from the cross, not by cords, but by nails cruelly driven into Thy feet and hands."

Father Jogues owed the relief from his tortures to a strange Indian who happened to come upon the scene. He seemed affected by the sight, and without uttering a word approached the sufferer and cut the cords. No one dared oppose him. The man was rewarded for his charitable act, as the sequel will prove. God, who blesses the slightest service rendered to the least of His little ones, will not forget what is done for His most faithful servants, and especially His apostolic men.

Two days were spent at this village, and then the captives were brought back to Andagaron, where sentence was at last to be pronounced on them. Thus were they for seven days* marched from village to village and from platform to platform. At this place they were told that they were to be burned alive that very day.

"Although there is something horrible in this mode of death," remarks Father Jogues, "the thought of God's will, and the hope of a better life, free from sin, alleviated all its rigors. I addressed my French and Huron companions for the last time, and exhorted them to persevere to the end, ever remembering in the midst of their sufferings of body and soul Him who had 'endured such opposition from sinners against Himself, that you be not wearied, fainting in your minds' (Heb. xii. 3). To-morrow we shall all be united in the bosom of God, to reign eternally."

Thus did Father Jogues strengthen the captives by his words, but he did not neglect the grace of the Sacraments. He had habituated them frequently to receive absolution, and to nourish their souls by constant pious aspirations to heaven. As they feared that they might

---

* Father Jogues gives this figure himself. Charlevoix ("Histoire de la Nouvelle France," i. p. 238) has by an oversight put seven weeks.

be separated from each other, they had agreed among themselves upon a certain sign, which meant "I desire absolution." They were to lay a hand on the breast and raise the eyes to heaven.

Meanwhile the sachems of the village were dissatisfied at the resolution adopted by the warriors. They insisted that no precipitate action should be taken, at least in regard to the French, in hope that this course would make the soldiers of the Canadian colony less eager in pursuing the Iroquois warriors. The first sentence was at last revoked, at least in part : only three Hurons were sentenced to die—Eustace at Tionnontoguen, Paul at Ossernenon, and Stephen (whose Indian name history has not preserved) at Andagaron, the place where they then were.

Eustace gave an admirable example of resignation and courage. They applied fire to almost every part of his body, and cut his throat with a knife. Father Jogues adds a remark that savors of his days spent in the classroom : "While Indians doomed to death usually give way to violent outbursts of fury against their executioners, and to the last breath cry, '*Exoriare aliquis nostris ex ossibus ultor*'—May an avenger arise from our bones.* Eustace, prompted by the teachings of Christianity, conjured the Hurons who witnessed his death not to be deterred by this event from treating for peace with the Mohawks, his persecutors and his murderers. Indeed, his death was an act of forgiveness. With Eustace perished his nephew, a wonderful young man, who, after his baptism, never ceased repeating, '*I shall be happy in heaven.*' He had promised his uncle that he would never abandon him, even in the greatest dangers ; and indeed, he was true to his word" (Relation, 1644).

Paul Ononchoraton was tomahawked, but not till

---

* Virgil's Æneid, Book iv. 625.

after he had passed through the ordeal of fire unflinchingly. He was a young man, only twenty-five years of age, but of admirable constancy and energy. The principles of faith and Christian hope alone inspired his courage, and made him despise death.

The Iroquois singled out as victims men of this stamp. It was not only to exhaust gradually the power of their enemies, but also to excite the emulation of their young braves, and afford them an example of how a warrior should die.

The good neophyte Paul had, during his last trials, given the servant of God a proof of his attachment—thus related by the latter: "When the Iroquois approached to tear out my nails, or subject me to some new torture, Paul would offer himself and entreat them to spare me and wreak their cruelty on him. May God repay him a hundredfold, and with usury, for his admirable charity that made him *lay down his life for his friends* (John xv. 13), and for those who *had begotten him in chains* (Philem. 10).

The death of the third captive was as holy and as courageous as that of his brethren. Yet it was happier in that he had the privilege of seeing Father Jogues by his side to suggest thoughts of faith, and to encourage him.

Such were these men, transformed by religion. They had but just abandoned their rude ways and their idolatrous prejudices; they were just born to the Faith, and were able to become its heroes. This glorious triumph, in which he had taken so active a part, caused Father Jogues to return heartfelt thanks to God. Deprived as he was of the crown of martyrdom, for which he longed, he saw himself doomed to a cruel slavery, the duration of which it was not in the power of man to measure. But this state presents to us with new lustre the virtue of the servant of God.

CHAPTER VII.

Captivity of Father Jogues—The Dutch Interpose—New Dangers—Murder of René Goupil—Consoling Dreams.

N the evening of the day when the great council had determined the fate of the prisoners, the Iroquois took William Couture, who retained strength enough to walk, to Tionnontoguen, the farthest town. When Indians spared a prisoner's life they gave him to a family which had lost a member in war, in order to replace him; and the head of the family to whose hands his fate was committed, obtained over the adopted prisoner the right of life and death. No one else dare strike him within the village. Father Jogues and René Goupil, who appeared much weaker, were detained in the first town, the residence of their captors. They were doomed to slavery.

After such long fasts, after so many nights of pain and sleeplessness, after so many blows and bruises and wounds; above all, after such inward trials, these two poor mutilated beings began to feel their sufferings fully, and were completely prostrated. They could scarcely stand or drag themselves about. Their hands were one festering wound, so utterly useless to them that they had to be fed like children. To recover their strength they had only a little corn grits, and occasionally a half-cooked piece of pumpkin: their bed was the bark of a tree, their blanket a tattered deerskin, greasy, and swarming with vermin. Their wounds, unbandaged and exposed, were night and day irritated by the sting of insects, against which they were helpless to defend themselves. Patience was their physician: but some women took pity on them; bandaged their hands in their way, and washed their wounds in cool water, which arrested and reduced the inflammation. But René, even more weakened than the missionary, and suffering from the effects of the blows he had received on his head, was rapidly failing. The savages saw it, and gave the prisoners some more substantial food; but it was merely some fish, and meat dried and reduced to powder, cooked with their corn-meal. By this simple means the two captives were restored to health.

The chiefs and sachems deliberated as to their position. Some proposed that they should be sent back to Three Rivers, in order to arrest a war which every day thinned the ranks of their warriors.

This project was on the point of being carried out, and men were actually selected to accompany them. At the same time, the Dutch at Rensselaerswyck, which was not forty miles from this town, having heard of the capture of several Frenchmen, desired to interpose, and obtain their deliverance. On the 7th of September, the eve of the Nativity of the Blessed Virgin, the commandant of the fort, Arendt Van Corlaer; his interpreter, Jean Labatie; and Jacob Jansen of Amsterdam, went as ambassadors to the town of Andagaron, and opened negotiations: they made flattering offers, and a more attractive promise of two hundred dollars; but to no avail. The Iroquois, under pretence of not understanding the terms of the parley,—in fact, unwilling either to displease their neighbors, or seemingly to yield to their offices,—only spoke of an exchange of prisoners with the French which was to be effected in a few days. Such was their intention undoubtedly; but an unforeseen circumstance prevented it, and rekindled all their fury and hatred against the

French. The violent had prevailed at the last council, and after the close of its stormy session the captives would have been put to death had they been found. Providence had permitted that they were then walking in the fields, conversing on pious subjects. They were sought, but in vain; after the first outburst of savage fury the minds of the Indians calmed down, and the danger was averted once more.

The change in the disposition of the Iroquois was caused by the news of a check sustained by a band of warriors—the very braves whom the prisoners had met on Lake Champlain, and by whom they had been so wantonly saluted. These braves, continuing their course, came to Fort Richelieu, which the French were then erecting at the mouth of the river of the Iroquois. The Indians thought it a favorable moment to overthrow that barrier. Their number, which was some three hundred, inspired complete confidence. They expected to crush this handful of soldiers, and profiting by this surprise, to demolish the work. It was only seven days since the first axe had been struck into a tree of that unbroken forest, but the inclosing palisade had already been raised strong enough to shelter those at work. Religion had come at the same time to bless the soil, and the missionary who accompanied the expedition had celebrated Mass on the 20th of August, the Feast of St. Bernard.

Lurking at first in the neighboring woods, the Iroquois formed three different bands, and at a given signal they fell with a war-whoop on the workmen. But, fortunately, Mr. de Montmagny had that day arrived with three well-armed barques to inspect and direct the works. From the deck of his brigantine he descried the Indians and guessed their plan. Taking a canoe, he reached the fort before the enemy. In a moment the little garrison was under arms, and, following Durocher, the commandant of the post, manned the palisade, ready for the

affray.* The Indian attack was made at different points
at once. An Iroquois chieftain was distinguished among
the rest by his tall figure, his particolored face, and red
deer-skin headpiece. He fought bravely at the head of
his party, and his example inspired his men. Suddenly a
ball stretched him lifeless on the ground. Almost at
the same moment two other Indians were killed and
several wounded. The assailants became demoralized:
some retreated, carrying the rest with them. A precipitate and disorderly flight ensued. Brave at a first onslaught, Indians are easily disconcerted, and their energy
fails them if they meet with a firm resistance. The
French sustained some loss. Corporal Deslauriers was
killed, and the Sieur Martial, the Governor's secretary,
who took part in the affair, was wounded.

After this repulse the Indians returned home, humili-
ated, and enraged at heart. On learning that the French
prisoners were still alive, they determined at any cost to
wash away in their blood the affront they had received,
and atone for it by this easy victory. Providence, as
we have seen, baffled their wicked design.

Father Jogues and his companion then entered upon
the ordinary routine of a captive's existence—a precarious situation, where life always hung on a thread.
Under the least pretext, the first comer might murder
them, provided it was not within the bounds of the town.
It was thus that good René was killed some time after.
In his captivity the pious young man wished to see God
glorified by all around him. Unable to address his
masters, whose language he could not speak, and who

---

* The military strength of Canada at this time may be noticed. It
was very insignificant. The garrison of Quebec consisted of fifteen
men, and cost the treasury 12,180 livres. Three Rivers had seventy,
and Montreal as many. An order of the Council of State (March 5,
1648) directs a captain and thirty men to be sent to the Hurons.
This made 115 men for the whole of Canada (Manuscript at the
Library of the Louvre).

would only have been provoked by his words, as he well
knew, he drew unto him the little children, and taught
them how to make the sign of the cross. An old man
caught him making the sign on the forehead of his grandchild, and even teaching the child to bless himself. The
sight aroused all his hatred and superstition. He called
one of his nephews and said, "Go kill that dog of a
Frenchman. The Hollanders tell us that the sign he has
made on my grandchild is not good. I fear lest some
evil will befall him." Unfortunately, the order was too
much to the taste of the young brave; he breathed only
vengeance since he learned that one of his relations had
been killed in the attack on Fort Richelieu. He had
only to find his victim outside the palisade, and unpro-
tected. An opportunity was soon found.

Full of gloomy forebodings Father Jogues endeavored
to maintain his disciple as well as himself in perfect
resignation to the will of God. When not at prayer, this was the ordinary subject of their conversation.
One evening the missionary and his disciple were walking in the woods near the town, when they saw the old
man's nephew and another young brave approaching,
and were ordered to enter their cabin at once. "I had
a presentiment," writes Father Jogues : "of what was
going to happen, and I said to Goupil, 'My dear brother,
let us recommend ourselves to our Lord and our good
Mother the Blessed Virgin : these men have some evil
purpose, I fear, . . . We had shortly before offered ourselves to our Lord with much earnestness, entreating
Him to accept our lives and our blood, and to unite them
to His life and blood for the salvation of these poor people !"

The two captives turned their steps towards the village,
all the way saying their rosary. They had recited four
decades, when, as they neared the gate, the two Iroquois
following, one of them raised a tomahawk which he
had concealed under his robe, and dealt a violent blow

on the head of poor René, who fell on his face, uttering the most holy name of Jesus. "Happily," adds the good Father, "we had often reminded one another to sanctify our last word at our death, by pronouncing this most holy name to gain the indulgence."

On beholding his companion fall lifeless, Father Jogues turned back, and seeing the reeking hatchet in the hand of the murderer, fell on his knees and uncovering his head, awaited the same fate, offering his life a sacrifice to God. But the Indian told him he had nothing to fear, for he belonged to another family. Disappointed in his hopes of a blessed martyrdom, Father Jogues rose, and hearkening only to his grief and love, threw himself on the body of "his dear René," as he calls him; he imparted to him a last absolution, as he was wont to do every other day; shed abundant tears over him, and pressed him to his heart. In him he had lost his spiritual son, his brother, the companion of his sufferings and labors, the only comfort of his captivity. He felt himself left to a dreary solitude.

"It was on the 29th of September, 1642," says Father Jogues, "that this angel of innocence and martyr of Jesus Christ was immolated, in his thirty-fifth year, for Him who had given His life for his ransom. He had consecrated his soul and his heart to God; his hand, his very life, to the welfare of the poor Indians."

The two murderers tore the missionary from the body of their victim, on which they dealt two blows with their tomahawks, for fear the first had not been effectual. Father Jogues was sent back to the family that had adopted him. The rest of that day and the following he did not go out, as he constantly expected a fate like René's; for he had learned that his adoptive family had also lost one of their young men in war: In place of ill-treatment, he met kindness at the hand of his master, who even examined the marks of blood on his person to see whether he had been wounded. He put his hand over the missionary's heart to discover what impressions it might betray; but on finding it perfectly calm, and beating no more quickly than usual, he warned him, "Do not go out of the town, unless in company with one of us. There are some young madmen who are bent on killing you. Be, then, on your guard."

Nor was this the only warning of danger that the servant of God had received : some told him openly; one Indian asked him for his shoes, as he soon would have no more need of them ; the good missionary gave them up with a smile.

However, on the second day after Goupil's murder, Father Jogues could not resist his desire to learn what had become of the corpse, for the purpose of giving it a proper burial. He set out to find it at the risk of his life ; for armed young braves might be seen lurking about, bent on mischief. An old man, with whom the missionary had dwelt, met him on the outskirts of the town, and divining his intention, tried to dissuade him: "Where are you going? You have no sense ; they are after you to take your life, and you are hunting for a carcass already half decayed ! Do you not see these young braves down there waiting to kill you?" The man of God here remarks, "I feared nothing, for life in the midst of so much anguish was only a torment; whereas death in the pursuit of such an act of charity, would be a real gain" (Phil. i. 21).

He therefore continued his way; but the old man directed a good Algonquin, who had been adopted by the Iroquois, to go with the missionary and to protect him. They searched together, and at last found the body: after the murder it had been turned over to the boys, who in their turn had stripped it, and by a rope fastened to its neck dragged it to the torrent that ran at the foot of the village. The sides had been torn by dogs. The pitiable condition of the corpse drew tears from Father Jogues, and awakened all his grief. All he could do for the moment was to lay the corpse in a deep eddy of the torrent, concealing it under stones, in order to keep it from being floated away, and protect it against famished animals. He intended to return the next day with a spade, and bury it secretly.

When he reached the cabin, two young braves requested him to accompany them to a neighboring town: the holy man readily detected their murderous design, but he answered humbly, "I am not my own; ask my master: if he consents, I am ready to go with you." This spirit of obedience saved him, for his master stoutly refused to let him go.

Father Jogues endeavored to pay the last offices of respect and religion to René's remains the next day; but his master, to save him from the treacherous designs of ill-disposed men, sent him in another direction to work in their field. But on the day after he succeeded in starting early to seek the precious remains. Let us hear him recount this act of fraternal devotion, which reveals all the affection of his generous soul: "I went to the spot where I had laid the remains. I climbed the hill, by the foot of which the torrent runs; I descended it. I went through the wood on the other side: my search was useless. In spite of the depth of the water, which came up to my waist,—for it had rained all night,—and in spite of the cold (it was the 1st of October), I sounded with my feet and with my staff to see whether the current had not carried the corpse farther along. I asked every Indian I saw whether he knew what had become of it; but as they are liars by nature, and always answer in the affirmative without any regard for the truth, they told me that it had been carried down by the current to the river near by, which was untrue. Oh, what sighs I uttered, what tears I shed, to mingle with the waters of the torrent, while I chanted to Thee, O my God, the psalms of Holy Church in the Office of the Dead!"

The fact was that the young braves who had seen Father Jogues hide the body of René, went stealthily, took it up, and carried it to a neighboring wood. "After the thaws," writes Father Jogues, "I went to the spot pointed out to me, and gathered some bones partly gnawed, left there by the dogs, wolves, and crows, and especially a skull, fractured in several places. I reverently kissed the hallowed relics, and hid them in the earth, that I may one day, if such is God's will, enrich with them a Christian and holy ground. He deserves the name of martyr, not only because he has been murdered by the enemies of God and His Church, and whilst laboring in ardent charity for his neighbors; but more than all because he was killed for being at prayer, and notably for making the sign of the cross."

Thus did Father Jogues spend the two first months of his captivity in almost constant fear and danger of death, and he admired how Divine Providence, notwithstanding the cunning and malice of his enemies, baffled their guilty projects. He mentions several remarkable incidents. One half-witted Indian insisted on having part of the blanket which served as a robe by day and a covering at night. "I would give it to you willingly," said the missionary, "but you know that it is not enough to protect me against the cold; and I would, moreover, be in a state of nudity, to which we are not accustomed. However, do as you choose." The reply, meek as it was, provoked the wretch, who took it as an insult. He darted off, bent on having his revenge on that *dog* of a Frenchman, as he termed him. He confided to his brother his plan of vengeance. They induced the missionary to enter the cabin at a certain hour, as the punishment was to be inflicted there, with the master's assent. The murderer of René, as an experienced hand, was chosen for the execution of their plans; but he could not be found, and the plan failed. Yet they thought to retrieve their mishap on the morrow, and discussed the matter in his very presence, not thinking he knew enough of the language to understand them. "I pretended," he writes, "not to understand they were plotting against me. 'I was as a dumb man, not opening my mouth: and I became as a man that heareth not; and that hath no reproofs in his mouth. For in thee, O Lord, have I hoped' (Ps. xxxvii. 14–16). I loved to recall to my mind Him 'Who was led as a lamb to the slaughter' (Acts viii. 34) and I wished to meet death with a prayer to God that He would not 'turn back the evils upon my enemies, and cut them off in His truth'" (Ps. liii. 7).

The next day two women were commissioned to conduct him to an adjoining field, under pretence of bringing back something, but in fact to deliver him into the hands of his murderer, who was already posted there. They had some pumpkins, corn, and other presents to pay the assassin. When Father Jogues descried the murderer of René at a distance, he once more commended his soul to God, and went forward boldly, as it were, to meet his sacrifice. But God would only accept the offering of his heart: as for himself, he felt in his humility that he had been deprived of this crown of martrydom because of his sins. The Indian passed him by harmlessly, ashamed, as it were, of his own wicked purpose.

In this precarious existence, and amid daily alarms, Father Jogues had no heart to apply himself to learn the language of the Iroquois: he thought that no benefit would accrue from his labor. He divided his hours between his duties as a slave, forced to provide for the wants of the cabin, and those of an apostle, bound to encourage and support the poor Hurons, his companions in captivity; and finally in practices of piety, the exercises of religion, reading, and prayer.

He thus relates his pious ingenuity to keep alive his fervor: "I avoided crowded places, and sought solitude: there I entreated God 'to make His face shine upon His servant' (Ps. cxviii. 135), and to 'grant him help from trouble' (Ps. cvii. 13). 'If I have become unto many as a wonder' (Ps. lxx. 7), I owe it only to God, who so wonderfully bore me up, and who, by a proof of His infinite goodness, often roused my drooping courage. I found a refuge in the Holy Scriptures—my only source 'in the trouble which hath encompassed me' (Ps. xxxi. 7). I venerated them, and desired to die while using them. Of all the books that we were carrying to the Hurons, I had saved only the Epistle of St. Paul to the Hebrews, with the comments of Mgr. Anthony Godeau, Bishop of Grasse. I always carried this book with me, as well as an indulgenced picture of St. Bruno, the illustrious founder of the Carthusians, and a little wooden cross I had myself made the best way I could. I wished that wherever I should meet death, which I never lost sight of, it should find me ready, resting on the Holy Scriptures, which had always been my greatest comfort; strengthened with the graces and indulgences of the Most Holy Church, my mother, whom I have always loved, but now more than ever; and lastly, armed with the cross of my Redeemer."

The devout missionary subsequently had the happiness of finding a "Following of Christ," and a "Little Office of the Blessed Virgin Mary." Thus he was able to add to his spiritual treasure. This was his only resource to compensate for his being deprived of the happiness of saying the Breviary and offering the Holy Sacrifice of Mass. But God did not forget His servant in his anguish, and more than once He comforted his soul abundantly in pious dreams, which the missionary regarded with gratitude as direct effects of the Divine goodness. We translate from the Latin one of those mysterious dreams, which did so much to rouse his courage and re-animate his confidence. It was only at the order of his Superior that he consented to relate what he humbly called his reveries. The words of Holy Writ, which flow from his pen as from a fountain, give it an additional charm. It seems as if his memory followed the lead of his heart. "I had left the town as usual, to give a freer vent to my feelings before Thee, O my God, to offer Thee my prayer, and 'to set my tears in Thy sight' (Ps. lv. 9). As I returned I found it all transformed: the palisades which inclosed it seemed changed into towers, with battlements and magnificent walls. Yet I saw nothing that appeared new in these structures; but it was an ancient city, already venerable for its antiquity. Whilst I was doubting whether this was our town, some Iroquois whom I knew assured me that it was. Almost bewildered, I advanced, and passed the first entrance, when, above the rising of the second, I perceived L N, engraved in large letters, with the figure of the Lamb that was slain. I was amazed, and could not conceive how barbarians who had no idea of our writing could have engraved those letters. While I was thus endeavoring to solve this problem, I saw above it a floating ribbon, with words explaining them: 'Laudent Nomen Ejus '—'Let them praise His name' (Ps. cxlix. 3). Then my soul was, as it were, flooded with a great light, which made me see in a most clear manner that the name of God is praised above all by those who endeavor in their trials to imitate the meekness of Him 'who opened not His mouth' to those who stripped Him, and who 'was led as a sheep to the slaughter' (Isaias liii. 7). Encouraged by this vision, I passed through a second gate, built of handsome stones, squared and polished. It was a portico vaulted over, large and imposing. I saw in its centre, yet a little on one side of the pathway, an armory full of arquebuses, arrows, and 'all the armor of valiant men' (Cant. iv. 4). I saw no soldiers; but I thought that I should, according to custom, salute the guard as a mark of respect. As I took off my cap towards them, a sentinel near by ordered me to halt. Now, whether I had my face turned, or that the novelty of all I saw had engrossed my entire attention, I did not see or hear him. The sentry challenged me again in a louder tone, 'Halt, I say.' Coming to my senses, I halted. The soldier said, 'Is this the way you obey the guard posted before the King's palace, that you have to be challenged twice? I will take you at once before our judge and our commandant [I heard these two titles of officer and magistrate], that your insolence may be punished as it deserves.' I replied, 'I assure you, my very dear friend, I halted as soon as I heard you.' Not satisfied with my explanation, he led the way to the judge. The gates of the palace were on the side where I stood, yet a little farther from the armory. I entered. The palace seemed to me like one of those halls called in Europe Golden Halls, where judgment is held, or, rather, like the halls in ancient monasteries known as chapters. It was all on a scale of great magnificence.

"In this hall I beheld a venerable man, full of majesty, like to 'the Ancient of Days' (Dan. vii. 9). He wore a scarlet robe of great beauty. He was not seated on his throne, but walked about with a most benign countenance, administering justice to his people. There was a crowd, as we see in Europe, of all ranks. I recognized some, who asked of me news about the Hurons. I said to myself, 'Good! they know me, and know that I have done nothing to deserve being brought before this court. I shall be treated more indulgently.'

"But when the judge heard the charge laid against me by the soldier, without a question he drew a rod from what appeared to be like the fasces the lictors carried before the Roman consuls, and scourged me long and unmercifully on the shoulders, then on the neck, lastly on the head, causing most intense pain. Though he used only one hand, I think I suffered as much as when I entered the first town of the Iroquois, when all the youth of the place came to meet us, and welcomed us so cruelly with blows from their clubs. I made no sign of complaint; I did not groan; I received every blow with perfect resignation; I endured it all with humility. Then my judge, seemingly struck with admiration at my patience, threw the rod aside, and embraced me most affectionately. The pain was calmed, and I felt overcome with an unspeakable and Divine consolation. In the transport of this celestial joy, I kissed the hand that had smitten me, and in the impulse of my delight I cried, 'Thy rod, O God my King, and Thy staff, they have comforted me' (Ps. xxii. 4).

"On that he led me to the door, and left me on the threshold. When I came to myself, after mature deliberation on what I had seen, I could not but attribute to God this uncommon experience, not only for the admirable connection of circumstances, though I had not thought of anything like it while awake, but for the ardent love I felt when my judge embraced me and I exclaimed, *Thy rod*. Months after, the mere remembrance drew tears from my eyes, and filled me with unspeakable consolation."

CHAPTER VIII.

THE attempts on the missionary's life ceased at last; animosity disappeared for a while, and he had an interval of peace, although there was no relaxation of the rigor of his captivity. Winter brought on additional labors and privations—it was the time for deer-hunting, an exercise that could please none but Indians. Father Jogues was given to a family as a servant, and set out with them in the latter part of October. The weather was severe, and the hunting-ground was more than sixty miles distant, and the march was made on foot. His wardrobe was in the most miserable plight—one shirt and one pair of drawers well worn out, his shoes broken, and his breeches and stockings so ragged that his legs were bare. His feet were soon bleeding from the sharp stones, the piercing briars, and reeds; yet all he had to suffer on the way was nothing compared to what he had to undergo during the hunting.

As he was considered of no avail for the chase, he was set apart for woman's work; that is, to cut wood and keep up the fires in the cabins. Game was abundant at first, and meat was about the only food of the hunters. The diet proved healthy to Father Jogues, and it helped him to recruit his strength; but he soon had to give it up when he saw the idolatrous practices of his masters. For no sooner was an animal taken, than a part—usually that considered the greatest delicacy—was raised aloft by one of the old men, who offered it to the demon of the hunt, saying, "Genius Aireskoï, behold, we offer thee meat: feast on it, eat it, and show us where the deer roam." .

After once hearing the idolatrous invocation, Father Jogues would never again touch meat, and said to the Indians, "I will never live on food offered to the devil." Thus he contented himself with a little sagamity and some parched grains of corn, and there was little even of that, for in the abundance of game the hunters despised Indian corn. "Often did I enter the cabin at night," says he, "without having tasted food the whole day, and I would find my Egyptians gluttonly 'seated over the flesh-pots' smoking full (Exod. xvi. 3); and although I might allege the best reasons for allowing myself to partake of their fare, I did not once, thank God, fail in my resolution. When suffering the pangs of hunger, I would say to God, 'We shall be filled with the good things of Thy house' (Ps. lxiv. 5); 'I shall be satisfied when Thy glory shall appear' (Ps. xvi. 15); Thou shalt fulfil the yearnings of Thy servant in the holy city of Thy celestial Jerusalem."

However, the ever-suspicious mind of the savages attributed Father Jogues' abstinence from meat to a mark of contempt of their deity, and they held him accountable for their ill-luck subsequently in their hunts. Their former feelings of pity were changed into abhorrence and hatred. His presence seemed irksome to them. His endeavor to learn Mohawk more perfectly was stopped. They would not give him any explanation or answer his questions any longer. They even refused to listen to him when he endeavored to tell them, as he had often done, the history of creation, of the fall of Adam, the deluge, of the last judgment, and of hell.

Nor was this the only occasion when the credulous superstition of this ignorant people exposed Father Jogues to great danger. One of the Iroquois who had fallen ill imagined, after a dream, that his recovery depended on certain ceremonies and dances, in which the missionary must take part, and he insisted that he should lend it his presence, holding his book of prayers in his hand. Now, a dream is so sacred an occurrence with the Indians, above all when in connection with sickness, that it was unheard of that any one should refuse to aid in its accomplishment. All the tribes of North America were slaves to this belief. The relations of the sick man called on Father Jogues and informed him that the man's recovery was in his hands. "You have only to do," said they, "what he has seen in his dream, and he is saved. It is very easy for you: you pray like that every day; his recovery will be a triumph for you." The Father smiled, and tried to make them see the folly of their system. They insisted; he refused. Other messengers called on him, and spoke of the cruelty of letting a man thus suffer and die, when it was such an easy thing to give him relief. It was all of no avail: the missionary could not join in their foolish notions, much less encourage them. Then the Indians resolved to employ force, and some stalwart young men were appointed to drag him to the dance. But Father Jogues, learning their design, escaped from their hands and fled to the woods. His agility was still such that they could not overtake him. This resolute course showed them how useless it was to try to overcome his opposition, and they gave him no further trouble.

Thus did the life of the missionary alternate between painful labor, privations of every kind, and continual annoyances. He could not pray any more in their presence, for they accused him of invoking evil spirits. He could kneel no more in their sight, for a posture so unusual to them became suspicious. Winter soon added its rigors to this life of suffering. Heavy falls of snow covered the frozen ground, and he was protected only by a wretched and scanty deer-skin. Yet the Indians had plenty of peltries for their trade, but never thought of giving him any. Sometimes, at night, while shivering with cold, he would succeed in drawing one of them over his body, but as soon as discovered it was taken from him amidst imprecations. He was continually benumbed with cold, and at last his skin was all chapped and raw. Nor was this all. His bodily sufferings were soon exceeded by interior anguish and pain, even more intense, which threw the servant of God into the deepest dejection. He beheld "the sorrows of hell encompass him" (Ps. cxiv. 3), "combats without, fears within" (2 Cor. vii. 5).

Let us hear him portray what then passed in his soul, and the remedy which faith supplied:

"I thought," he writes, "of my dear companions, whose blood had so lately covered me, and I heard a report that good William had also ended his life in most cruel torments, and that a like end was in store for me on our return to the town. Then the remembrance of my whole life rushed back to me, with all its unfaithfulness to God, and all its faults. I groaned to see myself die 'in the midst of my days' (Is. xxxviii. 10), as if rejected by the Lord, deprived of the sacraments of the Church, and with no good works to propitiate my Judge. Thus tormented with a desire to live and the fear of death, I groaned, and cried to my God, When shall my grief and my anguish come to an end? When wilt Thou 'see my abjection and my labor' (Ps. xxiv. 3); when wilt Thou give me 'calm after the storm' (Matt. viii. 26); when shall 'my sorrow be turned into joy?'" (John xvi. 20). Then he adds, in a lively sentiment of humility and confidence: "I should have perished unless the Lord 'had shortened the evil days' (Mark xiii. 20); but I had recourse to my support and ordinary refuge, the Holy Scriptures, of which I could recall some passages. They taught me to see in God His goodness, and made me alive to the fact that although deprived of all aids of piety, 'the just man liveth by faith' (Heb. x. 38). I often pondered on these words: 'I followed the running waters' (Ps. i. 3) to endeavor to quench my thirst (2 Esd. ix. 20). On the law of the Lord I meditated day and night (Ps. i. 2), for 'unless Thy law had been my meditation, I had then perhaps perished in my abjection' (Ps. cxviii. 92); and 'perhaps the water had swallowed us up' (Ps. cxxiii. 4).

"But 'Blessed be the Lord, who hath not given us to be a prey to the teeth' (Ps. cxxiii. 6) of my enemies, 'for now their hour seemed come and the power of darkness' (Luke xxii. 53). 'I was pressed out of measure above my strength, so that I was weary even of life' (2 Cor. i. 8). Meanwhile I repeated with Job, but in another sense, 'Although *God* should kill me, I will trust in Him'" (Job xiii. 15).

In this state of bodily suffering and spiritual desolation, Father Jogues' sole comfort was to retire to a little rustic oratory, which he had constructed in the woods, a short distance from the cabin. Hither he repaired as soon as he had done his work as a slave, by laying in a stock of wood for the day, and here, without fire or any shelter but some fir branches to shield him against the wind, he spent whole hours kneeling in the snow to converse with his God, at the foot of a large cross which he had cut in the bark of a tree. There he meditated and prayed, read the "Following of Christ," and roused himself to a holy fervor, by thinking that he was almost alone in loving and honoring the true God in that vast country.

He did even more. Like a good religious, he endeavored to follow as well as he could all the pious exercises of community life, and as it was just the time when he usually made his annual spiritual retreat, he devoted a certain number of days to perform its holy exercises.

Meanwhile the Indians had noticed his long and frequent absence. Accustomed to misinterpret all he did, they watched and followed him to make sure that he was not performing some witchcraft to injure them. They did not disturb him when they saw that he was simply engaged in prayer, but the young men amused themselves by trying to distract or alarm him. They rushed on him, brandishing their tomahawks as if to strike him, or fired arrows which fell around him. Sometimes they raised a yell from behind, as if to warn him of some great danger; at others they cut down trees near by, so as to graze him as they fell.

But nothing could divert the servant of God from his close colloquies with Heaven. He renewed his courage, and learned by experience that the Almighty seemed to choose that spot of predilection for bestowing favors on him. We take from one of the Latin notes written by him on his captivity the account of some of these favors, which proved a source of abundant consolation to him. "While in the place," says he, "which I had chosen as my retreat, I seemed to be in the company of several of our Fathers whom I had known in life, and whose virtue and merit I esteemed highly. I preserve a distinct recollection only of Father James Bertrix, Father Stephen Binet, and Father Coton vaguely. I besought them with all the ardor of my soul to commend me to the Cross, that it might receive me as the disciple of Him whom it had borne, and that it would not repulse a 'Citizen of the Cross.' (This idea had never entered my mind even in meditation). I was indeed born in Orleans, a city the cathedral church of which is dedicated to the Holy Cross."

"Another time, in the same solitude, I seemed, in my sleep, to be transported to the Cloister of the Holy Cross in my native city. Entering the store of a bookseller whom I knew, I asked him whether he had not some edifying book. He replied that he had one that he esteemed greatly—'The Lives of Illustrious Men.' I at once felt a great desire to see it, asking only to borrow it for a few days, promising to return it as soon as I had read it in my room with two or three excellent friends. The bookseller showed an unwillingness from the value he attached to the book. During this time the persons present were talking about tribulations and misfortunes, and each one told what he had undergone. I had the boldness to say myself, that I had suffered something for God's sake; but not seeing the book come which I desired so much, I asked one of the clerks to go and bring it to me. As if without his master's knowledge, the clerk went for the book and gave it to me. It had scarcely touched my hands when I heard a voice say distinctly, 'This book contains the lives of men illustrious for their piety, and stout hearts in war.' * I felt imbued with this thought, that it is only 'through many tribulations we must enter into the kingdom of God' (Acts xiv. 21). When I came out full of joy with my book, I saw the whole store full of crosses, and I said that I would return, as I wished to buy many of different kinds."

Another day in the same place, when he was more than usually depressed by the burthen of his sufferings, and the contempt which the Indians showed for him, as well as by the remorse of conscience and the anguish of his soul, he had the following dream : "I distinctly heard a voice, which reproached me for my perplexity, and recommended me to 'think of the Lord' only 'in goodness' (Wis. i. 1), blindly 'casting all my care upon Him' (1 Pet. v. 7). This, too, was the advice of St. Bernard, addressed to his monks : 'Serve the Lord with that feeling of love which casteth out fear, and does not even regard the merit.' These two counsels," continues Father Jogues, "suited my case, for I was giving way to excessive fear, but it was servile, not filial. I lacked con-

---

* Illustres pietate viros et fortia bello
Pectora.   VIRGIL.

fidence in God. I was distressed to see myself hurried to judgment almost in the midst of my course, without sending any good work before me, while I could but feel greatly saddened by my numerous infidelities to God.

"The effect of these words was to rouse my courage and fill me with such love for God, that in my transport, even before I awoke, I added these words of St. Bernard: 'Not unreasonably does He ask our life, who first gave us His own.'

"These pious thoughts so expanded my heart, that when the Indians proposed to return to the village, where I expected to meet death, I set out full of joy."

This homeward march soon began. The servant of God himself suggested it when he saw that his masters seemed loath to put up with him. He knew well that his charity and zeal would find opportunity for their exercise in the village. He accordingly asked permission to go back with some of the Indians, and his masters consented readily, as much to get rid of him, as to profit by his journey, making him carry to their friends a good load of dried meat.

Father Jogues submitted without a word to all they required, and started, loaded like a beast of burden. But if this eight days' march on foot through the snows of January, and so loaded down, was painful for nature, it was compensated by its influence on the heart of the apostle.

In this party was a woman carrying a heavy load on her back, and also a young child. They came to a deep and rapid torrent, which in that rigorous cold they could not attempt to cross by swimming. Fortunately there was a sort of bridge near, such as Indians understand making. It consisted of a tall pine tree which they had cut down, adroitly directing its descent so that it crossed from one bank to the other. The Indians boldly crossed this narrow path, but the poor woman, encumbered by her double burden, and alarmed at the swaying of this unsteady bridge, lost her balance and fell into the water. At that moment the strap which held her pack on her back, and which as usual passed over her forehead, slipped down to her neck, and choked her so that she could do nothing to save herself.

Father Jogues was following close behind. Seeing her fall, and her danger, he did not hesitate a moment or stop to count its risk to himself, but sprang into the water. By his courage and dexterity, he fortunately reached her and drew mother and child to the shore. It was none too soon, for the child was well-nigh drowned. The missionary hastened to regenerate it in the waters of baptism, and two days after its little soul went to heaven to pray for its deliverer.

Another of the missionary's companions on this journey was, though he did not recognize him, the old man who had instigated good René's death. On the way, won doubtless by the virtue of the man of God, he showed compassion for his condition. He one day invited him to share his meal ; but when he saw the missionary, before beginning to eat, make the sign of the cross and pray, he said earnestly, " Do not do that : the Dutch have told us that that sign is good for nothing, and we hate that action as they do. It caused your comrade to be killed, and will bring you to the same fate." " No matter," replied the missionary firmly, " I shall never cease to make it, because the Author of Life approves of it. Come what will, I am ready to die."

This resolute and frank liberty silenced the Indian, and instead of being offended at Father Jogues, he continued to show him kindness. It is a glory of virtue that it can triumph over its enemies.

On reaching the village, and executing the orders which he had received, Father Jogues' first care was to seek to obtain some clothes not only to resist the rigorous cold, but also to conform to rules of decency. He had no alternative but to assume the character of one of Christ's poor. He went from cabin to cabin begging something to cover him. In almost every one he met with nothing but insults and jeers. Yet one Indian did fling him a ragged old cloth; but a Dutchman who was just then on a trading visit to the Mohawks, struck with admiration at so much virtue and so much suffering, obtained for him a suitable dress.

The servant of God felt his destitution all the more keenly, because he saw the Indians every day wrapped up, in the most grotesque way, in all the stuffs and clothes they found in the packages intended for the Huron Mission. The sacred vestments had not been spared more than the rest, and this profanation deeply grieved his heart. He saw one Indian who had made himself leggins* from the knee to the ankle of two veils intended for covering the chalice at Holy Mass.

Father Jogues did not enjoy a long rest at the village. Those to whom he had brought presents from the hunting party wished to show their gratitude, and saw no better way than to send the bearer back with a good supply of corn.

It was hard for this man, exhausted by suffering and privation, to make the long march again, and return to a position of which he knew all the hardship. But Father Jogues regarded his slavery only with the eyes of faith, and without yielding to the repugnance of nature, he prepared to obey. Not only was the load assigned to him altogether beyond his strength, but the ground was covered with a glare of ice that made progress almost impossible. He set out, but slipped at every step, and fell frequently, without advancing on his journey. After useless efforts he saw that he could never reach the hunting camp and resolved to return.

Without giving him credit for his good-will, or considering the difficulty of travelling, the Indians loaded him with taunts and insults. They called him lazy, good-for-

---

* Indians are fond of adorning these richly.

nothing, deformed. They even reproached him with the scanty fare they allowed him. The servant of God bore it all with humble resignation, and without a reply.

He submitted even more willingly, when the Indians, to make his presence useful, assigned to him a task of which they had long wished to rid themselves. They appointed him to nurse a sick man whose body was one ulcer. The stench he exhaled and the horror he inspired drove all the Indians from him. This made him an object dear to the man of God, and what made his sacrifice more meritorious was the fact that he recognized in this man the one who had treated him so inhumanly when he entered the first Mohawk town, and who had torn out his nails. Father Jogues saw in this but a greater motive for remaining by him, and showing by his care what Christian charity can do.

However, the people of the cabin to which Father Jogues belonged, on returning from their winter hunt called him back to work for them. Their manner toward him had somewhat improved. His host's mother, whom he called "aunt," especially showed kindness to him. She began to admire and respect virtue such as had hitherto been unknown among these Indians. At last the other Indians gradually left him in peace, either tiring of this prolonged persecution, or coming at last to esteem him, overcome by his heroic patience.

As soon as Father Jogues saw calm restored around him, and found his masters exact less labor from him, he resumed his duties as a missionary. His first care was to acquire the language of the people thoroughly. This would enable him to make his presence among them useful, and fit him to become their future apostle. He devoted himself to study with great ardor, and as his owner's cabin was a general meeting-place, where the public affairs not only of the town, but in fact of the tribe, were discussed, he found opportunity to speak in regard to the faith and doctrines of the gospel with all the older men of the tribe. They plied him with questions as to the sun, the moon, the figures seen on its face ; on the size of the earth and of the ocean, the tides, etc. They wished to know whether there was not a place where the heavens touched the earth, whether heaven was a solid vault ; and question followed question without end.

The missionary endeavored to reply by adapting his explanation to their comprehension, and his answers excited their admiration wonderfully. He heard them say, " How we should have missed it if we had killed this prisoner, as we have so often been on the point of doing !" These conversations afforded the servant of God an opportunity of raising their minds by degrees from creatures to a knowledge of the Creator, and of refuting their absurd traditions, which ascribed the origin of the world to a tortoise. He gradually grew so bold as to tell them that the sun was not only not a God, or endowed with mind and life, but that if, delighted with its beauty, they took it to be a God, they should know how much the Lord of it is more beautiful than it (Wisd. xiii. 3). He showed them that their Aireskoï was only a demon, and the father of lies, by pretending to be the author and preserver of life and all good things.

If faith required of man only conviction of the mind, Father Jogues would easily have won a complete triumph ; but he found his teaching obstructed by the powerful chains of the passions, superstitious habits, and the intense aversion Indians feel for everything that is new. They readily admitted that he was right ; but as to adopting his teaching, they often would merely tell him : "All that is good for you, who live beyond the great lake [ocean], but not for us."

The devil, who had till then ruled as undisputed lord over this vast country, saw himself attacked, as it were, in his last lines, and redoubled his efforts to check the conquests of the Faith.

Yet, slave as he was, the apostolic ministry of Father

Jogues was not exercised in vain. The Almighty King of these nations, as of all others on earth, was already choosing His elect among them: not only among the children, numbers of whom were baptized by the servant of God when in danger of death, but also among the adults, several of whom became docile to the voice of grace, and sought the sacrament of regeneration. This was especially the case among the sick, who saw their last hour approach, and also among the wretched victims of war, condemned to undergo the horrors of the stake.

These labors did not satisfy the zeal of Father Jogues. Availing himself of the partial liberty allowed him by his owners, he visited the Huron captives in the neighboring towns, where, like the faithful Israelites, these Christians refused to bend the knee before Baal. He comforted them and sustained them by his pious counsels, and by enabling them to approach the sacrament of penance. How often he had reason to bless God when he beheld the salutary fruit which the preaching of the Gospel had already produced! He found hearts imbued with Christianity only for a few days, yet gifted with admirable purity, unshaken constancy, and a heroic resignation to God's will.

After spending two months in these pious exercises, Father Jogues was compelled to go on another journey. It was the season for fishing. He set out with his "aunt" and two other Indians. His duties were the same as on the hunting excursion, but his treatment was much milder. The fishing party halted on the banks of a little lake only four days' march from the town.*

The fish caught here were very small, but generally very abundant, though few at this time. They laid them up carefully for their summer supply, after cleaning and smoking them. They took as food at the time only the intestines, which they used to season their hominy.

---

* This was undoubtedly Saratoga Lake.

But Father Jogues was by this time inured to such fare, and he adds with simplicity when describing it, "Custom, hunger, and want of everything renders tolerable at least, if not agreeable, what nature often revolts at."

These excursions, away from the towns and the noise of the Iroquois, always had a charm for the servant of God. They afforded him time and opportunity for greater union with God. "How often in these journeys," he writes, "and in that quiet wilderness, 'did we sit by the rivers of Babylon, and weep while we remembered thee, Sion' (Ps. cxxxvi. 1.) not only exulting that Sion in heaven, but even thee, Jerusalem, praising thy God on earth. 'How often, though in a strange land, did we sing the canticle of the Lord,' and mountain and wildwood resounded with the praises of their Maker, which from their creation they had never heard! How often on the stately trees of the forest did I carve the most sacred name of Jesus, that seeing it the demons might fly, who tremble when they hear it! How often, too, did I not strip off the bark to form on them the Most Holy Cross of the Lord, that the foe might fly before it, and that by it Thou, O Lord my King, 'mightest reign in the midst of Thy enemies'—the enemies of Thy cross, the misbelievers and the pagans who dwell in that land, and the demons who rule so powerfully there! I rejoiced, too, that I had been led by the Lord into the wilderness, at the very time when the Church recalls the story of His Passion, so that I might more uninterruptedly remember the course of its bitterness and gall, and my soul pine away at the remembrance" (Jer. iii. 20).

As in his first excursion he had made a little oratory of branches in the woods at the foot of a huge tree, on which he had traced the form of the cross; hither, as soon as his work as a slave was done, he returned to commune with his God. "But," adds the pious missionary, "I was not long allowed to enjoy this holy repose: indeed, too many days had I passed, unharmed by my wonted terrors."

In fact a messenger had just come from the village to warn the fishing-party that Algonquins had been seen prowling around, and that they must return in haste to escape the danger. This alarm was merely a stratagem invented to bring the missionary back to the village, where all preparations had been made to put him to death.

The most unfavorable rumors were circulating as to the fate of a band of ten Mohawk warriors who had been out for a long time, and of whom there were no tidings. A neighboring tribe asserted that they had become victims to the cruelty of their enemies, and this news was confirmed by a prisoner who had recently fallen into the hands of the Iroquois. They immediately sacrificed him to the shade of one of the young warriors for whom they mourned, and who was a son of the master of the cabin to which Father Jogues belonged; but this victim did not seem noble enough in the eyes of the grief-stricken father: he wished the missionary also sacrificed.

His fate was decided; and the day of our Saviour's death would also have been his last, had not God, who had so often led him to the gates of death to draw him back as if by a miracle, permitted them to learn in time that the warriors were returning with twenty Abnaki captives, and that they were within a day's march of the town.

The missionary was no longer thought of, and on the arrival of the victors there was nothing but festivity and rejoicing. Five of the prisoners were doomed to the most fearful tortures, the women and children being reserved for slavery. These unhappy victims became immediately the object of the missionary's ardent zeal. He knew only a few words of their language, but one of the prisoners who spoke Huron acted as interpreter.

He instructed them without delay, and succeeded in baptizing them before their execution, which took place at Easter-tide.

This hideous spectacle was renewed at Pentecost. Three young women and some children were brought in, for the men had been killed in the battle. These poor creatures, stripped of their clothing, were mutilated and beaten as they entered the village. One of them was even, contrary to custom, burned all over the body, and then thrown on an immense pyre. She was instructed in the faith, and Father Jogues was on the alert for an opportunity to baptize her. Seeing her on the point of expiring, he ran up to her in the midst of the flames, as if going to give her a drink of water, and poured on her head the saving water, which cleansed her and secured her everlasting happiness.

Father Jogues witnessed on this occasion idolatrous practices of a character new to him, and of unheard cruelty. Every time that the fire was applied to the body of this poor woman, one of the sachems raised his voice, crying, "Aireskoi, we offer thee this victim, which we burn in thy honor. Sate thyself on her flesh, and make us ever victorious over our enemies." Her body, cut up, was distributed through the different villages and eaten.

This bloody sacrifice was apparently, in the eyes of the Iroquois, a reparation due their god, and the fulfilment of a vow. They believed that they had incurred his displeasure, because they had not eaten human flesh for six months; and in a solemn sacrifice of two bears, which they made in his honor, Father Jogues heard them, and not without a shudder, utter these words: "Justly dost thou punish us, O Aireskoi! Lo! this long time we have taken no captives. . . . We have sinned against thee in that we ate not the last captives thrown into our hands; but, if we shall ever again capture any, we promise thee to devour them as we now consume these two bears."

These sad scenes were frequently repeated at this time before the eyes of Father Jogues, and they plunged his soul into the deepest affliction. But, in the hope of being useful to these unfortunate victims, he remained to attend them in their tortures, neglecting no means to sustain and encourage them by thoughts of faith.

In a profound sentiment of humility he looked upon himself as the cause of all these woes. "I certainly," says he, "felt in my own person this punishment deserved for my sins, and pronounced of old by God to His people when He said 'their solemnities, their new-moons, and all their festival-times' . . . 'shall be turned into mourning and lamentation' (Osee ii. 11; Amos viii. 10), as Easter, and Whitsuntide, and the Nativity of St. John the Baptist each brought sorrows on me, which increased to agony.' . . . 'Wo is me, wherefore was I born to see the ruin of my people?' (1 Mach. ii. 7.) Verily, in these and like heartrending cares, 'my life is wasted with grief, and my years with sighs' (Ps. xxx. 2); 'for the Lord hath corrected me for mine iniquity and hath made my soul waste away as a spider' (xxxviii. 12). 'He hath filled me with bitterness, he hath inebriated me with wormwood' (Lament. iii. 15); 'because the comforter, the relief of my soul, is far from me' (i. 16); 'but in all these things we overcome,' and by the favor of God will overcome, 'because of Him that hath loved us' (Rom. viii. 37), until 'He come that is to come, and will not delay' (Heb. x. 37); 'until my day like that of a hireling come' (Job vii. 1), or 'my change be made' (xiv. 14)."

CHAPTER IX.

Steps taken by the Chevalier de Montmagny to deliver Father Jogues—The Missionary's Letters — His Resignation —A Journey—Unexpected Meeting—Consolation.

THE deepest anxiety prevailed for a long time at Quebec as to the fate of Father Jogues. The report of his death spread, and even reached France, where it produced the deepest impression. He was mourned for by his family and fellow-religious, who yet envied his happiness and his glory.

The news that he was still alive was brought to Quebec by a Huron who had shared his captivity, Joseph Theondechoren, to whom allusion has already been made. This good Christian had followed his owners in an excursion which they made to the banks of the St. Lawrence. There he succeeded in baffling their vigilance, and escaped from their hands. After a series of hardships and dangers, he reached Three Rivers.

The Chevalier de Montmagny, anxious to learn what was going on in the Iroquois country, and especially to obtain tidings of Father Jogues, summoned the fugitive before him. The detailed and affecting story of the sufferings undergone by the man of God, and the danger which still hourly threatened him, affected the Governor all the more, because he felt himself utterly unable to rescue him. The re-enforcements expected from France had not arrived, and he feared that any vigorous action against such bold enemies, instead of intimidating them, if they were not crushed, would only increase their exasperation and hasten the death of all the prisoners. He wished, at all hazards, to save the life of a missionary whose virtue and experience might prove so useful in winning over these savages. He accordingly sought a favorable opportunity for treating prudently this delicate matter, and when he found one shortly after, he seized it, but without avail.

On the 19th of October, 1642, a Sokoki * Indian, highly esteemed in his tribe, was taken by the Algonquins near Three Rivers. They condemned him to pass through all the horrors of Indian torture. They had already torn out his nails and cut off two of his fingers; one of his feet had been pierced with a sharp stick, and his whole body had been seamed with awls. Four young men had tied his wrists with running knots, and drew it so cruelly that the flesh was cut to the bone. The pain was so intense that, notwithstanding his apparent impassibility, he fell unconscious, and did not come to till water had been thrown in his face.

As soon as the Governor heard of the prisoner's arrival at Sillery, he hastened there with the intention of rescuing him from death. A motive of humanity and religion prompted his interference to prevent this act of cruel barbarity, and, independently of this, he had another motive, as worthy of his heart as of his faith. By means of this prisoner, whose nation was in alliance with the Iroquois, he hoped to obtain the deliverance of the missionary, whose wretched fate the whole colony and the very Indians deplored. The Chevalier de Montmagny accordingly asked and obtained the freedom of this captive.

The Hospital Nuns received the unfortunate man into their establishment at Sillery. His wounds were in a horrible condition; worms and putrefaction made him an object of disgust and pity; but the case did not baffle the motherly care of active charity.

---

* A tribe living near the western border of Maine.

When the patient, cured of his wounds, was able to travel, he was loaded with presents, and the only return asked of him was that he should urge the chiefs of his tribe to interpose with their allies, the Iroquois, in order to obtain the liberation of Father Jogues.

After having been so near death, the Sokoki returned to his country, full of joy, to relate all the kindness and liberality shown him. Praise of Onontio, the great chief of the French, and of the black-gowns was constantly on his lips, and all who heard him soon began to share his gratitude. For, brutish as they were, these Indians warmly entered into the feelings of one of their tribe, when gratitude was to be shown for a favor or vengeance taken for a wrong.

The Sokokis proved it. Every man felt indebted to the generous benefactors of their countryman, and they prepared at once to carry out his wishes. A solemn embassy set out in the month of April to ask the Mohawks to set Father Jogues free, and they offered the usual presents to give weight to their words.

The Mohawks received the deputies with the usual ceremonial in a public audience. The Sokoki orator detailed at length the object of his coming, and the claims of the French on their friendship. His natural eloquence inspired him with arguments best able to produce an impression, and he concluded by saying, "My tribe think that they cannot do too much to please men so generous, and as they know how highly the French esteem Ondesonk, here is a belt of many thousand beads of wampum to cut his bonds." With these words he produced a letter from the Governor of Quebec, which he solemnly placed in the hands of Father Jogues, with every mark of respect and esteem.

The next day the Mohawk sachems assembled to deliberate and announce their reply. It was not long delayed, and it justified their reputation for perfidy and cunning: they accepted the presents and promised to set the prisoner at liberty, and they said that they claimed for themselves the honor of escorting Father Jogues back to the French colony, but that they could not do so just at that moment. These words were only a new deception. They were forgotten as soon as the ambassadors departed.

Yet the demonstration of the Sokokis on behalf of Father Jogues had not been altogether fruitless. It exalted considerably in the eyes of the Iroquois the importance of the missionary, and they began to treat him with more respect.

If public dangers seemed thus provided against, Father Jogues was not yet safe from private hate or vengeance. One day he saw a half-crazy Indian enter his cabin, who rushed upon him and dealt him two blows on the head with a war-club. The missionary was struck to the ground; and if the assassin's arm raised for a third blow had not been checked, his life would have ended there. The guilty man retired calmly, without punishment or even a reproach.

The only satisfaction that the servant of God received was the tears of his aunt, whose devotedness and affection seemed to increase daily, while she lamented her inability to protect him. When she could foresee a danger, she never lost a moment in warning him and aiding him to escape it; but as she was in constant apprehension that he would be suddenly attacked, and saw that the sachems had really no intention of keeping the promise they had made to the Sokokis, she at last advised Father Jogues to escape, as the only means of ending his fearful captivity, and almost certain death.

It was not, however, his own deliverance that preoccupied Father Jogues; above that he held the interest of religion and his country, and he soon bore noble testimony to this heroic feeling.

Having learned that other steps were proposed for his relief, he desired his state of mind to be clearly known; and listening only to patriotism, he resolved to write to the Governor of Canada, and suggest measures which might prove fatal to himself, but which were most advantageous to the colony. Providence afforded him a favorable opportunity of transmitting his letter to the banks of the St. Lawrence.

During the summer a party of warriors from his village prepared to march to the banks of the great river in order to lie in wait for the French and their allies, and one of them took his letter. According to the custom of the Indians, he should have inserted this letter on the cleft top of a stick, to be planted on the trail usually taken by travellers. Whatever his motive was, he chose to do something more. He approached Fort Richelieu.

On the 15th of August, 1643, the soldiers in the fort perceived a solitary Indian approaching them on the river. Before letting him come near, they asked his tribe and his business. "I am an Iroquois," he replied, "and I come as bearer of the word of Ondesonk, the black-gown." On this statement he was permitted to enter freely, and he really handed in a letter of the missionary addressed to the Chevalier de Montmagny.

As he showed a desire to depart, the commandant of the post compelled him to wait for some time, so as to give the Governor an opportunity to send back an answer to the missionary. Then a cannon was fired to announce that the truce was over. Alarmed at this signal, which they took for an attack on them, the Iroquois fled precipitately, abandoning their comrade. This, as we shall see, gave new life to the hatred against Father Jogues.

His letter to the Governor was written partly in Latin, partly in French, and partly in Huron, so as to make it almost unintelligible if it fell into the enemy's hands. The following is a translation of it, from a copy preserved in the archives of the Gesù at Rome :

"MY LORD : This is the fourth* letter I have written since my detention as a prisoner in the hands of the Iroquois. Time and paper both fail me, and prevent my repeating here what I have said elsewhere at greater length.

"We are still alive. Henry, taken prisoner by the Iroquois near Montreal, on St. John's Eve, has been brought among us. He did not indeed run the gauntlet on entering the village, nor have his fingers been cut off, as ours were. He and the Hurons brought in with him are still alive.

"Fear constantly and everywhere the ambuscades of these men, for bands of braves leave the village every day to go on the war-path, and you must not think that the river† will be free from these savages before the end of autumn.

"They are here to the number of seven hundred; possess three hundred guns, which they use with great skill; and know several routes to reach the station of Three Rivers. Fort Richelieu arrests them indeed somewhat, but yet does not entirely prevent their raids.

"If the Iroquois had known that the Sokoki prisoner was indebted to the French for his deliverance from the hands of the Algonquins, they would, they say, have spared the French who have been taken and killed near Montreal. But it was already midwinter when this news came to their knowledge.

"However, a new party has just taken the field. The chief is the very same who commanded the expedition which took us prisoners. They intend to attack the French no less than the Algonquins.

"Do not, I beg you, take me personally into consideration, and let no sympathy for me prevent your taking

---

* The three other letters mentioned by Father Jogues did not reach their address.

† The St. Lawrence.

any measure that seems to you best fitted to advance the greater glory of God.

"So far as I can divine, it is the design of the Iroquois to capture all the Hurons, if it is possible; to put the chiefs and a great part of the nation to death, and with the rest to form one nation and one country.

"I shed tears over the lot of these unfortunate people, most of whom are already Christians, the rest cate-chumens, and well disposed to receive baptism.

"When will it be possible to apply a remedy at last to so many evils? Perhaps when there are no more prisoners to take.

"I have here a Relation* written by our Fathers on what had occurred among the Hurons, and some letters written by the same Fathers. The Iroquois captured them from the Hurons and handed them to me.

"The Dutch have made several efforts to deliver us, but always to no purpose. They are now renewing their attempts; but I think it will be with the same result.

"I form a resolution, which daily becomes more de-cided, to remain here as long as it pleases Our Lord, and not to seek to achieve my liberty, even if an oppor-tunity offers. I do not wish to deprive the French, Hurons, and Algonquins of the benefit they receive from my ministry. I have administered baptism here to some, several of whom have already soared to heaven.

"My only consolation amid my sufferings is to think of the most holy will of God, to which I most willingly submit mine.

"I beg your Excellency to have the kindness to have prayers said and Masses celebrated for us all, and especially for him who is in Our Lord,

"Sir, your most humble and most obedient servant,

"ISAAC JOGUES,
"*of the Society of Jesus.*"

---

* It was the Annual Relation of the Huron Mission for 1642. It was taken by the Iroquois from a convoy of Hurons, who were carry-ing it to Quebec.

Father Vincent, the Superior in Canada, when inserting this letter in the Relation of the Missions for 1644, adds with holy admiration : "There is more juice here than words. The tissue is excellent, although the hand that formed these letters is all mangled. His style is more sublime than that which emanates from the most pompous schools of rhetoric. . . . Although his words have drawn tears from our eyes, they have nevertheless increased the joy of our hearts. Some of us rather envy than compassionate him."

To this letter, a beautiful monument of the ardent zeal and heroic patriotism of the servant of God, we must add, as a complement, the close of that from which we have drawn a part of the details of his captivity, and which he wrote to his Provincial in France on the 5th of August, 1643. He had at the time, while on a journey with his owners, stopped at the Dutch post of Rensselaerswyck, called also Fort Orange.*

"Although I could in all probability escape either through the Europeans or the Indian nations around us, did I wish to fly, yet on this cross to which our Lord has nailed me, with Himself (Gal. ii. 19), am I resolved by His grace to live and die. For who in my absence would console the French captives ? who absolve the penitent ? who remind the christened Huron of his duty ? who instruct the prisoners constantly brought in ? who baptize them dying, encourage them in their torments ? who cleanse the infants in the saving waters ? who provide for the salvation of the dying adult, the instruction of those in health ? Indeed I cannot but think it a peculiar interposition of divine goodness, that while a nation, fallen from the true Catholic religion, barred the entrance of the Faith to these regions on one side, and on the other, a fierce war between savage nations, and on their account with the French, I should have fallen into the

---

* Our present Albany.

hands of these Indians, who by the will of God reluctantly, and I may say against their will, have thus far spared my life, that through me, though unworthy, those might be instructed, believe, and be baptized, who are pre-destined to eternal life. Since the time when I was taken, I have baptized seventy persons, children, young people and old, of five different nations and languages, that of 'every tribe, and people, and tongue, they might stand in the sight of the Lamb' (Apoc. vii. 9).

"Therefore do I daily bow my knee to my Lord and to the Father of my Lord, that if it be for His glory, He may confound all the designs of the Europeans and savages for ransoming me or sending me back to the whites ; for many of the Indians speak of my being restored, and the Dutch, among whom I write this, have frequently of-fered, and now again are offering, to rescue me and my companions. I have visited them twice, and have been most kindly welcomed ; they leave no stone unturned to effect our deliverance, and have made many presents to the Indians with whom I am, to induce them to treat me humanely.

"But I am now weary of so long and so prolix a letter; I therefore earnestly beg your Reverence ever to recog-nize me, though unworthy, as one of yours; for though a savage in dress and manner, and almost without God in so tossed a life, yet as I have ever lived a son of the most holy Church of Rome and of the Society, so do I wish to die. Obtain for me from God, Reverend Father, by your holy sacrifices, that though I have hitherto but ill-em-ployed the means He gave me to attain the highest sanc-tity, I may at least employ well this last occasion which He offers me. Your bounty, surely, owes this to a son who has recourse to you; for I lead a truly wretched life, where every virtue is in danger: Faith in the dense darkness of paganism, Hope in so long and hard trials, Charity amid so much corruption, deprived of all the sacraments. Purity is not, indeed, endangered here by delights, but is tried, amid this promiscuous and intimate intercourse of both sexes, by the perfect liberty of all in hearing and doing what they please; and, most of all, in their constant nakedness. For here, willing or not, you must often see what elsewhere is shut out, not only from wandering, but even from curious eyes. Hence I daily groan to my God, begging Him not to leave me without help amid the dead;—begging Him, I say, that amid such impurity and such superstitious worship of the devil to which He has exposed me, naked as it were, and un-armed, 'my heart may be undefiled in His justifica-tions' (Ps. cxviii. 80), so that when that good Shep-herd shall come, 'who will gather together the dispersed of Israel' (Ps. cxlvi. 2), 'He may gather us from among the nations to bless His holy name. Amen! Amen!' (Ps. cv. 47.)

"Your Reverence's most humble servant and son in Christ,   ISAAC JOGUES.

"Permit me through your Reverence to salute all my dear Fathers and Brothers whom I tenderly love and cherish in Christ, and to commend myself to their holy sacrifices and prayers.

"Your most humble servant and son in Christ,
"ISAAC JOGUES.

"RENSSELAERSWYCK, in New Netherland, August 5, 1643."

The repugnance which Father Jogues manifested for seeing his term of captivity end, had no other motive than the desire to advance more efficaciously the Glory of God. But when he saw that he could not possibly continue his zealous and charitable work, he did not re-fuse to profit by the circumstances which Divine Provi-dence disposed, in order to escape from the hands of his executioners. This was soon to come to pass; yet God first brought about one of those incidents which display the goodness of the Almighty for His elect, and which afford His apostles their richest reward here below.

A band of Iroquois chiefs had been selected to visit, as representatives of the nation, a small tribe in the neighborhood, which they regarded as a tributary, and from which they expected some aid. Father Jogues' master was one of the party, and he took his slave with him. The distance to be travelled was nearly two hundred miles. The march was a painful one: the Indians set out as usual without any provisions, and contrary to their expectations found no game on their route, and were compelled to subsist on poor insipid berries they gathered in the woods. The object of the Indians in taking the missionary with them was to make an ostentatious display of their power over other nations—even over Europeans; but the Lord had other designs. He was going to reward a charitable act.

On reaching the town, Father Jogues at once proceeded to visit the cabins, in order to baptize dying children and to instruct the sick whom he found inclined to hearken to him. What was his surprise, on entering one of the first cabins he reached, to hear a young man stretched on the ground and racked by pain, address him by name?

"Do you not recognize me, Ondesonk," said the dying man; "do you not remember the good turn I did you in the Iroquois country, and how it relieved you?" "I do not recollect ever to have seen you," replied the Father; "but that matters not: I thank you, since you did me a service. What did you do for me?" "It was in the third Mohawk town," said the young man, "when you were hung up, and could no longer endure your intense sufferings: do you recollect an Indian coming up and cutting the ropes?" "Yes, indeed," replied the missionary; "many a time have I blessed the Lord for inspiring him to do that charitable act. I have never met him since, and I should be happy to see him, and, if I could, show him all my gratitude."

"I did it myself," replied the sick man.

On hearing this, Father Jogues clasped him to his breast, kissed him tenderly, shedding tears of gratitude and compassion. "How grieved I am," said he, "to find you in this pitiable condition! Why can I not relieve and help you? Without knowing who you were, I have often prayed to the Master of Life for you. You see my extreme poverty; yet I wish to do you a greater favor than you did me."

The Indian listened with astonishment. Then the missionary told him of God, the creator and rewarder; of Jesus Christ and His sufferings, of eternity and its rewards. While he spoke, God acted interiorly on the well-disposed heart; and, like the eunuch in the Acts of the Apostles, the sick man soon asked, "What must I do to please the Master of Life?" "Believe in Him," said the missionary, "and in His only Son, who died for us, and receive baptism."

The soul of the neophyte opened to the light, and the minister of Jesus Christ had the consolation of instructing him and receiving proof of his faith. He became a Christian, and as the disease made rapid progress, Father Jogues ere long saw him depart to heaven, full of hope, and with no earthly regret. Thus did God reward a hundredfold the man who took pity on His servant.

CHAPTER X.

THE hour of deliverance approached; once more
Father Jogues accompanied his owners to a fish-
ing-station on the banks of the Hudson, about
twenty miles from Rensselaerswyck. It was this providential excursion which afforded him the means of escape. We will hear him relate his flight in detail, in a
letter * which he wrote from that Dutch post to Father
Charles Lalemant on the 30th of August, 1643.

"On the very day of the feast of our Holy Father
Ignatius (July 31), I left the village where I was a prisoner to follow and accompany some Iroquois who were
going first to trade, then to fish. Having got through
their traffic, they proceeded to a place seven or eight
leagues below the Dutch post,† which is on the river
where we were fishing. While arranging our weirs for
the fish, a report reached us that an Iroquois war-party,
returned from the Huron land, had killed five or six on
the spot, and brought in four prisoners, two of whom
had been already burned at our village with more than
common cruelty.

"At these tidings my heart was rent with most keen and
bitter grief, that I had not seen, consoled, or baptized
these poor victims. Fearful that something of the kind
might happen again during my absence, I went to a good
old woman, who from her age and her care of me, as well

---

* Relation for 1643, p. 75.   † Rensselaerswyck.

as from her compassion for my sufferings, called me her nephew, as I called her aunt. 'Aunt,' said I, 'I would much rather go back to our cabin; I am very lonesome here.' I did not indeed expect more comfort or less pain at the village, where I suffered a continual martyr-dom—compelled to witness before my eyes the horrible cruelties they perpetrate—but my heart could not bear that one should die without my affording him baptism. 'Go, nephew,' said this good woman, 'go, if you are tired of this place, and take something to eat on the way.' I accordingly embarked in the first canoe going up to the village, always conducted and always accom-panied by Iroquois.

"On reaching the Dutch post through which we had to pass, I learned that our village was furious against the French, and that they only awaited my return to burn me. The reason of all was this: Among the war-parties against the French, Algonquins, and Hurons was one that resolved to go and prowl around Fort Richelieu to spy the French and their Indian allies. A certain Huron of this band, taken by the Iroquois and naturalized among them, came to ask me for letters to carry to the French, hoping perhaps to surprise some one by this bait; but as I had no doubt the French would be on their guard, I saw the importance of giving them some inkling of the designs, arms, and treachery of our enemy. I found means to get a bit of paper to write on. The Dutch did me this charity.

"I knew well the danger to which I exposed myself. I was well aware that if any mishap befell the party I should be made responsible, and the blame thrown on my letters. I foresaw my death, but it seemed to me sweet and agreeable, employed for the public good, and the consolation of our French, and the poor Indians who listen to the word of Jesus Christ. My heart was undis-turbed by fear at the sight of all that might happen—God's glory was concerned.

"So I gave my letter to the young brave, who never returned. The story given by his comrades is that he carried it to Fort Richelieu, and that as soon as the French saw it, they fired their cannon at them; that, alarmed at this, most of them took to flight all naked, leaving one of their canoes, in which were three arquebuses, powder, ball, and other articles. When this news was brought into the village, the cry was raised that my letter had caused them to be treated so. The rumor spread around; it reached my ears; I was taunted with the mishap; they talked of nothing but burning me; and had I been found in the village when these braves returned, fire, rage, and cruelty had deprived me of my life.

"To increase my misfortune, another party, returning from the neighborhood of Montreal, where they had laid an ambush for the French, said that two of their party had been killed and two wounded. All made me guilty of these mishaps. They were now beside themselves with rage, and impatient for my return. All these reports I heard, offering myself unreservedly to our Lord, and resigning myself, all in all, to His most holy will.

"The commander of the Dutch post where we were, aware of the evil design of the savages, and aware, too, that the Chevalier de Montmagny had prevented the Canada Indians from coming to kill the Dutch, had offered me means of escape. 'Here,' said he, 'lies a vessel at anchor,* to sail in a few days. Get privately on board. It is bound first to Virginia, whence it will carry you to Bordeaux or Rochelle, where it must stop.' Thanking him with much respect and courtesy, I told him that the Iroquois would suspect them of favoring my escape, and perhaps do some injury to their people. 'No, no,' he replied; 'do not fear; get on board; it is a

---

* The States-General of Holland had sent orders to all the commandants in New Netherland to deliver Father Jogues, the Queen-Regent of France having requested it in the most urgent manner.

fine opportunity, and you will never find a surer way of escaping.'

"At these words my heart was perplexed. I doubted whether it was not for the greater glory of our Lord to expose myself to the danger of savage fury and flames, in order to aid in the salvation of some soul. I therefore replied, 'This affair, sir, seems to me so important that I cannot give you an answer on this spot; give me, if you please, to-night to think it over. I will recommend it to our Lord; I will examine the reasons on both sides, and will tell you my final resolution in the morning.' Greatly astonished, he granted my request. The night I spent in prayer, earnestly imploring our Lord not to let me adopt a conclusion myself, but to give me light to know His most holy will; that in all and through all, even to the stake itself, I would follow it. The reasons to retain me in the country were the consideration of the French and Indians; I loved them, and felt so great a desire to serve them, that I had resolved to pass the rest of my days in this captivity for their salvation; but now I beheld the face of affairs entirely changed.

" First, as for the three Frenchmen, brought prisoners like myself into the country, one—René Goupil—had already been massacred at my feet. This young man was as pure as an angel. Henry, taken at Montreal, had fled to the woods; because while he was beholding the cruelties perpetrated on two Hurons roasted alive, some Iroquois told him that they would treat him so, and me too, as soon as I got back. This threat made him resolve to run the risk of starving in the woods, or being devoured by some wild beast, rather than endure the torments inflicted by these half-demons. He had not been seen for seven days. As to William Couture, I could scarcely see any means of being of service to him, for he had been put in a village at a distance from mine, and the Indians kept him so busy here and there that I could no longer find him. He had, moreover, himself told me, 'Father, try to escape; as soon as I see no more of you I will manage to get off. You know well that I remain in this captivity only for your sake; do your best, then, to escape, for I cannot think of my own liberty or life till I see you in safety.' Besides, this good young friend had been given to an old man, who assured him that he would let him go in peace if I could effect my deliverance; so that I no longer saw any reason to remain on account of the French.

"As to the Indians, instructing them was now out of the question and almost hopeless; for the whole country was so excited against me that I no longer found means to speak to them or gain them; and the Algonquins and Hurons kept aloof from me, as a victim destined to the flames, because they feared to come in for a share of the rage and hatred which the Iroquois bore me. I saw, too, that I had some knowledge of their language, that I knew their country and their strength, and that I could perhaps contribute better to their salvation in other ways than by remaining among them. All this knowledge, it occurred to me, would die with me if I did not escape. The wretches, too, had so little intention of giving us up, that they committed an act of perfidy against the right and custom of all these nations. An Indian of the country of the Sokokis, allies of the Iroquois, having been taken by the upper Algonquins and brought to Three Rivers or Quebec as a prisoner, was delivered and set at liberty by the intervention of the Governor of New France, at the solicitation of our Fathers. The good Indian, seeing that the French had saved his life, sent beautiful presents in the month of April to deliver at least one of the French. The Iroquois retained the presents without setting one of us at liberty; a treachery perhaps unexampled among these tribes, for they invariably observe the law, that whoso touches or accepts the present made him, must execute what is asked by the present. Accordingly, when they do not wish to grant what is desired, they send back the presents, or make others in their stead.

"But to return to my purpose. Having weighed before God, with all possible abstraction from self, the reasons for remaining among the Indians, and those for leaving, I concluded that our Lord would be more pleased with my taking the opportunity to escape.

"As soon as it was day I went to salute the Dutch Governor, and told him the resolution I had come to before God; he called for the officers of the ship, told them his intentions, and exhorted them to receive and conceal me —in a word, to carry me over to Europe. They replied that if I could once set foot in their vessel, I was safe; I should not leave it till I reached Bordeaux or Rochelle. 'Cheer up, then,' said the Governor; 'return with the Indians, and this evening, or in the night, steal off quietly and make for the river; there you will find a little boat, which I will have ready to take you to the ship.' After most humble thanks to all these gentlemen, I left the Dutch, the better to conceal my design. In the evening I retired with ten or twelve Iroquois to a barn,* where we spent the night. Before lying down, I went out to see where I could most easily escape. The dogs, then let loose, ran at me, and a large and powerful one snapped at my bare leg and bit it severely.†

"I immediately entered the barn; the Iroquois closed the door securely, and to guard me better, came and lay beside me, especially one who was in a manner appointed to watch me. Seeing myself beset with these mis-

---

* The barn, about one hundred feet long, belonged to a Dutchman whose wife was an Iroquois. One end served as the house of the family: the domestic animals were kept in the other end; the open space in the middle was left to the companions of Father Jogues. (MS. of Father Buteux).

† The farmer, roused by the noise, came with a candle to examine the wound. Moved by pity, he tried to dress it, but the only remedy he applied was a hair of the dog that bit him. (Same MS.).

haps, and the barn well shut and surrounded by dogs that would betray me if I attempted to go out, I almost thought that I could not escape. I sweetly complained to my God, that having given the thought of escaping, 'He hath shut up my way with square stones, and in a spacious place my feet' (Lament. iii. 9). This whole night also I spent without sleep; towards day I heard the cocks crow; soon after a servant of the Dutch farmer who had received us into his barn, entered by some door I did not see. I went up to him softly, and not understanding his Flemish, made him a sign to stop the dogs barking. He immediately went out, and I after him, as soon as I had taken my little luggage, consisting of a Little Office of the Blessed Virgin, an Imitation of Christ, and a wooden cross, which I had made to keep me in mind of my Saviour's sufferings. Having got out of the barn without making any noise or waking my guards, I climbed over a fence which inclosed the house, and ran straight to the river where the ship was; it was as much as my wounded leg could do, for the distance was a good quarter of a league. I found the boat as I had been told, but, as the tide had gone down, it was high and dry. I pushed it to get it to the water, but finding it too heavy, I called to the ship to send me their boat to take me on board. There was no answer; I do not know whether they heard me; be that as it may, no one appeared, and day was now beginning to reveal to the Iroquois the robbery which I had made of myself, and I feared to be surprised in my innocent crime. Weary of hallooing, I returned to my boat, and praying to the Almighty to increase my strength, I succeeded at last so well, by working it slowly on and pushing stoutly, that f got it into the water. As soon as it floated, I jumped in and reached the vessel alone, unperceived by any Iroquois. I was immediately lodged in the bottom of the hold, and to hide me they put a large box on the hatch. I was two days and two nights in the hold of this ship, in such a state that I expected to be suffocated and die of the stench, when I remembered poor Jonas, and prayed Our Lord 'that I might not flee from His face' (Jonas i. 3), nor depart from His will; but on the contrary, 'that he would infatuate all counsels' (2 Kings xv. 31) that were not for His glory, and keep me in the land of these heathen if He did not approve my retreat and flight.

"The second night of my voluntary imprisonment, the minister of the Hollanders * came to tell me that the Iroquois had made much trouble, and that the Dutch settlers were afraid that they would set fire to their houses and kill their cattle. They have reason to fear them, for they are armed with good arquebuses. 'If,' I replied, 'for my sake this great tempest is upon you, cast me into the sea' (Jonas i. 12). If this trouble has been caused by me, I am ready to appease it at the loss of my life. I never wished to escape to the injury of the least man in the colony.

"At last, then, I had to leave my den; the sailors took umbrage, saying 'that they had pledged their word in case I could set foot on the ship, and that they were now taking me off at the very moment when they should have brought me, had I not been there; that I had put my life in danger by escaping on their promise, and that, cost what it might, they must stick to it.' This honest bluntness touched me, but I begged them to let me go, as the captain, who had opened to me the doorway of escaping, now asked me back. I was taken to his house,

---

* The name of this benefactor of Father Jogues deserves to be recorded. It was John Megapolensis; he was the first minister of the place. He came from Holland with his wife and four children, and the States-General fixed the sum for his maintenance. This circumstance of a Jesuit being saved by a Protestant minister is one of the most striking episodes in this history. Domine Megapolensis is the author of a short but interesting account of the Mohawks.

where he kept me concealed. These comings and go-ings were done by night, so that I was not discovered. In all this proceeding I might have urged my own rea-sons, but it was not for me to speak in my own cause, but rather to follow the commands of others; I cheer-fully submitted. At last the captain told me that we must yield calmly to the storm, and wait till the minds of the Indians were appeased: in this advice all con-curred. Here, then, I am a voluntary prisoner in his house, whence I write this. If you ask my thoughts in all this affair, I will tell you first, that the vessel which had wished to save me has gone off without me; second, that if our Lord does not in an almost miraculous way protect me, the Indians, who come and go here every moment, will discover me; and if they ever believe that I am still here, I must necessarily be restored to their hands.

"Now, when they had such fury against me before my flight, how will they treat me when I fall again into their power? I shall die by no ordinary death; their fire, rage, and new-devised cruelties will wring out my life. Blessed be God's name forever! We are ever in the bosom of His Divine and adorable Providence. *Vestri capilli capitis numerati sunt, nolite timere, multis passeribus meliores estis vos; quorum unus non cadet super terram sine patre vestro,*—' Yea, the very hairs of your head are num-bered. Fear not, therefore; you are of more value than many sparrows,' ' not one of whom falls to the earth without your Father' (Matt. x. 30).

"I have been hidden ten or twelve days, and it is hardly possible that an evil day will not come upon me.

"In the third place, you will see our great need of your prayers, and of the holy sacrifices of all our Fathers. Give us this alms, *Ut reddat me Dominus, idoneum ad se amandum, fortem ad patiendum, constantem ad perseverandum in suo amore et servitio,*—' that the Lord may render me fit to love Him, patient to endure, constant to persevere in

His holy love and service.' This and a little New Testament from Europe are my sole desires. Pray for these poor nations that burn and eat each other, that they may come to a knowledge of their Creator, and render Him the tribute of their love. *Memor sum vestri in vinculis meis,*—'I am mindful of you in my bonds;' captivity cannot enchain my remembrance.

"I am, in heart and affection, etc."

"RENSSELAERSWYCK, August 30, 1643."

While the commandant at Rensselaerswyck sought to appease the Indians, who, numbering only ten or twelve, could not excite in his mind any serious alarm, he was perplexed to see a delegation come from the Mohawk town about the middle of September to demand explanations. The towns had been greatly excited when the flight of the servant of God became known. The Dutch were known to be accomplices, and the Mohawks wished to hold them responsible.

The deputies, who had been selected from the leading chiefs, came fully armed, and determined to get their prisoner back, willingly or by force. The case seemed desperate, but the commandant of the fort was not be intimidated by threats; he sturdily maintained his position, refusing to surrender him.

The clamor redoubled, and after several stormy interviews, they were on the point of resorting to violence, when the brave Dutch captain boldly advanced to the spokesman of the Mohawk party and said to him firmly, "The Frenchman you are seeking is under my protection. I cannot give him up. If I surrendered him to you, I would be false to my own honor and humanity. You yourselves ought to be glad to have a motive for justifying your conduct in the eyes of your countrymen, and preventing them from committing a crime. You like our nation. Well, you must know that there are rights of protection which allied nations must respect. To set these at defiance without some plausible reason would lead to a rupture that would bring on us endless bloody wars. The course I have followed is sanctioned by all the Dutch; you esteem them enough, I think, to yield to their wishes; but to give you full satisfaction, here is gold for the ransom of your prisoner." With this he offered them three hundred livres.

These words, uttered in a tone of authority, which the crisis suggested to a generous heart, prevailed : the Iroquois chief, influenced by the sight of the money, agreed to a settlement, and withdrew with his party.

Though he had been ransomed, Father Jogues found that he was not yet free. The Dutch had fears as to the permanence of a peace so hastily made, and a new opportunity of sending him to Europe was impatiently awaited.

The commandant then committed his guest to the care of an old Dutchman, faithful, but hard, avaricious, and unpitying. He lodged the missionary in a wretched garret, where hunger, thirst, heat, and fear of the Iroquois made every moment a torture ; but there too the servant of God cast himself into the hands of Providence, like a child in the arms of its mother.

This guardian, the commissary of the settlement, had no care or respect for the missionary. He took him up water every fortnight in a pail used to make lye. The heat of the month of August and the taint of the vessel made the water so vile that the disgusting liquid caused the poor prisoner violent pains in the stomach. His food was so scanty that it barely sufficed to keep him alive. A little black bread and rancid butter, stewed pumpkin, but no meat, was his ordinary diet, contrary to the commandant's orders, who sent him from time to time a dish from his own table, and who charged the man to provide the missionary with all he required, but his orders were disregarded.

This almost complete isolation lasted six weeks : Father Jogues spent them in converse with God and His Saints. The Protestant minister sometimes came to see him. One day he asked him how he was treated, and whether he required anything. The missionary, who had hitherto kept silence, and would have continued to do so, had he not been directly questioned, replied that very little was brought to him. "I was afraid so," replied the minister; "the old fellow is an arrant miser, and keeps what is sent to you." This was the fact. The commandant on learning the truth, sent Father Jogues bread and meat, which were after that time delivered to him without passing through the hands of the faithless host.

A torment more painful than abstinence imperilled the life of Father Jogues. While he was on the vessel a plaster made of ointment for scurf had been put on his injured leg. It poisoned the wound, and gangrene was setting in when the surgeon of the settlement was called, and succeeded in checking the progress of the evil.

Independently of these physical sufferings the poor Father was in constant alarm, and unable to leave his hiding-place, as the Iroquois were all the while prowling about the court of the fort, and often spent the night there. He says in one of his letters, that he did not see how the savages had failed a hundred times to one to see him. The garret was divided into two rooms by thin boards, so badly set up that there was a finger's width between them. You could easily see from one side what was in the other ; and one of these was his room. Now the commissary kept in the outer room a part of the goods and provisions which he sold. The Iroquois came there constantly during the day, and were separated from their prisoner by a mere partition of lath. The missionary at these times hid behind some empty casks, remaining there on some occasions three or four consecutive hours, crouched down and motionless ; a position which inflicted "a gehenna of torture," full of dread of being betrayed by the slightest movement, and discovered by his implacable enemies.

After this long trial, to which Divine Providence wished to subject the virtue of His servant, the hour of deliverance arrived at the moment when it was least expected.

The Governor of New Netherland resided at New Amsterdam, now New York, one hundred and forty-two miles below Rensselaerswyck. William Kieft, the fifth Director-General of this rising colony, of which he assumed the administration March 23, 1638, on hearing of the missionary's sad condition and the dangers which surrounded him, ordered the commandant to send him down by the first vessel, with all the precautions prudence could suggest.

There was just then a vessel lying there which was to sail down the river the next day. The preparations required little time. The minister and some of the leading inhabitants accompanied Father Jogues, who embarked secretly. On the sail down the river, which took six days, he received marks of cordial sympathy and benevolence from his travelling companions. Domine Megapolensis showed constant kindness toward him, and wished to give a little entertainment to the crew in his honor, in order to celebrate his happy deliverance. "Especially," relates the hero of the adventure, " did he insist, when we came to an island to which he wished to give my name. Amid the noise of cannon and bottles each showed his esteem after his own fashion."

Domine Megapolensis neglected no means of exciting in their hearts a frank and hearty joy, and Father Jogues, whom he called a very learned man, met these touching marks of friendship with cordial gratitude. All admired his modesty as much as his humility.

The Governor at Manhattan Island gave him a most honorable reception, invited him to his table, and seated him beside the pastor. He also provided for his pressing wants, and gave him suitable clothing to replace the ragged and half-savage costume in which he was attired.

The presence of a Jesuit, a confessor of the Catholic faith, amid a Protestant community excited lively curiosity. All flocked to see him, and they manifested the deepest feeling on hearing an account of the hardships which he had undergone. Some asked him what reward the members of the Company of New France* would pay him, for they imagined that he had been treated so on account of their trade. Father Jogues undeceived them, and explained the sanctity of his apostolic ministry. "No thought of earthly or transitory interest," said he, "induced me to leave my own country; I sought but one object, even when exposing myself to the dangers into which I fell, and that was to announce the Gospel to those who knew it not."

A young man employed by a merchant in that country, seeing him one day, ran to him, fell at his feet, and covered his mutilated hands with kisses. He cried with streaming eyes, "Martyr of Jesus Christ! Martyr of Jesus Christ!" The missionary, confused and affected, embraced him affectionately. He sought to escape these demonstrations, which wounded his humility. He asked this man who sought to honor him whether he was a Calvinist. "No," he replied, expressing himself as well as he could, "I am a Pole and a Lutheran." Father Jogues was unable to render any spiritual service to this well-disposed soul; he could not make himself understood.

He had the same difficulty with a woman of Portuguese birth. On entering a house near the fort he was

---

* The Company of New France, founded in 1627, under the name of the Company of One Hundred Associates, was projected by Richelieu. It entered into all the rights and duties of the mercantile companies which had till then monopolized the Canada trade, and who thought more of their own interests than of those of the colony.

agreeably surprised to see on the chimney-piece a picture of the Blessed Virgin and one of St. Aloysius Gonzaga; he made inquiry, and found that the mistress of the house was the wife of the ensign, and a Catholic. Unfortunately she knew none of the languages which Father Jogues spoke.

He found greater consolation in his intercourse with a good Irish Catholic, who arrived during his stay from the Virginia coast. When he heard that there was a Catholic priest in the place, it was his first and urgent duty to show the servant of God all the interest he felt in his condition, and to profit by his ministry to approach the Sacraments. From him Father Jogues learned something of the progress of the Faith in the colony of Maryland, on the shores of the Chesapeake. Founded a few years before by Lord Baltimore to afford Catholics of the British Isles a place where they could enjoy religious liberty and peaceably live in the Faith, it received its name in honor of Queen Henrietta Maria. Two Jesuit Fathers, Andrew White* and John Altham, had accompanied the first settlers to aid them spiritually and labor in converting the Indians.

Meanwhile Father Jogues was constantly awaiting an opportunity to proceed to Europe. In the month of November the Governor cheerfully offered him a passage in a little vessel of fifty tons which he was despatching in all haste to the Dutch Government to lay before it grave occurrences which had taken place, and which threatened to compromise seriously the future of the colony.

A force of sixty well-armed settlers had undertaken to exact reparation for the death of a Hollander whom a drunken Indian had killed with an arrow. They went

---

* After twelve years' labor in the colony, a Protestant revolution caused him to be sent back to England as a prisoner in 1645, and he died there in 1656, at the age of seventy-seven.

out to surprise a band of Indians of the same tribe who had fled to a small island, and they massacred eighty. This was the signal for a bloody war.

The Indians retaliated, and caused immense destruction in the colony. The Dutch then resolved to crush them. The Indians were pursued with such ferocity that more than sixteen hundred perished in battle; the rest made peace. But this result was more fatal than advantageous to the Dutch. They soon felt that they had alienated all the Indians and lost confidence with them.

It was important to lay the whole condition before the States as soon as possible.

Accustomed to see in all things the action of Providence, Father Jogues thanked God for the opportunity it afforded him of returning to Europe, and, furnished with a letter of recommendation from the Governor, he embarked for Europe on the 5th of November; but all the precautions taken to facilitate the voyage could not shield him from new annoyances and sufferings, which the Almighty seemed constantly to raise up before him, in order to give greater lustre to his virtue.

CHAPTER XI.

FATHER JOGUES had an uncomfortable voyage. The rough, prejudiced sailors did not show him the compassion manifested to him in the Dutch colony. They regarded the penniless Jesuit as an unwelcome burden. Some ropes on deck were his cabin and berth. When the sea was too rough he had to take refuge in the hold with a swarm of cats and a most offensive cargo. With no food but that given the sailors, exposed to damp and cold, in very light clothing, and not yet fully recovered from his hardships, privations, and wounds, he continued his life of sacrifice and danger in this small craft, which was tossed by every motion of the waves.

As they neared the coast of Europe new trials arose. They encountered a violent gale as they entered the British Channel, and finding it necessary to seek refuge in an English port, steered for Falmouth in Cornwall, which still held out for Charles I. Two Parliament vessels cruising off the coast gave chase to the Dutch vessel to intercept it ; but it eluded them and entered the port, where it anchored, towards the close of December, 1643.

To recruit after such a voyage nearly all the ship's people went ashore for the night, leaving Father Jogues alone with a sailor who was in charge of the vessel. In the middle of the night it was boarded by prowlers, who came to steal. They imagined that a vessel did not come that distance without bringing some valuables. But they were baffled, in spite of their search and threats. They even put a pistol at Father Jogues' head, but did not otherwise maltreat him. They contented themselves with carrying off his hat, but took all the baggage of the Dutch.

As soon as day broke Father Jogues hastened to report to the captain what had happened, and while he was in pursuit of the thieves, the missionary met a French sailor, who, seeing that he was a fellow-countryman, invited him to breakfast, and gave him an old coat and a sailor's cap. When he learned his adventures, and found that he was conversing with a priest of the Society of Jesus, who was anxious to return to France, he was much affected, and set to work to secure a passage for him.

He soon had the good-fortune to find a small vessel clearing for Brittany, which agreed to take the missionary on board.

Although a friend of the Frenchman, the Dutch captain did not like this, and was loth to let his passenger go unless he paid his fare. He yielded at last to their remonstrances, and trusting to a promise that he should be indemnified on his arrival in Holland, allowed Father Jogues to proceed directly to France.

The holy missionary embarked on Christmas eve on this vessel, a collier, which put him ashore the next morning on the coast of Lower Brittany, near Saint-Pol de Leon.*

What must not have been his joy to find himself once more on Catholic soil! What sighs of gratitude and

---

* Father Jogues says that he landed between Brest and Saint-Pol de Leon. As the distance between the two places is nearly twenty-five miles, the exact spot cannot be determined, but as it required five days to reach Rennes on horseback, we must suppose that he landed near Saint-Pol de Leon.

love did there not rise from his heart to thank God for having rescued him from so many perils and restored him to liberty!

His first thought was to go and prostrate himself at the foot of the altar, and partake of the holy Eucharist, of which he had been deprived for thirteen months and more. He made his way to the nearest cottage in sight, to ask the way to the church.

On learning that the ill-clad, unknown stranger was anxious to receive holy communion, the pious villagers, touched by his venerable air and his exhausted looks, lent him a hat and a short cloak to enable him to go to communion more becomingly. They had taken him for some poor Irish Catholic flying from persecution, and this thought increased the interest which his pious wish inspired; they pressed him to come back and take some refreshment after he had satisfied his devotion.

It was the great festival of Christmas. The good peasants were all out in their holiday garb, preparing to attend the services of the solemnity. It was a happiness to take the new-comer to the church. Joy filled the heart of the servant of God to see himself surrounded by these thoroughly Catholic Breton folk, but it was still greater when he was enabled to approach the Sacraments of Penance and the Eucharist, and join in offering the Sacrifice of the Mass. He then remembered with lively gratitude the long days of his cruel captivity, and that prolonged isolation amid heathen savages or people estranged from the Church. "At that moment," he said subsequently, "I seemed to begin once more to live, and to enjoy all the happiness of my deliverance."

Father Jogues returned to his hosts after the service, in order to take a little food, so necessary in his fatigued and exhausted condition. The sight of his mutilated hands excited the curiosity of these good peasants, and they asked him without ceremony how such a misfortune had befallen him. The missionary then related to them his long story, and these hearts, full of lively faith, heard with deep respect and admiration the touching story of those long sufferings endured for religion. It was not mere compassion, but a genuine veneration, which they experienced in the presence of the man of God. He has himself related how deeply he was touched when he saw the two daughters of this poor family show him their pity according to their means, and ask a remembrance in his prayers. "They came," he says, "to offer me their alms of a few sous, perhaps their whole store, with so much humility and modesty, that my soul was moved to tears."

However, Father Jogues had promised the captain who had brought him to Brittany that he would return to his vessel after he had performed his devotions. He had scarcely reached it when a merchant from Rennes, named Berson, whom business had brought to that part, came on board to arrange some affairs with the captain.

Father Jogues perceived him, and ascertaining whence he came, regarded his presence at that place as providential. Seizing a favorable moment, he approached Berson, and touching him gently asked him to take pity on him.

On seeing a man so attenuated and so ill-clad, Berson took him for a beggar, and offered him a sou, which he refused. Berson offered two, which were again refused. After hesitating a moment, between fear and hope, Father Jogues resolved to make himself known, and whispered to Berson, "My very dear sir, take compassion on me. I am a Jesuit Father."

Surprised and affected, Berson promised to help him. Till he had transacted his business, he sent Father Jogues to one of his friends, who lived in a little town about ten miles distant, where he joined him the next day.* He immediately arranged to take Father Jogues

---

* The account in Creuxius (Historia Canadensis), which has not been followed by Charlevoix, is very confused as to what happened in Eng-

to the nearest Jesuit college, that at Rennes, regarding it as a special favor that he could act as his guide.*

After five days' travel, Father Jogues, on the 5th of January, 1644, knocked at the door of the college, where he was to meet his brethren of the Society once more. It was early in the morning, and the porter had no suspicion who the ill-clad man in the sailor-cap might be; but hearing that the stranger wished to see the Father Rector to give him some information from Canada, the Brother-porter at once went to notify the head of the house. The Rector was just putting on his vestments to say Mass, but yielding to a feeling of pity as much as of curiosity, he preferred to defer the holy sacrifice for a moment. "Perhaps," he said to himself, "this poor man is in great need; perhaps he brings us some important intelligence from the noble apostles of those wild parts."

The Rector accordingly hastened down to the parlor to see this traveller, who handed him the letters of recommendation given him by the Dutch Governor of New Netherland. But without stopping to read them, the Superior plied him with questions as to the country from which he came, the condition of the Mission, and especially about Father Jogues. "Do you know him?" "Very well," replied the stranger. "We have learned," continued the Rector, "his capture by the Iroquois, his captivity and sufferings ; but we do not know what fate has befallen him. Is he dead, or is he still alive?" "He is alive, he is free, and it is he himself who is addressing you," said Father Jogues, falling at his Superior's feet and asking his blessing. The Rector clasped him to his heart, and took him into the house, where the whole

---

land and on the Breton coast. A typographical error, *huronicum* for *brittanicum*, increases the obscurity.

* The college at Rennes was founded in 1606, and soon became very flourishing. In 1641 it had 1484 pupils, and was exceeded only by Clermont College, Paris, which had 1800; that of Rouen, which had 1968; and La Flèche, which had more than two thousand.

community soon gathered to salute the heroic missionary. He had many questions to answer, much sympathy to receive, many to share his joy. Every one wished to kiss with respect the scarred hands and hear the account of his affecting captivity. How happy is the moment when a brother tried by so many disasters, and given up for lost, is found once more!

Amid these transports of holy joy, all led the holy missionary to the foot of the altar, still in his sailor garb, to render just and fervent thanksgiving to God for this wonderful series of signal benefits.

Although they repeat some of the events already related, the reader will peruse with interest two letters written by Father Jogues after his arrival at Rennes, as they lay open his saintly soul.

One is addressed to a friend on the very day of his arrival.

"At last my sins rendered me unworthy to die among the Iroquois! I am still alive, and God wills it so for my amendment. At least I recognize it as a great favor that He has permitted me to endure something. 'It is good for me that Thou hast humbled me; that I may learn Thy justifications' (Ps. cxviii. 71).

"I sailed on the 5th of November from the Dutch settlement on a barque of fifty tons, which brought me to Falmouth, England, on Christmas eve, and I reached Lower Brittany, between Brest and Saint-Pol de Leon, on Christmas day, in time to have the consolation of hearing Mass and performing my devotions. A good merchant who met me brought me to Rennes, paying my expenses, and I arrived here to-day, Feast of the Epiphany.

"What a happiness, after living so long among savages, and being thrown among Calvinists, Lutherans, Anabaptists, and Puritans, to find myself among the servants of God in the Catholic Church, and to see myself in the Society of Jesus! It is a slight idea of the joy we shall one day enjoy in heaven, if it please God, when 'He will gather together the dispersed of Israel' (Ps. cxlvi. 2).

"When will God withdraw His hand from our poor French and our poor Indians? 'Woe is me: why was I born to see the ruin of my people?' (1 Mac. ii. 7.) My sins and the infidelities of my past life have made weighty indeed the hand of God's majesty justly incensed against us.

"I beg Your Reverence to obtain for me of our Lord a perfect conversion, and that this little chastisement which He has given me may serve, as He designed, to render me better. Father Raymbault, Father Dolebeau, and Father Davost, are then dead?* They were ripe for heaven, and New France has in one year lost three persons who had labored greatly there.

"I do not know whether a copy of the 'Relation of the Hurons' has been received this year. It was sent down to the French in the month of June, and was given to me in the Iroquois country with a large package of letters which our Fathers on the Huron Mission were sending to France. Had I thought that God designed to deliver me, I would have brought it with me when I went to visit the Dutch. All was left in the cabin where I lived.

---

* Father Dolebeau came to Canada in 1640, and remained from that time at the mission of Miscou, on the Gulf of St. Lawrence. Ill-health compelled him to sail for France in 1643, but the vessel was captured by three of the enemy's frigates, and while they were plundering it, the magazine took fire and blew up. All on board perished. Some historians confound the Jesuit Father Dolebeau with a Recollect Father Dolbeau, who arrived in Canada in 1615, and returned to France in 1629.

Father Ambrose Davost came to Canada in 1632 with Father Anthony Daniel, and was employed at first at St. Anne, on the Island of Cape Breton. He was then successively on the Huron Mission at Quebec and Montreal. Suffering greatly from scurvy, he was sent back to France in 1643, but died on the way, and the ocean was his grave also.

"The next time I will write a longer letter; let this suffice for the first day of my arrival.

"RENNES, January 5, 1644."

The second letter of Father Jogues was addressed to Father Charles Lalemant, then Procurator of the Canada Mission at Paris.

"RENNES, January 6, 1644.

"'Now I know in very deed that the Lord hath sent His angels and hath delivered me out of the hand of Herod, and from all the expectation of the people of the Jews' (Acts xii. 11). The Iroquois came to the Dutch post about the middle of September, and made a great deal of disturbance, but at last received the presents made by the captain who had me concealed. They amounted to about three hundred livres, which I will en-endeavor to repay. All things being quieted, I was sent to Manhattan, where the Governor of the country resides. He received me very kindly, gave me clothes, and passage in a vessel which crossed the ocean in mid-winter.

"Having reached England, I got on a collier's vessel, which brought me to Lower Brittany, with a night-cap on my head, in utter want of everything, as you landed at St. Sebastian, but not after two shipwrecks." *

The mother of Father Jogues was still alive, and it is easy to understand the anguish and perplexity of her motherly heart when she heard of the sufferings of her beloved son. He hastened to write to her the day after he reached Rennes, but the letter has not been preserved to our time.

The missionary did not remain long at Rennes. His

---

* Father Jogues alludes to two shipwrecks of Father Charles Lalemant. The first occurred on his unfortunate attempt to carry supplies to his brethren in Canada in 1629. A storm prevented the vessel from entering the Gulf of St. Lawrence, and drove it on the south side of Cape Breton. Father Noyrot and Brother Malo lost their lives. When returning to Europe that same year Father Charles Lalemant was wrecked on the coast of Spain.

Superior summoned him to Paris, where all impatiently expected him. Everywhere he received the same welcome and excited the same interest. He was justly regarded as a Confessor of the Faith, and the marks of his victory on his mutilated body were lovingly venerated by all.

Queen Anne of Austria, when she heard of the arrival of the missionary, whose virtues and travails she knew, said in the presence of the courtiers, "Romances are written every day which are a tissue of fictions : here is one that is true, and that combines the wonderful with the most admirable heroism." She wished to see the missionary, and was moved to tears on beholding the scarcely healed wounds inflicted by the cruelty of the Iroquois. The sentiment she experienced was like that displayed by Constantine to the Fathers of the Council of Nice, when he respectfully kissed the wounds of those glorious defenders of the Faith.

While Father Jogues remained in France a petition was forwarded to Rome to obtain from the Sovereign Pontiff faculty for him to say Mass, notwithstanding the mutilated condition of his hands. The reputation of the servant of God and the account of his combats had already reached the Eternal City. The Sovereign Pontiff, Urban VIII., filled with admiration at such heroic courage, replied in these famous words : "*Indignum esset Christi martyrem, Christi non bibere sanguinem*"—"It would be unjust that a martyr for Christ should not drink the blood of Christ."

The humble missionary was pained at the notoriety and the honors paid him. People came out of devotion to hear his Mass, where all admired his humility, modesty, and piety. The more people spoke about him, the more deeply he seemed impressed with his own nothingness; and far from wishing to speak of his past sufferings, it was a torture for him to hear others converse about it, or to be obliged to show his maimed and distorted fingers as a curiosity. His Superiors were even obliged to recommend that his sensitiveness on this point should be respected.

A soldier does not display the wounds he receives in the service of his country more proudly than the servant of God strove to hide the wounds which covered his body and which, like St. Paul, he might call the stigmata of Christ.

The repugnance of Father Jogues to be seen abroad was the chief motive why he resisted the entreaties of his family, who were anxious to enjoy his presence, and to see more intimately his virtues, which were so generally recognized. Like Xavier, his model, he would not yield to their pious wishes. This lawful consolation seemed to him incompatible with the career of sacrifice that he had embraced, and the apostolic ministry which Providence had confided to him. Moreover, if his modesty had something to undergo in the seclusion of houses of his own order, how could it but shrink in dread from what must be experienced if he appeared publicly in places where he was so well known ?

This truly apostolic heart, from all the testimonies of admiration, friendship, and veneration lavished on him, drew only one conclusion—that he must return to the field of battle where he had fought so valiantly. He longed for his beloved Mission, with which he had formed so close an alliance, cemented by his blood. One of his confidential friends, who knew his ideas intimately, said of him, " He is as cheerful as though he had suffered nothing ; he is as zealous to return to the Hurons, amid all the dangers, as though he considered the dangers a shelter and a port."

His Superiors did not wish to thwart his holy desire : he had shown himself worthy of so noble a heritage, and his heart always cherished the fond hope that he would receive the crown of martyrdom, which he had seen so often glittering above his head.

Father Jogues had spent only a few months in France when, in the spring of 1644, he resolved to take advantage of a ship which was clearing at Rochelle for Canada, and he embarked once more for his Mission.

His heart was more inflamed than ever with the desire to labor for God's glory. The signal benefits that he had received seemed to bind him more closely to the divine service, and to require a more generous and complete sacrifice of himself than ever. The voyage afforded him more than one occasion to practise this zeal, and he did not let them pass unimproved.

The vessel which bore him had scarcely lost sight of the shores of France when the discontented sailors mutinied against the captain, and formed a plot to compel him to put back, on the pretext that the vessel was unseaworthy. After experiencing very violent winds, they believed that she could not safely make a long voyage; at all events, they resolved not to make it at their risk and peril.

These murmurs reached the ears of Father Jogues, and he easily saw how far this germ of insubordination might carry the men. He interposed without hesitation, and by his prudence and the ascendancy acquired by his virtue, his words of peace found hearers. The men's minds settled down, and order and harmony soon prevailed in the ship. The presence of the holy priest inspired all with confidence, and seemed a more efficacious security than all the resources of human prudence. They soon had tokens of God's special protection.

In the midst of the voyage the ship was assailed by a furious storm. Hell seemed to have let loose all the fury of the elements, and the danger seemed so great, even to men the most inured to the sea, that all gave up hope, and at once raised the fearful cry, " We must go down!"

At that moment Father Jogues, kneeling in his cabin, was piously reading the Holy Scriptures. The noise which he heard on deck recalled him from his consoling contemplation, and he ran up his mind full of a passage of the prophet Isaias, which he had just read, where God reproaches His people with their prevarication. He repeated the passage aloud in an animated tone, to produce in all hearts the thought of God, and induce them to recur to His mercy.

His words produced fruit even in the most hardened hearts. Alarmed at the presence of what seemed imminent death, and touched by grace, these men were the first to fall at the missionary's feet, to avow their faults and implore pardon for them. God seemed to await the cry of repentance to turn away the thunders of His wrath and reduce the demon to impotence. The storm soon passed away. A favorable wind impelled the ship and brought it to the desired haven. Late in June Father Jogues was able to embrace his brethren in Quebec, and rejoice with them and all the inhabitants on the ways of Providence towards him.

The servant of God immediately placed himself in the hands of the Rev. Father Vimont, the Superior of the Mission, to resume his apostolical labors. He was at once sent to Ville Marie, as Montreal is called in the language of religion, one hundred and fifty miles above Quebec. Indians of various tribes were beginning to frequent this place, and Father Jogues' familiarity with their languages might prove of great use.

The foundation of this post dated back barely two years. It was the western frontier post of the French, and of course the most exposed. It had been established in a delightful and fertile spot on the south side of Montreal Island, which had been visited by Jacques Cartier in 1534. He gave the name of Mont-royal to the high mountain that rises from its shore, and which towers above the surrounding country like a king over his subjects. At its foot the hardy navigator found the great Indian village of Hochelaga, where he was received with the highest honor.

When Champlain reached this spot in 1611 the Indian town had utterly vanished, but the beauty of the site, the fertile soil, the teeming woods and waters, the facility it enjoyed for communicating with all parts of the country, struck the able commander, and he marked the spot as a post to be occupied as soon as possible. He seemed to foresee the future importance of that city, and the great strides it was to make. In commerce, wealth, and population—now exceeding 150,000 souls—Montreal is the most important city in Canada.

The foundation of this city was exclusively religious in its character. A great servant of God, the venerable Mr. Olier, founder of the Sulpitians, impelled by the Spirit of God, gathered several zealous hearts to form in Canada an active centre for propagating religion among the Indian inhabitants of those parts. They were to exclude from their plan every motive of interest, and all human considerations.

The execution of this project was confided to a brave and virtuous gentleman, Mr. de Maisonneuve, and he arrived at the spot on the 17th of May, 1642, with the first forty settlers, all animated with the same courage and the same religious sentiment. They came in arms, for at that time, in the very heat of the Iroquois war, men had to be as ready to handle the musket as the plough.

To take possession, they planted the banner of France and the symbol of Faith. Father Vimont had accompanied them, and the very first day he offered the holy sacrifice in a humble bark chapel, to consecrate to God the soil over which Satan had till then reigned as master.

Born under such auspices, the little colony expanded under the salutary influence of religion, and always retained that characteristic. Faith and piety formed its soul; peace and harmony reigned there. Hence a chronicler of that time could say in truth, "If till now this wilderness has been the domain of demons, it is now inhabited by angels."

When Father Jogues arrived in Montreal, the bark lodges had been replaced by substantial wooden houses. A small hospital had already been erected, as well as a chapel and missionary's house.*

The servant of God immediately began his labors among the Indian travellers, who frequently landed at this place, but he also devoted himself to maintain the fervor of the little colony. Three years after, Father Jerome Lalemant was to give this high testimony in regard to his stay at this post: "His memory still lives there. The odor of his virtues always revives and consoles all who had the happiness to know him and hold intercourse with him."

The successful beginnings of Ville Marie were in strange contrast with the agitation and panic then prevailing through the whole colony. The Iroquois war had assumed an alarming character of boldness and fury. They infested every road. They seemed to have arranged their plan of attack on a more extended scale than ever, and with a strategic skill not to be expected among Indians. Their warriors divided into ten bands, were posted in a line covering all the ways of travel. They had learned to occupy points from which they could discern canoes or travellers ten or twelve miles off without being themselves observed, and they never made an attack unless they thought they were superior in numbers.

It was insecure to travel even in the country of the Hurons, and the Algonquins no longer dared to come down to Quebec. "I would almost as soon be besieged

---

* The Jesuit Fathers had charge of the church in this rising city only during its first fifteen years,—that is to say, till the arrival of the Sulpitians sent by Mr. Olier, who became seigneurs and pastors of the whole island.

by phantoms as by Iroquois," wrote Father Vimont. "One is scarcely more visible than the other. When they are at a distance, we suppose them to be at our very doors; and they pounce on their prey when we imagine them to be in their own country."

This difficulty had for three years prevented the French from sending any supplies to the missionaries in the Huron country, and the Superior at Quebec rightly considered that they must be in great distress. Their clothes were falling in tatters, and their provisions were exhausted. In the spring of 1644 it was decided to make an attempt to carry them some relief.

There was then at Quebec a young missionary from the Roman province, Father Joseph Bressani, who had just arrived for the Canada Mission, for which he had petitioned earnestly. He had made such an impression for virtue and courage, that he was deemed fit to lead this perilous expedition; but his Indian apostolate was to begin by captivity and his preaching by suffering.

A young Frenchman and some Christian Hurons formed his escort. To be ready for any event, they had all prepared for this voyage as if they were to meet death on the way. The Governor distributed arquebuses among them; but the joy caused by this present, which was at that time made only to Christians, was the innocent cause of their ruin. Their constant firing betrayed them to some Iroquois who formed an ambuscade on the banks of Lake Saint-Pierre. They arranged their plan of surprise deliberately, so as to fall on the convoy without giving the Hurons time to defend themselves. And so it turned out. One single Huron fell in the attack. Father Bressani and all the neophytes were taken prisoners and condemned to horrible tortures. But after four months' captivity the missionary*

---

* Like Father Jogues, Father Bressani was the historian of his own sufferings. His account, full of touching simplicity, is contained in an interesting history of the Huron Mission which he published at

was ransomed by the Dutch of Rensselaerswyck and sent to Europe.

The news of the capture of Father Bressani and of his neophytes filled the French colony with consternation. Deprived of all succor from Europe, the Governor was powerless to punish the Iroquois or lay down the law to them. The few soldiers at his command barely enabled him to maintain the posts occupied by the French so as to secure their respect. Fortunately the Iroquois were not aware of the real weakness of the colony.

In this precarious situation Governor Montmagny saw no resource except in a treaty of peace with these cruel enemies, but he wished to make one that would not detract from the honor of France. Fortunately for the colony, a powerful party among the Iroquois also inclined to peace, and made no secret of its wishes. They saw that war was sapping the strength of the nation: their warriors gradually disappeared, with none to succeed them, so that the victories would ultimately become disasters. They had, moreover, at that moment an obstinate war to maintain against a powerful nation in the South, and a diversion would be fatal to them.

When these dispositions were known, the Governor sought an opportunity to open negotiations without compromising the dignity of France, and he found one soon after, in the latter part of the month of May.

Two Iroquois warriors had been captured by the Algonquins, and according to custom they were con-

---

Macerata, in Italian, in 1653. A French translation appeared in Montreal, Canada, in 1852. Father Bressani returned to Canada in 1646, and remained till the destruction of the Huron Mission three years afterwards. On returning to the Roman province he produced great fruit as a missionary, due less to his eloquence than to his fame as an Indian missionary, and the glorious scars seen on his hands. Michaud's "Bibliographie Universelle" and Didot's "Biographie Generale" make two distinct men of the missionary, under the names Brassoni and Bressani; and Father Patrignani in his Menology incorrectly gives his name as Bresciani.

demned to the stake. The Governor interposed, and having obtained their deliverance, sent them home as a testimony of his good-will, and to induce them to labor to secure peace. He then endeavored to induce the Hurons, who had so much to dread from the war with the Iroquois, to take a similar step. He asked some of their warriors to set free an Iroquois prisoner who had fallen into their hands, and even made them presents to obtain it. The pride of the Hurons took offence, and thirst for vengeance made them obstinate. When he proposed it, one of the chiefs made a reply which from any but the mouth of a savage would have been an insult, whilst it revealed a pride of character and the depth of the wound inflicted on his nation: "I am a man of war, and not a trader; I have come to fight, not to barter. It is my glory to take back not presents, but prisoners. I will not touch your hatchets and kettles. If you are so anxious to have this prisoner, take him. I am strong enough to go and capture another. If I lose my life they will say in my country, 'Onontio took their prisoner, and they doomed themselves to death to capture another.'"

Charles, a Christian Huron, interposed in this contention and spoke with more modesty and reason: "Be not angry, Onontio," said he; "it is not to thwart you that we act so; but our honor and our life are at stake. We have promised our sachems to place in their hands any prisoner whom we took. As the soldiers around you obey your command, so we must obey those who command us. What reply could we make to the reproach of the whole country, if when they knew we had made prisoners, they should see in our hands only hatchets and kettles? We should be condemned as men of no sense to decide a matter of this kind without the direction of the sachems. You wish peace; so do we; and our sachems do not oppose it. If we released our prisoner, our life would be compromised. The Iroquois are everywhere on our route. If we meet them we need fear nothing, as we can show our prisoner unharmed, whom we wish to deliver to our sachems as a means of securing peace."

To this judicious and well-considered speech there was no reply. The Governor saw how much was to be gained by allowing the Hurons to take the first step. He did no more than urge them earnestly to do so, and in fact the Huron sachems did send the prisoner back to his tribe.

This generous conduct of the French and their allies bore its fruit. The Mohawks also were stimulated to show their generosity, and as a token of their good-will they set at liberty William Couture, the young Frenchman who was a fellow-prisoner with Father Jogues, and sent him home accompanied by three Iroquois, who were appointed to open negotiations for peace.

The arrival of this embassy was an event for the colony. It reached Three Rivers on the 5th of July, 1644. The whole French and Indian population flocked to the shore. Kiotsaeton, whom the French nicknamed Le Crochet, was the chief of the embassy. He was supported by Chief Atogouaekouan, or the Great Spoon. "The latter," says Father Le Jeune, "was of fine stature, well-formed, bold and eloquent, but treacherous and a mocker."

Kiotsaeton was attired in his richest garments. Ornaments of every kind and color decked his head, his neck, and his wrists. He stopped his canoe before reaching the land, and before stepping ashore rose in the bow and said to the crowd, "I have left my country to come and see you. I was told that I came to seek death, and that I should never again see my native soil: I feared naught. I have willingly exposed my life for the sake of peace. I come in all confidence to bring you the thoughts of the Iroquois."

The cannon of the fort saluted the arrival of the Iroquois. All was done to give an exalted idea of the power and magnificence of the French. The hero of the hour, however, was good Couture, who had long been given up for dead. Every one manifested his joy, and blessed the Lord with him on his happy deliverance. Towards the end his captivity had ceased to be rigorous. "The Iroquois held him in esteem and reputation; and he assumed the air of a chief, having acquired this credit by his prudence and wisdom," says the Venerable Mother Mary of the Incarnation, in one of her letters, "so amiable is virtue even among savages."

The negotiations for peace brought Father Jogues once more on the scene. He was summoned to Three Rivers to aid in following them up. Without ceasing to be an apostle, he was about to become a negotiator For him it was the path of martyrdom.

CHAPTER XII

Great Assembly at Three Rivers—The Treaty of Peace—Father Jogues among the Iroquois—A Toilsome Journey—He Returns to Three Rivers.

N the 12th of July, 1644, a solemn assembly was convened at Three Rivers, in the open square of the fort. The Governor-General presided, having beside him Mr. de Champflour, commandant of the city, and Father Vimont, representing Rev. Father Lalemant, Superior of the Missions, who had been detained among the Hurons. Sails from the shipping formed a vast tent. A short distance before the arm-chair of the Chevalier de Montmagny was a seat covered with spruce bark for the Iroquois. Behind them stood the Algonquins, the Montagnais, and the Attikamègues. Hurons and French intermingled were arrayed on either side.

The Iroquois had planted two poles in the middle of the open space, and the cord between them was to hold the seventeen wampum belts,* which were their word.

This curious and animated scene depicts to the life the manners and character of the Indian. A slave of the

---

* The Indians in this part of America made beads of the clam-shell, which the English called *wampum*, from its Algonquin name, and the French *porcelaine*, from " porcella," the scientific name. The polished glassy shell was broken into pieces, rubbed into beads, and pierced. Of these they made single strings or collars, which served as adornment and a pledge and guarantee in solemn transactions. Beads introduced by Europeans soon took the place of shells. The Iroquois Confederacy still preserve ancient wampum belts received in negotiations from the French.

senses, everything must speak to his eyes. He invests all his words with imagery; and his imagination, ever in contact with nature, borrows thence, in most cases, its comparisons and illustrations. Good sense, eloquence, and noble thought do not depend on education merely, and under the rough exterior of these children of the forest are often found the crafty diplomatist and the pathetic orator.

When all were seated Kiotsaeton rose. He was at once seen to be a man accustomed to such duties, and he discharged them with a dignity that savored nothing of barbarism; his memory seemed marvellous. He readily explained the meaning of each belt, and the article of the treaty which it symbolized, as fluently as though he had a written document in his hands. Metaphors and figures flowed as from a fountain, accompanied by expressive and pantomimic gestures.

Taking up the first collar, he addressed the Governor-General: "Onontio, give ear to my voice. I am the mouth of my whole nation. You hear all the Iroquois when you listen to my words. My heart has no crooked thoughts; my intentions are upright. We wish to forget all our war-cries and change them to songs of joy." Then he began to chant and gesticulate as he strode up and down, his comrades beating time with a *hé* in cadence, and strongly aspirated, sounded from the depth of the chest.

Kiotsaeton often looked up to the sun, and grasped his arms with his hands, as if to press out their warlike strength, which had kept them so long equipped for war. He soon resumed a calmer manner, and continued: "This belt which I present to you thanks you for sparing the life of my brother, Tokrahenchiaron, whom you rescued from the fire and the teeth of the Hurons; but why did you let him set out alone? If his canoe had capsized who was there to help him right it? If he had drowned or perished by any other accident you would have heard no news of peace, and would perhaps have blamed us for a fault that was all on your own side."

After hanging this belt on the cord, he took a second, tied it around Couture's arm, then turning to the Governor said: "Father, this belt brings back your subject; but I was far from saying, 'Take this canoe and go back to Quebec.' My mind would not have been at ease till I heard positive tidings of his safe arrival. My brother whom you sent back suffered much, and encountered many dangers. He had to carry his baggage alone; to paddle all day, and drag his canoe around the rapids. He had at the same time to be always on his guard against being surprised."

Animated gesticulations accompanied all these words. Sometimes you saw an Indian pushing his canoe along with a pole, sometimes keeping off a wave or avoiding a rock with his paddle. At one moment he was exhausted and out of breath, then he regained courage and rested for a time. Then he began to march like a man making a portage, and pretended to stumble over a stone, after which, as if lamed, he limped along in pain. "If you had even helped him to get beyond the most difficult places! Indeed, Father, I do not know where your mind was when you sent back one of your children in that way, alone and unaided. I did not act so with Couture. I told him, 'Come, nephew, follow me. I will restore you to your family at the risk of my life.'"

Each belt had thus its particular object. The fourth declared that the Iroquois renounced all thoughts of vengeance for their brethren slain by the Algonquins in the spring, and he gave his thought this ingenious turn: "As I came hither I passed by the field of the last battle, where these two brothers were taken prisoners. I marched as fast as I could, so as not to see the blood of my countrymen shed by Piescaret* and the Algonquins.

* A famous Algonquin chief.

As their bodies are still unburied, I turned away my eyes, that my wrath should not be enkindled."

He began to strike the ground and to listen; then he went on: "I have heard the voice of my ancestors slain of old by the Algonquins; they saw me burning for revenge; they said to me gently, 'Be good, grandson; hearken not to resentment. It would be useless to try and deliver us from death. Think of the living and work for them; avert the sword from above their heads, and the fire kindled to consume them.'"

The fifth belt drove off the enemies' canoes. The sixth smoothed the rapids on the way to the country of the Iroquois. The eighth was to build a road.

"You would have said," writes Father Vimont, "that he was felling trees, lopping off branches, clearing away woods, filling up the hollow spots with earth." "There," said he, "is the road all clean, smooth, and straight." He stooped towards the ground, looking to see whether there were no thorns or wood, whether there was any inequality that one could stumble over. "It is all ready," he added; "the smoke of our cabins can be seen from Quebec to the end of our country.* All obstacles are removed."

The tenth belt, larger and finer than the rest, proclaimed peace between the French, Algonquins, and Mohawks; and as a symbol of this union, the orator, while still speaking, took a Frenchman and an Algonquin and bound their arms together with the belt.

The eleventh belt promised a hospitable board. "We have fish and game in plenty," said the orator. "Our forests teem with stags, moose, deer, bears, and beavers. Drive away the filthy hogs that defile your houses and feed only on filth."

The twelfth belt banished all suspicions of perfidy that were ascribed to them. The ambassador rose and beat

* More than three hundred miles.

the air as if to scatter and drive away the clouds. "Let the sun and truth shine everywhere!" he cried.

The thirteenth and fourteenth were addressed to the Hurons. "You formerly wished to make peace: five years ago you had in your hands a bagful of belts and other presents to ask our friendship. What prevented you? Your bag will fall to the ground; your presents will be broken and scattered: then you will lose heart. Why do you wait so long?"

The fifteenth present was of much deeper interest than the rest; and in spite of all the cunning eloquence of Kiotsaeton he would have given grounds for the charge of duplicity if in his position he did not seek in some way to extenuate, as far as possible, the cruel conduct of his countrymen.

He endeavored to justify their treatment of Father Jogues and Father Bressani. "We wished to bring them both back to you, but we could not accomplish our design. One escaped from our hands, in spite of us, and the other insisted on being given up to the Dutch. We yielded to his desire. We regret, not that they are free, but that we don't know what has become of them. Perhaps at the very moment that I am speaking of them they have been swallowed up in the waves or have fallen victims to some cruel enemy; but the Mohawks did not intend to put them to death."

The Iroquois chief did not know that Father Jogues was actually present at the meeting. At these words the missionary could not help smiling. "For all these fine words," said the missionary to those near him, "the stake was prepared and the executioners were in waiting. If God had not rescued me from their hands, I should have been well and thoroughly burned, and have endured a hundred deaths in one; but let him talk."

The seventeenth present had reference to Honateniate, one of the two Iroquois prisoners rescued from the Algonquins, and kept as hostages by the Governor till the return of the one who had gone to carry to his country-men the first words of peace. His old mother had already lost her eldest son in the war, and Father Jogues had been given to her to replace him. Having ascertained that her second son was still alive, she had gone to Kiotsaeton before he set out, and given him a belt which she had often worn, and with all a mother's love had begged him to offer it to the one who had saved her son's life.

At the beginning of his captivity this young man had been oppressed with a deadly fear and melancholy. Nothing could divert his mind, and he seemed the prey of the gloomiest despair. When he learned that Father Jogues was at Three Rivers, he recalled his virtue, and his mother's regard for him, and endeavored to see the missionary. As soon as he perceived Father Jogues he showed the liveliest feelings of joy; he seemed to have found alike family and freedom. The missionary consoled him, and restored his soul to peace and hope.

A Huron who was not well disposed to the French, witnessing this imposing assemblage, endeavored to fill the mind of the Iroquois chief with distrust, and to inspire him with suspicions as to the sincerity of their intentions. The Mohawk shrewdly replied : "I have my face painted and striped on one side; the other is clean and neat : on one side I do not see clearly; on the other my sight is good. The painted side is the Huron side. I do not see a bit there. The clean side is for the French: I see there as clear as noon." The Huron slunk away abashed, without another word.

Two days after, the Chevalier de Montmagny made his reply, with the same pomp observed at the first session, and at the same time offered fourteen presents. The famous Piescaret, who had long been the terror of the Iroquois, spoke for the Algonquins, and Noel Negabamat, the fervent chief of Sillery, spoke for the Montagnais. The other nations had no spokesmen.

Three discharges of cannon proclaimed the end of the session. "It was," said the Governor, "to drive away the evil air, and to carry the news of peace to all the land." He then gave a great banquet to the ambassadors, and several speeches were made there, for nothing makes Indians more loquacious and eloquent than good-cheer, and with them no important matter is transacted without a banquet.

A mysterious incident, which seemed to prove the insincerity of the Iroquois intentions, nearly broke off the negotiations. After the public banquet the chief Kiotsaeton solicited a private interview with the Governor, saying that he had a present to make him. When he was in the Chevalier's presence he told him that he intended to conclude peace only with the French and Hurons, but he did not wish to include the Algonquins.*

This unexpected statement displeased the Chevalier de Montmagny, who refused the present, and would not even look at it; he declared that he would never consent to any such condition. The Mohawk chief was displeased at this refusal, and the treaty was on the point of being broken off. Time was taken for reflection, and the Governor in a second secret interview found a middle course. He explained to the Iroquois that there were two kinds of Algonquins—the Christians who were like French, and unless they were included he would never make peace; the others, who were more independent, and whose interests were not so closely united with the French, should alone be excluded from the peace. This distinction satisfied the ambassador, and the Algonquins in question were admitted into the convention. The Mohawks made this condition known in their country, but the French did not openly avow it.

The happy results of this first assembly spread joy through the colony, and revived hope everywhere. Yet

---

* Jesuit Journal.

it was only a preliminary of peace. The Iroquois ambassadors were to secure the approval of the treaty by the sachems of their nation, and then return with more ample powers.

On the other hand, Governor de Montmagny wished the nations in alliance with the French, who were to share as fully as themselves in the benefits of the peace, to take an active part in its conclusion. They were all convoked to, meet in September, and more than four hundred Indians then gathered at Three Rivers—Hurons, Attikamègues, Montagnais, Algonquins of the Island, etc. Four Iroquois ambassadors, always attended by Couture, who acted as interpreter, arrived at the place of meeting, and great assemblies were then held, in which all the Indian allies of the French without exception took part.

All passed in order and perfect harmony. Unfortunately only the Mohawk canton of the Iroquois league took part in these negotiations; and notwithstanding the hopes which the Mohawks gave of bringing in the other cantons, they not only did not bind themselves to it, but some of their warriors were seen attacking the Algonquins and French near Montreal, or making raids into the country of the Hurons.

But peace was really concluded with the Mohawks, though the final ratification did not take place till May, 1646. In one of these meetings the famous Kiotsaeton, to show all his sympathy for the French, offered the missionaries a wampum belt to console them for the death of Father de Noüe,* who had been found

---

* Father de Noüe died February 2, 1646, at the age of sixty-three. He went on foot by the frozen river from Three Rivers to Fort Richelieu to extend his ministry to the little garrison. A snow-storm completely concealed the horizon, and he lost his way. He was found frozen to death on the shore, ten miles beyond the fort. He was on his knees, his hands clasped on his breast, and his eyes open, raised to heaven. He died as a martyr of duty and charity.

frozen to death in the month of February. "Here," he said, "is something to warm the spot where the cold froze the good Father. Put this present in your bosom to divert your thoughts, which might sadden you."

Songs, dances, feasts, followed the solemn assemblies; and men who had been arrayed against each other in such bitter war were seen exulting in a common joy. They were seen hunting together, and in peace, in the very parts where they had laid their deadly ambuscades. But they soon dispersed in different directions—some to seek the remote shores of Lake Huron, others to strike northward to their hunting-grounds, and the Iroquois to return to their castles on the Mohawk River.

Up to this time Couture* alone had borne the word of the French to the Iroquois, but rather as interpreter than as ambassador. The Governor felt that to give greater importance to this treaty its conclusion should be confided to envoys of a higher rank.

He cast his eyes on Father Jogues, who, during the long negotiations for peace, had returned to Montreal, and was continuing his labors there. The knowledge which he possessed of the language and manners of the Iroquois seemed to mark him out in advance for this dangerous commission. He had purchased it dearly enough. Moreover, he was going to fulfil a religious as well as a political duty. He was not only the bearer of the words of the French Governor, but went to prepare the way for the Gospel.

The thought of confiding this apostleship to Father Jogues preoccupied the Superior of the Canada Mission

---

* Couture went to Canada in his youth, and was at first employed on the Huron Mission, and appears in 1640 in the list of *donnés*. In the catalogue of employments he is sometimes put down as joiner, sometimes *ad multa*, showing that he was ready in many capacities. He negotiated the peace which put an end to his captivity. Being released from his engagement as a *donné*, he married, and was the head of a large family. He died in 1702, at the age of ninety-four.

from the moment that he saw the project of peace with the Iroquois take a favorable turn. The hardships and danger attending the enterprise required that it should be treated with the utmost prudence and maturity. We see it the topic of serious consultation in the month of January, 1646, between Father Jerome Lalemant, Superior of the Mission, and Fathers Vimont, De Quen, d'Eudemare, and Peter Pijart, who were then in Quebec. We find the result entered in these terms in the Register of the Superior in that city: "Omnium consensu approbata profectio"—"All unanimously approved the departure."

When the peace had become a reality, Father Lalemant imparted to Father Jogues the wish to confide the Mission to him. We do not know in what terms the Superior asked Father Jogues to make this act of heroic devotedness; but we are so happy as to possess the reply of the servant of God—as worthy of his humility as of his magnanimity.

"MONTREAL, April, 1646.

"REVEREND FATHER : The letter which it has pleased your Reverence to write found me in my retreat and in the exercises which I had begun, there being no canoe to carry our letters. I chose this time, because the Indians, being at the chase, allow us to enjoy a greater silence.

"Would you believe that, on opening your letter, my heart was at first seized with a kind of fear that what I desire, and what my soul should earnestly desire, might not arrive. Poor nature, mindful of the past, trembled; but our Lord, by His goodness, has given, and will again restore it calm.

"Yes, Father, I will all that our Lord wills, and I will it at the peril of a thousand lives. Oh! how I should regret to lose so glorious an occasion, when it may depend only on me that some souls be saved! I hope that His goodness, which has not abandoned me in the hour of trial, will aid me still. He and I are able to trample pown every difficulty that can oppose the project.

"It is much to be '*in medio nationis pravæ*,' without Mass, without Altar, without Confession, without Sacraments; but His holy will and Divine Providence so will it.

"He who, by His holy grace, preserved us without these helps for eighteen or twenty months, will not refuse us the same favor, for we do not thrust ourselves into this work, but undertake this voyage solely to please Him, without consulting all the repugnances of nature.

"As to all these comings and goings of the Iroquois, what I can say is, that I see very few from the first two towns; yet it is with them chiefly that we are concerned, as the last killed were of these villages. Scarcely any have come, except from the last village, where Couture was; and they profess, at least in words, not to come as warriors in these parts. It is not, however, with these last that we must dwell, but with those whom we do not see.

"I thank you affectionately for sending me your Huron principles. Send the rest when you please. What I need is chiefly prayers, formularies for confession, *et ejusdem generis*. I will thereby become your debtor, as I am already on so many grounds. I owe your Reverence the account of the 'Capture and Death of good René Goupil,' which I should have sent already. If the bearer of this give me time, I will send it by him.

"If God wills that I go to the Iroquois, my companion must be virtuous, docile, courageous, and willing to suffer something for God. It would be well for him to know how to make canoes, so that we can go and return without calling on the Indians."

Father Lalemant had not presumed too much on the courage of Father Jogues. He wrote on this point in the Relation of 1645: "He was ready before the proposition was made to him. He who had borne the weight of the war was not a man to recoil in peace. He was very glad to test their friendship after experiencing the rage of their hatred. He was not ignorant of the inconstancy of these savages or of the difficulty of the roads. He saw the dangers into which he plunged; but he who runs no risk for God will never deal wholesale in the riches of heaven."

The Iroquois ambassadors were pleased with the selection; and the French Governor, heartily applauding it, gave him an official character, associating with Father Jogues the lay-negotiator whom he had chosen, Mr. John Bourdon, a good and devoted man, the engineer of the colony.*

On seeing Father Jogues embark, the Christian Algonquins expressed their fears, and advised the missionary not to speak of the Faith in his first intercourse. "There is nothing," said they, "more repulsive at first than this doctrine, which seems to exterminate all that men hold dearest, and as your long robe preaches as much as your lips, it will be more prudent to travel in a shorter habit."

This advice, dictated by prudence, was followed. It was right to treat the sick as sick, and to humor the susceptibilities of prejudiced and irritable people. After the example of the Apostle, the evangelical laborer must be ready to bend to circumstances, and to " become all things to all men," that he may gain them all to Christ.

"When I speak of an Iroquois mission," said Father Jerome Lalemant, announcing in France in the Relation of 1646 the departure of Father Jogues, "it seems to me that I am talking of some dream; and yet it is a reality. With good reason we have given it the name of ' Mission of the Martyrs;' for, besides the cruelty which these savages have already inflicted on some persons devoted to the salvation of souls, besides the pains and hardships

---

* John Bourdon had been in Canada since 1634, and enjoyed a high repute for probity and intelligence. After being engineer, he became Attorney-General of New France. He took an active part in pushing discoveries on the coast of Labrador and in Esquimaux Bay.

which those appointed for this mission must encounter, we can say in truth, that it has already been ensanguined with the blood of a martyr, inasmuch as the Frenchman (René Goupil) who was killed at the feet of Father Jogues lost his life for having formed the sign of our Faith on some little Iroquois children. If we are permitted to conjecture in matters that seem highly probable, we may believe that the designs we have formed against the empire of Satan will not bear fruit till they are irrigated with the blood of some other martyrs."

The whole colony was piously affected at the moment when this grave step was taken, in the result of which religion and the prosperity of New France were so deeply interested. Public prayers were immediately begun in all the churches to assure its success.

Father Jogues and Mr. Bourdon set out from Three Rivers on the 16th of May, with four Mohawk deputies who were to be their guides and introduce them to the sachems. Two Algonquins appointed by their nation to present to the Iroquois presents in the name of the tribe to confirm the peace went also.

Notwithstanding the heat, the voyage up the river of the Iroquois through Lake Champlain and Lake George was accomplished happily. It was while crossing this last lake on the 30th of May, the feast of Corpus Christi, that Father Jogues gave it the name of *Lac Saint-Sacrement*** (Lake of the Blessed Sacrament), which was retained by the French while they ruled Canada. The Iroquois called

---

* Spofford in his Gazetteer, and other early American writers, ignorant of the circumstances attending the giving of the name, state that it was given on account of the purity of the water, confounding Baptism with the Holy Eucharist. Yet this explanation was for years the only one given in English and American works. The present name, Lake George, due to some ambitious individual, or flatterer of the English king, was given not long before the English conquest of Canada. Mr. John G. Shea and Mr. Francis Parkman have proposed that it be called "Lake Jogues."

this sheet of water Andiatarocte (Where the Lake closes).

After reaching the extremity of this lake the travellers had to make the hardest part of their journey, and it had to be made on foot. With so small a party, and bearing presents which constituted a considerable weight, they had to look forward to a task severe enough to exhaust the stoutest men. The Algonquins were the first to be discouraged. They decided to leave behind a part of the twenty-four elk-skins which they were appointed to carry, and they left them on the shore of the lake, where they carefully concealed them, according to Indian custom. As for Father Jogues, he was, according to Mr. Bourdon, indefatigable. However, after two days' march the Iroquois guides abandoned the idea of going directly to the Mohawk town. Seeing their companions exhausted they began to fear that they would be reproached with not having sufficiently considered the strength of their new allies. Accordingly, striking westward, they took up their march for a place called Ossaragué or Beaver Dam, a favorite resort of the Mohawks, from its abounding in fish. There they hoped to find some aid in carrying their baggage; and they were not disappointed.

This swerving from their direct route, which seemed merely fortuitous, was really a providential protection of His elect by our Lord. At this spot Father Jogues found Teresa, the young Christian Huron girl who had been taken at the same time as himself, and who had since remained a prisoner in the hands of the Mohawks. The presence of the missionary filled her with joy. She approached the tribunal of penance, and the words of the Father quickened her sentiments of faith and piety. Her confidence revived when she learned all that had been done at Quebec for her deliverance. "Courage!" said the holy priest to her; "you shall be happy in heaven if you persevere."

Her virtue had not diminished during her two years'

captivity. The lessons of her good teachers, the nuns, had borne fruit, and far from being ashamed of her baptism, she gloried in it. As she had been deprived of her rosary, she recited the prayers every day on her fingers, or marked the decades with pebbles. She sometimes said to her uncle, the wise and pious Joseph Teondechoren, who was a captive with her for some months, but succeeded in escaping, "If my mothers saw me with these wicked Mohawks who know not God, they would feel great pity for me." But if the Ursulines did not see their pupil, they did not forget her; their affection increased with her dangers, and was attested not only by their prayers, but by their exertions in her behalf.

On the 4th of June our travellers descended the Hudson River and made a short stay at the Dutch settlement of Rensselaerswyck, where the commandant of Fort Orange received them with great courtesy. The Chevalier de Montmagny had given Father Jogues letters saluting and thanking the Dutch Governor, and the servant of God was only too happy to be able to express in person his gratitude to those who had saved his life. The ambassadors after two days' rest* continued their journey, accompanied by several Iroquois who happened to be at the settlement, and who divided the baggage among them. At last on the evening of the next day, the little caravan entered the Iroquois town of Oneougiouré, formerly Osserion, to which Father Jogues gave the name of the Holy Trinity. Two whole days were scarcely enough to gratify the curiosity of the people of the country. They flocked from all parts to see the deputies. Those who had formerly persecuted and tortured the missionary, pretended to have lost all recollection of it, and those who could not resist a feeling of compassion at the sight of his tortures and resignation showed their

---

*The Relation of 1646 says the 16th, but the context enables the reader to correct this typographical error.

pleasure and happiness, on seeing him again under such different conditions, and invested with so honorable a title.

On the 10th of June a general assembly of the sachems and chiefs of the country was held to receive the ambassadors. It was brilliant and solemn. The presents, arranged in Indian style before the crowd of spectators, attested the magnificence of the King of France, and his pacific intentions.

Father Jogues, who was appointed to bear the word of the Governor and of the French, was able to adapt himself in his language and manner to the ideas of this nation. Amid a deep silence he raised his voice, and after expressing the universal joy excited in the colony by the sight of the Iroquois deputies, and the news of the peace concluded between them, the French, Hurons, and Algonquins, he exclaimed, "The council-fire is kindled at Three Rivers. It shall never be extinguished. The French shall be your brethren : your enemies shall be their enemies, and their arm shall be outstretched to defend you. We were glad when we heard that you had flung far from you the scalps of the Algonquins and Montagnais whom the Sokokis massacred last year.* Here are five thou-

---

* The Sokokis had taken up arms against the Algonquins, and had penetrated even to Quebec, scalping some Indians of that nation under its very walls When they heard of the steps taken towards a general peace, they wished to prevent any between the Iroquois and the Algonquins. Brandishing their bloody trophies, they sent ambassadors to the Iroquois. A council was held, and the Sokoki orator said, " I have long heard you say that the Algonquins were your irreconcilable enemies, and that you hated them even beyond the grave ; so that if you could meet them in the next world your war would be eternal. We are your allies ; we share your feelings and your interest. Here are scalps of Algonquins whom we massacred: it is a present that must gladden your heart. At the same time I give you this belt, which will serve as a chain to bind us closely together;" and the Sokoki laid a great wampum belt on the ground.

The Iroquois were indignant at this proposal. One of the chiefs

sand beads of wampum to break the fetters of the young Frenchman who is still among you, and another belt of five thousand for Teresa, that they may both be set at liberty and may soon arrive at Quebec."

This harangue was listened to with the deepest attention and the presents were gratefully received. The Wolf clan, the most powerful in the nation, which had shown Father Jogues kindness and respect during his captivity, received a special present.

The missionary ambassador then spoke for the Algonquins, who had no acquaintance with the Mohawk language. They were, moreover, timid, and somewhat ashamed, because they had left part of their presents behind. They had only ten elk-skins. Father Jogues excused them on account of a wound received by one of their young men, as well as of the weight of the burden and the difficulty of the way. The assembly seemed satisfied, and replied to the Algonquins by two presents; it also made two to the Hurons.

The reply to Onontio and the French, which was the very life of this negotiation, was given with much pomp and solemnity. They lavished every mark of the sincerest friendship. The French prisoner was released; and the Indians hung on him a wampum belt of two thousand beads. "Here," said they, "is the bond which retained him. Take the prisoner and his chain, and do Onontio's pleasure towards him." As to Teresa, who

---

rejecting the presents, replied: "We are surprised at your boldness and temerity. You cast shame in our face. We consider you as treacherous men. Onontio, with whom we have treated of peace, is not a child. If we looked upon you with favor, he would have reason to say, 'The Mohawks have not killed our allies, but their axe has. I thought I was treating with real men; I have treated only with impostors.' This is not all. The Algonquins, learning that the scalps of their brethren hang in our cabins, would scalp all the people in their country. This is the fruit of your boldness. Withdraw, then, and hide your scalps. As we have only one heart, we wish to have only one tongue."

was married, they replied that she should be set free in the village where she lived. "Here is a belt of fifteen hundred beads," they added, "to guarantee our words."

The Wolf clan made its special present; thirty-six fathoms of wampum assured the French that they should always have an abode among them; and addressing Father Jogues, they said, "You shall always have among us a mat to rest on and a fire to warm you."

Father Jogues had perceived in the crowd some Iroquois of the other cantons, and among others, Onondagas. He made them publicly a present of a thousand beads of wampum. "We wish," he said to the chief, "to salute you in your own country; take this present to smooth the way, and that no one may be astonished at our visit. Moreover, we have three paths to reach you—one by the Mohawk, the other by the great lake which you call Ontario,* the third by the Huron country."

These words seemed to surprise the Mohawks. "It is better," said one of the sachems to him, "that you take the route Onontio has traced. The others are too dangerous; you would find only warriors—men with painted faces, always brandishing the hatchet and axe; they desire only to slay. There is no road surer than that which leads here."

The orator, who had merely wished to make the Mohawks feel that the French could be independent of them if they chose to open intercourse with the other cantons, continued his speech and offered his present. The Onondagas accepted it, promising to convey it to the sachems and chiefs of their nation.

The missionary had not amid these political negotiations lost sight of the object of his desire and the secret aim of his coming. He administered the sacraments to

---

* Ontario means "beautiful lake." This sheet of water was called also by the French Lac Saint-Louis, Lac Frontenac, Lac des Iroquois, Lake Cataracoui. It also bore the name of Lake Skanadario.

several Christian captives, Huron and Algonquin, and taught them to bear their cross with merit. He visited and relieved the sick, and opened heaven to several dying children.

When the official meetings were over, the Mohawks advised Father Jogues not to prolong his stay among them. They hastened his departure, " because," they said, "a band of Iroquois from the upper country had started to lay ambuscades for the Hurons who were going down to the French posts. They were to follow the St. Lawrence and ascend the river of the Iroquois. We do not believe that they will harm you if they meet you, but we feel uneasy about your two Algonquin companions."

The Father expressed his astonishment : " How ! do you permit them to make war on your own land ?" " We have notified them," was the reply. " What then ?" added the French envoy. " Do they treat your words with contempt ? Do you not see that all the mischief they do will be laid to your charge ?" They seemed to open their eyes to the unreasonableness of their conduct, and promised to oppose, as the best remedy, everything that could impair their loyalty.

Be that as it may, the commissioners having discharged their duties, took the advice of the Mohawks, and prepared to return. They left the town of the Trinity on the 16th of June, and marched to Lac Saint-Sacrement. There they made bark canoes, and on the 29th—the Feast of St. Peter and St. Paul—they landed at Three Rivers, and on the 3d of July reached Quebec.*

---

* A contemporary manuscript, the Journal of the Superior of the Jesuits at Quebec, informs us that Father Jogues wrote a detailed account of this embassy. This document was lost, with no little of the Jesuit archives, after the English Government took possession of them, when the last member of the Society of Jesus died in Canada in 1800.

CHAPTER XIII.

**Third Visit of Father Jogues to the Mohawks—Ill-treatment—
Division of Opinion in the Tribe—Father Jogues is put to
Death—Punishment of his Murderer.**

THE success of his visit inspired Father Jogues with
fresh ardor. To continue a work which opened
under such consoling auspices, he thought of going to spend the winter among the Iroquois. In the
candid desires of his heart, he already beheld them listening to his words, submitting to the teachings of his
Divine Master, embracing the Faith, and becoming one
of its glorious triumphs after having been its most in-
superable barrier. He thanked God for having chosen
him to be the instrument of such a merciful Providence
towards them, and in this sweet hope he rejoiced in
anticipation of the day when he should present to God,
as his beloved children, those who had hitherto been
his enemies and torturers.

But always impenetrable in His designs, the Almighty
was about to demand of him a higher testimony than is
borne by words: He wished the last drop of that generous blood which had already flowed for His glory.
Having entered the way of the cross, the minister of Christ
was not to tread any other, and his noble soul will never
falter. If he had not, like some of his brethren, the consolation of seeing the fruit of his exertions, he will none
the less bless the name of Him for whose sake he labored. He knew that he who sows and he who waters may
merit as much as he who gathers in the harvest.

The prospect of the missionary's again visiting the

Mohawk country seemed improbable.   Yet it was discussed on the 9th of July in a consultation held by Father
Lalemant with Fathers Le Jeune and Vimont, at which
Father Jogues was present, as being the one best versed
in the whole matter.   The success of the attempt
seemed so doubtful that the project of wintering there
was suspended, "unless some favorable opportunity
offers."   Meanwhile Father Jogues was sent back to
Montreal to resume his services among the Indians.

Soon after affairs took a favorable turn, although we
do not know how or why.   The fact is stated in the
Journal of the Superior at Quebec, under the date of
July 21.   Father Lalemant summoned Fathers Le Jeune,
Vimont, and De Quen to an important consultation, as
he calls it, and the decision arrived at is expressed in
these simple words: "Father Jogues' wintering among
the Iroquois decided upon."   Yet the resolution was not
immediately carried out.   There were preparations to
be made and companions to be selected.

Father Jogues did not go down to Quebec till the
month of August, and it was not till the 27th of September that he took up his route for the Iroquois.   He was
accompanied by a young Frenchman, John De La Lande,
and by some Hurons, who were to take charge of his
canoe and baggage, and who availed themselves of this
opportunity to visit some of their kindred in captivity.
But soon alarmed at the rashness of this undertaking,
or disheartened by the dangers of navigation and the
hardships of the roads, these Hurons, all except one,
abandoned the missionary on the way.   As for him, he
saw only a duty to fulfil, and he advanced full of confidence.   Independently of the religious object proposed,
he had also the mission to maintain the peace so solemnly
concluded, and he promised himself that he would profit
by it to cultivate the seed which he had already sown
on that ungrateful soil.

Among the Mohawks the feeling towards him was no

longer the same, and a great hostile excitement prevailed in their minds. A violent animosity, born of distrust, had succeeded to their peaceful intentions. The cause was this :

When he left the Mohawk country at the close of the embassy, Father Jogues, who already nourished the idea and desire of returning, left a small box with his host, containing his scanty travelling outfit and some religious articles. He left it as a token that he would return, and to avoid the trouble of carrying it back and forth. This deposit seemed mysterious to several of these ignorant and suspicious minds. They did not conceal their apprehensions. They beheld in it a secret charm, which was to work their ruin and misfortune for the whole country.

Perceiving this provoking prejudice, the servant of God had endeavored to dispel them by spreading before them the articles which excited their fears. He opened his trunk and exposed all its contents to the crowd; but in minds once misled truth finds its way with more difficulty than falsehood.

At first they seemed to believe him, yet no sooner had he departed than their fears increased and became confirmed. The most dreaded scourges seemed to pour upon the country. First came a contagious disease, which swept off many victims; and then appeared swarms of worms, which destroyed almost the whole harvest. It did not require all this to give calumny a triumph, and to excite men's minds to the highest degree. The trunk, the supposed instrument of witchcraft, was thrown into the river, no one venturing to open it ; and for a month before the missionary's arrival the enemies of the French and of Christianity had succeeded in spreading everywhere hatred and vengeance against the man who was looked upon as the author of all the woes.

Unaware of this hostile feeling, Father Jogues had presentiments of evil during his journey, and did not dissemble the danger of his mission. Before setting out, he wrote to a Jesuit in France, to whom he confided the secrets of his heart, and imparted his apprehensions to him. This precious monument of his zeal for God's glory and his love for the cross proves that he did not conceal from himself any of the risks which he was about to run, and that he exposed himself to them with a cool intrepidity equalled only by his obedience and self-abnegation.

"Alas, my dear Father, when shall I begin to love and serve Him whose love for us had no beginning? When shall I begin to give myself entirely to Him, who has given Himself unreservedly to me? Although I am very miserable, and have so misused the graces our Lord has done me in this country, I do not despair, as He takes care to render me better by giving me new occasions to die to self, and unite myself inseparably to Him.

"The Iroquois have come to make some presents to our Governor to ransom some prisoners he held, and to treat of peace with him in the name of the whole country. It has been concluded, to the great joy of the French. It will last as long as pleases the Almighty.

"To maintain it, and see what can be done for the instruction of these tribes, it is here deemed expedient to send some Father. I have reason to think I shall be sent, having some knowledge of the language and country. You see what need I have of the powerful aid of prayers, being amidst these savages. I will have to remain among them, almost without liberty to pray, without Mass, without Sacraments, and be responsible for every accident among the Iroquois, French, Algonquins, and others. But what do I say? My hope is in God, who needs not us to accomplish His designs. We must endeavor to be faithful to Him, and not spoil His work by our shortcomings. I trust you will obtain me this favor of our Lord, that, having led so wretched a life till now, I may at last begin to serve Him better.

"My heart tells me that if I have the happiness of being employed in this mission, *Ibo et non redibo;* but I shall be happy if our Lord will complete the sacrifice where He has begun it, and make the little blood I have shed in that land the earnest of what I would give from every vein of my body and my heart.

"In a word, this people is 'a bloody spouse to me,'—'in my blood have I espoused it to me' (Exod. iv. 25). May our good Master, who has purchased them in His blood, open to them the door of His Gospel, as well as to the four allied nations near them.

"Adieu, dear Father; pray Him to unite me inseparably to Him.   ISAAC JOGUES, S. J."

These well-founded presentiments, and the desertion of his companions almost at the very outset of the voyage, ought to have disheartened him completely. Far from it. The thought and sight of death will not make him falter; he will march on as though he were going to fulfil his most ardent desires.

Meanwhile the public calamities had acted violently on this people. They excited to madness and fury these fierce and credulous savages. In natural events they beheld only effects of duplicity and ill-will, and they forgot their recent promises of friendship. The agitation kept increasing. The most sensible and prudent wished the peace maintained, but the turbulent and irascible prevailed; and it was decided to renew the war against the French, the Hurons, and the Algonquins, who were regarded as treacherous men, plotting the ruin of the Iroquois.

A war-party immediately took the field, aiming at Montreal, and surprised two Frenchmen in the vicinity of that city. Another band marched against Fort Richelieu, and came upon Father Jogues two days' march from their village. They fell upon the missionary and his companion, stripped them of their garments, loaded them with insults, and led them off as prisoners. On the 19th of October, 1646, these warriors made their triumphal entry into the town where the servant of God had already passed a captivity of thirteen months.*

From all sides threats of death sounded in their ears. Blows from fists and clubs soon accompanied these gloomy heralds of their execution. "You shall die to-morrow," they were told; "do not fear—you shall not be burned; your heads shall fall beneath our tomahawks, and we will set them upon the palisades around our village to show them for many a day to your brethren whom we capture."

Father Jogues endeavored to show them how unworth-ily they were acting, reminding them of his confidence in placing himself in their hands, the invitations they had given him to come and live among them, the promises which they had solemnly made, the manner in which the French had acted towards them, their treaty, their plighted word, and finally the unhappy results that war would draw down upon them. All was vain: a gloomy silence told him that he was speaking to men who would not hear.

This was not all: one furious savage sliced bits of flesh from his arms and back and devoured them, saying, "Let us see whether this white flesh is the flesh of a Manitou"!

The courage of the sufferer did not flinch. "No," he replied; "I am only a man like you all, but I fear neither death nor torments. Why do you put me to death? I have come to your country to cement peace, make the earth solid, and teach you the way to heaven, and you

---

* The Relation of 1668 (like the missionary in his letter of May 2d) speaks of eighteen months' captivity. It places his death at Ganda-ouagué (the Ossernenon of Father Jogues), the site of which General John S. Clark has unmistakably shown to be the Indian town still to be traced at Auriesville. Father Martin now recognizes Auriesville to be the place of the death of Father Jogues.

treat me like a wild beast ! Fear the chastisement of the Master of life."*

Meanwhile a division arose in the tribe. The families of the Wolf and Tortoise† wished to save the lives of the prisoners, and made every effort to rescue them. "Kill us," they said to their opponents, "rather than butcher in this way men who have done us no harm, and who come to us by faith of a treaty;" but the Bear family stubbornly insisted that they must die.

It was a grave question, affecting the whole nation. It was referred to a great council of sachems and chiefs, which met at Tionnontogen, the largest of the Mohawk towns, situated several miles farther west. Here the peace party prevailed. It was decided that the prisoners should enjoy life and liberty; but the party who thirsted for their blood did not wait for the result of this resolution, and their crime was accomplished when the delegates to the council returned to prevent it.

On the 18th of October some Mohawks of the Bear family had secretly formed a wicked plot to execute by themselves, and by their own private authority, this odious crime.

On the evening of the 18th‡ these Indians went to Father Jogues and perfidiously invited him to take a meal in their cabin. Accustomed to see in everything a mysterious disposition of Divine Providence, the servant of God followed them humbly. It was the hour of his last sacrifice. But sudden as was the blow which struck him,

---

* Manuscript of Father De Quen.

† Each Iroquois nation was made up of groups or families, each taking its name in most cases from some animal. To these families belonged the right of appointing sachems, who presided in the great councils of the League. These sachems retain to this day the hereditary names borne hundreds of years ago. Each family had also its war-chiefs.

‡ Charlevoix incorrectly gives the 17th as the date; but see the Relation for 1646–47, which is supported by the Manuscript of 1652 and the letter of Father J. Lalemant in the Archives at the Gesù.

it was not unexpected by the faithful missionary. He kept himself always ready for any event. At the moment when Father Jogues crossed the threshold of the cabin they dealt him a blow with a tomahawk which laid him dead. His head was immediately cut off and set up on one of the palisades encircling the place, the face turned towards the road by which he had come.

Early the next morning his companion* and the Huron who had guided them met the same fate, and their bodies were cast into the river. This assassination was publicly condemned by the principal sachem of the nation. "That blow of the tomahawk," he said, "can bring us only misfortune." But his power to punish the crime could extend no further.

Kiotsaeton, one of the deputies to the peace negotiations in 1643, spoke boldly against this criminal perfidy, and by the freedom of his language became an object of suspicion to the wicked clan. Another Iroquois, surnamed by the French "le Berger," also endeavored to thwart the murder of the missionary. He was impelled to do so by a sense of gratitude; for, having been taken prisoner by the Algonquins, he owed liberty and life to the interposition of Governor de Montmagny. But his efforts to prevent the tragic end of Father Jogues were in vain. When he saw the murderer raise his axe to strike him he tried to ward off the blow, and received a wound in the arm. This charitable act drew on him heavenly blessings: he had the happiness to die a Christian, and with sentiments of deep piety, during a voyage to France.†

---

*This young Frenchman, John De La Lande, was a native of Dieppe. He undertook this journey simply from religious motives. The desire of contributing to the glory of God, even at the risk of his life, had impelled him to ask. as a favor, permission to accompany the intrepid missionary. He found a crown worthy the aspiration of a heart full of faith.

†This Indian had fallen into the hands of the Christian Algonquins when religion was beginning to bring the Indian to more humane

The old woman to whom Father Jogues belonged during his captivity, who had taken care of him, and whom he called his aunt, also opposed with resolution the project for his death. "You must kill me at the same blow," she said. It was in vain; her brother, who was very far from sharing her feelings, was even one of the accomplices in his death, and betrayed the victim.

There were other proofs, too, of the division that prevailed among the Mohawks after this deplorable execution. A chief who had a Huron prisoner in his hands was so indignant at the conduct of his countrymen, that he set him free, and sent him to tell the French that he would not make war on them, and that the Algonquins alone were his enemies.

The death of Father Jogues was not known in Canada for a long time. A rumor came, but in a vague form, on the report of some women who had escaped from the Iroquois country, and on that of the Huron who had been set at liberty. It was, however, soon suspected, and

---

ideas. When this captive was solemnly received at the village of Sillery a chief told him, "Do not fear ill-treatment: we have abandoned that cruel custom." When Berger saw his bonds broken he could scarcely believe his eyes. He was treated with kindness when he expected to undergo horrible tortures. The Governor, to whom his case was referred, declared him free, praised his courage, expressed friendship for him, and gave him presents. The Iroquois at once exclaimed, "This goes well; my body is delivered from death, I am saved from the fire. Onontio, you gave me life: I thank you for it; I shall never forget it. My whole tribe shall be grateful. The land is about to become beautiful; the rivers shall be calm and smooth; peace will make us all friends. Now I have no shade in my eyes. The souls of my ancestors slain by the Algonquins have vanished. I have them beneath my feet. Onontio, men must avow that you are good and that we are bad, but our anger is extinguished." Then he began to dance and sing in cadence. He suddenly stopped, seized a hatchet and brandished it, gesticulating like a furious man. At last, throwing away the hatchet, he said, "My fury is overcome. I lay down my arms. I am your friend forever." He kept his word, and always remained faithful to the French.

justly, when Iroquois war-parties were seen once more infesting the great river and renewing their depredations and cruelties.

A letter from William Kieft, Governor of New Netherland, addressed to the Chevalier de Montmagny at last confirmed all the apprehensions entertained. Although dated in the month of November, 1646, it did not arrive till June in the following year.

According to the Manuscript of 1652, it read :

"MONSIEUR, MONSIEUR :

"I wrote a reply to that which you were pleased to honor me with by Father Jogues, dated May 15th, and I sent it to Fort Orange to deliver it to said F. de Jogues; but he not having returned as expected, it was not immediately sent. This will serve, then, to thank your Excellency for your remembrance of me, which I shall endeavor to return, if it please God to give me an opportunity. I send this through the Northern quarters, either by means of the English or Monsieur d'Aulnay,* in order to advise you of the massacre of F. Isaac de Jogues and his companion, perpetrated by the barbarous and inhuman Maquaas, or Iroquois; as also of their design to surprise you, under color of a visit, as you will see by the enclosed letter, which, though badly written and spelled, will, to our great regret, give you all the particulars. I am sorry that the subject of this is not more agreeable ; but the importance of the affair has not permitted me to be silent. Our minister above† carefully inquired of the chiefs of this *canaille* their reasons for the wretched act, but he could get no answer from them but this, that the said Father had left, among some articles that he had left in their keeping, a devil, who had caused all their corn or maize to be eaten up by worms. This is all I can

---

* D'Aulnay de Charnisé was then French commandant in Acadia.
† At Rensselaerswyck.

at present write to your Lordship. Praying God to vouchsafe to guard you and yours from this treacherous nation, and assuring you that I am

"Your most humble and obedient servant,

"WILLIAM KIEFT.

"FORT AMSTERDAM, in New Netherland, November 14, 1646."

The letter inclosed, written by Labatie, the Dutch interpreter, was addressed to Mr. La Montagne, a Huguenot doctor living on Manhattan Island, who held the highest place in the Colonial Council after the Director-General; we give it with his style, according to the Manuscript of 1652.*

"Praised be God, at Fort Orange!

"MONSIEUR, MONSIEUR LA MONTAGNE:

"I have not wished to lose this occasion of letting you know my state of health. I am in good health, thank God, and pray God that it may be so with you and your children.

"I have not much more to tell you, but how the French arrived the seventeenth of this present month at the Maquaas fort. This is to let you know how those ungrateful barbarians did not wait till they were fairly arrived at their cabins, where they were stripped all naked, without shirt, only they gave each a breech-cloth.

"The very day of their coming they began to threaten them, and immediately with fists and clubs, saying: 'You shall die to-morrow! Do not be astonished, we shall not burn you; take courage; we shall strike you with an axe, and put your heads on the palisade, that your

---

* The Relation of 1647, which Charlevoix follows, says that this letter was addressed to Mr. Bourdon, Father Jogues' companion on his first embassy. This does not agree with the contemporary manuscripts in our possession. The address bears the name of M. Lamontagne, and the context shows that Labatie saw no way of communicating with the French colony.

brothers may see you yet, when we take them.' You must know that it was only the Bear nation that killed them. Knowing that the Wolf and Tortoise tribes have done all that they could to save their lives, and said against the Bear, 'Kill us first;' but, alas, they are no longer alive. Know, then, that the eighteenth, in the evening, they came to call Isaac to supper. He got up and went away with the savage to the Bear's lodge; as entering the lodge, there was a traitor with his hatchet behind the door. On entering, he split open his head, and at the same time cut off his head and put it on the palisade. The next morning early he did the same with the other, and threw their bodies into the river. Monsieur, I have not been able to know or hear from any savage why they killed them.

"Besides this, according to their envy and enterprise, they are going with three or four hundred men to try and surprise the French, to do the same as they did to the others; but God grant they don't accomplish their design.

"It would be desirable that Monsieur should be warned, but there is no way to do it from here. Monsieur, I have no more to write, but I remain

"Your very humble and affectionate servant and friend,
                    "JEAN LABATIE.

"Monsieur, I beg you (give) my baisemains (respects) to the Governor.

"Written at Fort Orange, Oct. 30, 1646."

The Mohawks carried to the Dutch the missal, ritual. breeches, and cassock of Father Jogues, in hopes, doubtless, of obtaining some reward. When the Dutch blamed them for massacring the Frenchman in such a way, they justified themselves by a falsehood aggravated by a calumny. They replied that the Jesuits did not think as they did, and that they always had their arms ready to kill the Dutch.

God did not permit that the remains of the servant of God should be recovered and preserved for our veneration, but He glorified him by visiting a signal vengeance on his murderers, and those of his companions, and by the favors with which He has honored his name, as we shall see.

The two young men who had put good René Goupil to death before the eyes of the missionary were soon seized with a disorder unknown in the country, and died wretchedly. The woman who through a cowardly submission had cruelly cut off Father Jogues' thumb, as well as those who mangled his fingers with their teeth to crush out the bones, were all killed in succession soon after.

The epidemic which spread in the country served as an instrument of divine justice, and found many victims among the most bloodthirsty Iroquois.

The assassin of Father Jogues merited a more exemplary punishment; but this chastisement was at the same time a token of great mercy. God seems to have wished to show, by one more example, the full power of the prayer of the just man imploring pardon for his persecutors.

In fact, on the 16th of October, 1647, John Amiot,* a young Frenchman, brought in to Sillery an Iroquois whom he had just captured near Three Rivers. As the Algonquins of that Mission had to avenge the death of some of their people recently cut off by the Iroquois, the Governor consented that an example should be made, and delivered the prisoner to the Indians to undergo his fate, forbidding the Algonquins, however, to prolong his tortures or eat his flesh. He was obeyed. The prisoner did not suffer an hour. He was put out of misery, and his body was thrown into the river. During the eight or ten

---

* John Amiot had served in his youth on the Huron Mission. He was alike brave and virtuous. More than once he commanded parties in pursuit of the Iroquois He was drowned with Francis Marguerie before Three Rivers, in 1648.

days which preceded his execution the missionaries bestowed every care on the prisoner, in order to prepare him to die well. He listened with docility, and soon astonished them by the remarkable evidence of his faith, and his repentance for his sins.

A twofold interest attached to his fate: it had just been discovered that he had been the murderer of the servant of God. In conversation he had related at length the persecutions and cruel treatment to which the Iroquois had subjected the French, and especially Father Jogues, whose virtue he extolled. He described, as an eye-witness, the sudden outburst of one part of the village against the missionary, and he declared that his death was the work of but a few fanatics, who acted in defiance of the judgment of the assembly of the three towns.

He was asked the name of the murderer of John De La Lande, and he gave it on the spot ; but when they wished him to reveal the name of the one who had tomahawked Father Jogues, he hung his head and remained silent, as though ashamed of his crime. The Huron who had escaped from the Mohawks and had just arrived was cognizant of all the tragical events. He recognized the murderer, and the guilty man did not attempt to deny his crime. He seemed to think only of detesting and expiating it.

He was soon deemed worthy to receive baptism, and in sign of peace and union with his victim he received at the sacred font the name of Isaac.*

These happy dispositions did not diminish for a moment. During his execution he uttered no complaint. His lips pronounced no taunts to his torturers, and he made neither bravado nor threats as victims generally

---

* In the Register of the Sillery Mission, under the date of September 16, is this entry in the handwriting of Father Druillettes: "Baptisavi Isaacum captivum Agnonguerronon (vulgo Iroquois) mox comburendum."

do. Amid his pains he was heard exclaiming, "Jesus, Jesus!" He had said shortly before, "Antaiok [the Indian name of the Frenchman who had taken him] is the cause of my going to heaven. I am satisfied, and thank him."

God employed men to execute His justice upon him, at the same time that He granted his soul the benefit of His most mysterious mercies.

The death of the servant of God which we have related was doubtless the immediate result of those odious suspicions of witchcraft of which the Mohawks believed themselves victims. Futile and ridiculous as they seem to us, they were of a nature to exercise a powerful influence on ignorant and superstitious minds. When the material interests of a gross people are affected, inasmuch as they know no life but that of the senses, they can be easily driven to the most violent excesses. Like brutes, they dream only of violence when they think themselves wounded; but less clear-sighted than animals, they are blinded by prejudice and ignorance, and then often mistake falsehood for truth, and crime itself for an act of virtue.

In this tragic termination of an apostolic life there is something more, when it is studied by the light of faith. Is it not the heroic consummation of a life of sacrifice, which we admire as a martyr's death?

When Father Charles Garnier, then a missionary among the Hurons, and soon to be himself a victim to the hatred of the Iroquois, announced the death to one of his brothers in France, he did not hesitate to say, "Hi sunt martyres caritatis et obedientiæ"—"These are martyrs of charity and obedience."

Father Jerome Lalemant, then Superior of the Canada Mission, expresses himself in as decisive a manner in the Relation of the Missions for 1647. "We have respected this death," says he, "as the death of a martyr. Although we were separated from one another when we learned it, several Fathers, without any previous consultation, found that they could not bring themselves to offer a requiem Mass for him, but they presented the adorable sacrifice in thanksgiving for the benefits which God had bestowed upon him. Seculars who knew him best, and religious houses also, respected this death, and were all inclined to invoke him rather than pray for his soul.

"In fact, it is the thought of several learned men (and this thought is more than reasonable) that he is really a martyr in the eyes of God, who bears testimony before heaven and earth, and who esteems the Faith and the preaching of the Gospel more than his own life, losing it in the perils into which he plunges for Christ's sake, protesting before His face that he wishes to die in order to make His Name known. This is a martyr's death in the sight of the angels. And it was with this view that Father Jogues gave his life to Jesus Christ and for Jesus Christ.

"I say even more: he not only took the means to proclaim the Gospel, which caused his death, but we can also aver that he was killed out of hatred for the doctrine of Christ.

"In fact, the Algonquins, the Hurons, and subsequently the Iroquois, persuaded by their captives, have had, and some of them still have, an extreme hatred and horror of our doctrine, saying that it causes their death, and contains charms and spells, which cause the destruction of their grain, and produce contagious and epidemic diseases, such as now begin to ravage the Iroquois. It is on this ground that we have been on the point of being massacred in every place where we have been, and even at present we are not without the hope of enjoying that happiness some day.

"Now, just as formerly in the primitive Church, the children of Jesus Christ were reproached with causing misfortunes everywhere, and some were put to death on

that pretext, so are we persecuted because by our doctrine, which is only that of Jesus Christ, we depopulate
their countries, as they assert, and it was on this pretext
that they put Father Jogues to death.   We may therefore regard him as a martyr before God."

The proper tribunals at Rome * have it now under
consideration whether proof exists to decide juridically
the martyrdom of the servant of God—that is, to prove
that his murderers were impelled by a hatred of the
Faith in putting him to death ; but we can meanwhile
console ourselves with the testimony of St. Cyprian,
who said to the Thibaritans (Epist. 56), " You are not
alone, for wherever you go you are with God.   If flying
to the wilderness, if hiding in the mountains, you are
slain by robbers or devoured by a wild beast, or con-
sumed by hunger, thirst, or cold, or swept away by the
storm, what difference does the battle-field make ?
Jesus Christ contemplates you from heaven on high as
His soldiers battling for the glory of His Name, and you
shall have the same reward as he who has all the glory
of the combat, for an obscure death is not less glorious
than that which has the publicity of a triumph. For the
certainty of martyrdom it is enough to have as a witness Him who tries and crowns the martyr."

---

* Petitions for the Introduction of the Cause of Beatification of
René Goupil, Father Isaac Jogues, and the Iroquois virgin Catherine
Tegakwita have been recently presented to the Holy See in great
number.   See note at end of volume.

CHAPTER XIV.

Virtues of Father Jogues—Favors obtained by his Intercession.

WE should not do full justice to the virtues of Father Jogues if we passed over in silence some more interior traits which have been passed by in the narrative, and which have been transmitted by his confidant and friend, Father Buteux, whose manuscripts have fortunately escaped destruction. We must first recognize that he possessed in a high degree the happy qualities, which, according to Father de Brébeuf, ought to characterize a Huron missionary. "To convert them," said he, "requires not so much learning as goodness and solid virtue. The four elements of an apostolic man in New France are affability, humility, patience, and generous charity. Too ardent a zeal burns more than it warms, and spoils everything. It requires great magnanimity and condescendence to attract these Indians gradually. They do not grasp our theology readily, but they understand perfectly our humility and affability, and are won by them" (Relation for 1636).

HUMILITY AND MORTIFICATION.

We readily borrow from Father Buteux this beautiful thought, which he places at the head of his notes on the virtue of Father Jogues. "I have always thought that what was said and related in writing as to the lives of the Saints was the smallest and least considerable part of what they had done, and that scarcely anything was

said of their interior, which is nevertheless the noblest
ornament of their life. 'Omnis gloria filiæ regis ab intus'
—'All the glory of the king's daughter is within' (Ps.
xliv. 14). I thought that their humility made them conceal the most wonderful external things that they had
done, such as miracles, or great sufferings and torments
which they had endured for the love of God. I was
confirmed in this thought last year, when I resided with
Father Jogues the greater part of the year. The solitude
in which we were, and the familiar conversations which I
had with him, caused me to admire his virtue and to discover many things which his humility had never shown,
and nevertheless I should not have known all that I shall
say, if I had not used the power which obedience gave
me over him—who was, however, my superior in everything and for everything.

"Humility is one of the virtues which I most admired
in him. It prevented my obtaining many details as to
his sufferings and struggles; he did not like to speak of
them. When urging him one day to tell me something
of what God had made his soul undergo in his captivity,
I could draw from him only these three words: 'Dies
isti mali' —'They were wretched days.'

"To hear him, the Society of Jesus had never had a
member less capable than himself of serving God, nor a
heart so ungrateful and unfaithful to grace. He deemed
himself unworthy of the habit which he wore. When he
spoke of the favor which God had done him, to suffer
for His love, he sighed over the little profit he had derived from it, and his tears flowed abundantly. One of
his great faults, with which he bitterly reproached himself, was that he had felt some pleasure in the thought
of death as the term of his fearful sufferings.

"How could I wring any words that seemed to convey the slightest praise from the lips of a man who
always concealed himself in the shadow, in order to
cover up the signal graces which he had received from

heaven—who was convinced that he did no good, and that what came from others was always better? He questioned me as a novice would have done as to the manner in which he should make his meditation and his thanksgiving after Mass. Shortly before his departure for Quebec he wrote me that he would have liked to spend another year with me in order to exercise himself more solidly in virtue than he had done; 'yet,' he added, 'I would like better to return for the third time to the Iroquois country.'

"I had to employ stratagems to obtain of him the information I succeeded in gathering: not but that he had the perfect submission of obedience, but because he had so low an opinion of himself, that it seemed impossible for him to speak of himself except with contempt. He seemed afflicted and constrained when any esteem was shown him because he had suffered so much for Christ, and when people asked to see his mutilated hands.

"On his return to France, the Queen had to repeat her invitation twice before he could decide to appear before her. He could not persuade himself that she really desired it."

In a moment of unreserve he made with simplicity this touching and humble avowal : "God gave me from my tenderest youth this pious regard for those who chastised me, as I only too often deserved it. When I was a schoolboy I took the ferule, and when I could even the hand of the one who corrected me, to kiss it as a sign of affectionate gratitude. But I did so especially among the Iroquois, where, after life was granted to us, I did not fail to kiss for several days in succession the posts supporting the stage or scaffold on which we had suffered; and the sight of that place of torture was a subject of consolation, thanksgiving, and gratitude to Our Lord for the favor He had done me there."

The last year of his life he spent in Montreal, and as though he had a presentiment of his approaching death, he desired to make a more immediate preparation for it by instituting a general review of his conscience from his earliest years. "In this confession," says Father Buteux, who received the avowal of his faults, "he showed all the humility and candor of a child."

He could not bear to see any deference or special attention paid to him, such as the feeble state of his health seemed to call for. "I do not need anything," he said ; "I do not wish when I go back among the Iroquois that my wretched nature shall turn its head towards these houses, where it has found so much ease. I want only things absolutely necessary. Why should I give myself these indulgences that I must look for in vain hereafter ? God forbid that I should pamper the inclinations of my body by granting it what it cannot always have !"

His fervor seemed to increase daily, and his devotion to the Blessed Sacrament was the powerful means which he employed to nourish his virtue. It was before this hidden God that he loved to perform his spiritual exercises; neither severe cold, nor excessive heat, nor importunate insects could divert him from his pious practices. He heard all the masses that were said, and yet he lamented his tepidity. He longed, he said, to make up for the time when he had been unable to offer that Divine Sacrifice, and to supply, in anticipation, for the time when he might be again deprived of that happiness.

Father Jogues' courage in suffering inspired Father Buteux with this reflection: "I undertake this narrative," says he, "first to show slack and cowardly souls, like my own, how wrong we are to fly from pain and mortification under the pretext of health, since this Father, who has endured so much, is as sound and whole as ever; and secondly, to give holy and courageous souls an occasion to praise God and thank Him that He has still in these times servants and faithful souls who 'fill up those things that are wanting of the sufferings of Christ'" (Col. i. 24).

CHARITY AND CHASTITY.

His ardent charity for his brethren and for the Indians is conspicuous in what we have related. Never amid his sufferings and all the refinements of cruelty adopted by his torturers did he feel the least aversion for them. On the contrary, he felt sentiments of love and compassion for the Iroquois; he desired their salvation, and prayed incessantly for them. It was one of his consolations to think that he had been the first to shed his blood for God's glory amid that heathen nation, in the hope that this holocaust would hasten their conversion.

The blindness of these people and their opposition to the Faith deeply afflicted his soul. He regarded their excessive cruelty to him with the compassionate pity of a mother afflicted by the sight of a child seized with insanity. On other occasions he considered them as the rod of the Lord, appointed to punish his sins, and he bowed with submission beneath His hand while adoring His judgments.

His chastity, as angelic as his charity, excited the admiration of the very savages. Like a vigilant sentinel, he was always in arms to defend it. The rigorous treatment to which he subjected his body, already so cruelly tortured by these Indians, proves clearly that he had never regarded it, except as a slave to be kept under, because its revolt was always to be feared. The state of almost perfect nudity in which he was left during a part of his captivity was a more painful cross to him than all his other sufferings.

A Dutch Protestant entering the cabin where he was one day addressed some indecent words to him, and spoke ironically of his shamefacedness. The servant of God found in his zeal strength to denounce such language. He showed the man the impropriety and sin of his conduct so clearly, that the Indians did him justice, and declared openly that the French were not lewd and dissolute, like the Dutch. His virtue thus exalted his whole nation.

OBEDIENCE AND ZEAL.

On entering the religious state Father Jogues had fully comprehended the true value of obedience, and the assistance he would find in its practice. Naturally timid, fearful, and even pusillanimous, he became bold and intrepid when he fulfilled the will of his superiors. They knew this so well, that in difficult conjunctures they felt that they could rely on him as on a rock. When he heard the word "Go," he knew no obstacle, he perceived no danger. But, on the other hand, if he had a decision to make by himself, he stopped to examine minutely the slightest difficulties, while at the voice of his superiors he considered only how to execute a command and the will of God.

This disposition did not escape the eye of the Indians. On seeing him so docile to the voice of his masters, and so firm in everything that concerned the glory of God, they said to him, "Indeed, Ondesonk, it would have been a pity to kill you, for you act the master when you think proper, and the obedient child when a reasonable order is given you."

In fact he was always ready to obey the meanest Indian in lawful things, however humiliating they might be, but he could withstand the most powerful of them when he thought God's interests were at stake. It was by these qualities that he was able to acquire a complete mastery over several of them. They listened to him willingly, and at last respected him. One of the most influential sachems deemed it an honor to be visited by him, and when he expected the missionary he prepared beforehand to welcome him as well as he could, and treat him properly.

The holy courage with which Father Jogues arrayed himself against evil practices which he hoped to correct, excited the admiration of the most sensible Indians, and they often said to him, "You speak too boldly: you will get killed. If here, where you are a prisoner and with none to sustain you, you resist us, what would you do if you were free and among your own people? You surely would not speak in favor of the Iroquois." They were ignorant alike of evangelical charity and intrepidity.

In the visits which Father Jogues made to the Dutch during his captivity they invited him frequently to take a little of those spirituous liquors which the Indians called *fire-water*, and which they pressed on the natives so nefariously in their trade. He constantly refused to taste it, to show them his aversion for that drink which caused drunkenness, debauchery, and a host of disorders.

During his captivity he had the consolation of baptizing more than sixty persons, for he let slip no opportunity which Providence offered him of opening to souls the gates of heaven.

His masters took him one day to a neighboring town to witness the dances and games. He followed them, but with another object than enjoyment. As soon as he got there he slipped away from the crowd and the noise, and glided into the cabins to comfort the sick and dying, and administer baptism. In one of these dwellings he found five little children prostrated by the same disease, and ready to expire. Their parents had run off to the merry-making, so that he had ample leisure to discharge his ministry and regenerate them by the sacrament. Three days after he ascertained that they had all gone to heaven.

The zeal of which Father Jogues' whole life was the constant expression was the real chain which kept him so long a prisoner among the Mohawks. Several opportunities of escape had been given him, but he always repelled the idea as a temptation, on account of the good to souls which he was effecting. If at last he consented to escape, it was, as we have seen, on account of the well-grounded fear lest his death should compromise the interests of the Faith. It was, on the other hand, his consolation to think that he might perhaps be able some day to evangelize those districts which he had bedewed with his blood.

The Lord did, indeed, grant him the favor to return, but it was to complete his sacrifice on the spot where he had so heroically begun it. The blood of the martyr was not shed in vain. He made that impious land fruitful. Some years after, Faith went there to plant her standard, and all Christian virtues were seen flourishing.

Another precious fruit of this magnanimous sacrifice was to increase the ardor of his brethren and excite in their hearts a holy emulation of zeal and virtue. Father Jerome Lalemant wrote soon after: "The rage of the Iroquois will not make the mystery of Christ's cross useless. We shall be captured, we shall be massacred, we shall be burned: so be it. The noblest death is not on a bed. I do not see one here who hangs his head. On the contrary, all ask to go up to the Hurons, and all protest that the fires of the Iroquois are one of their motives for undertaking the dangerous journey" (Relation, 1647).

The death of the servant of God was only the prelude of the terrible trials through which the young Canadian Church was to pass. It was its bloodiest, but also its most glorious epoch.

Emboldened by impunity and success, the Iroquois spread on all sides, carrying terror and destruction everywhere. The Hurons and their missionaries were the most sorely tried. In 1647 one of their towns was utterly destroyed, with all its inhabitants. The Iroquois made the whole country one vast ruin. Fathers de Brébeuf, Gabriel Lalemant, Charles Garnier, Anthony Daniel, perished by their hands, as well as a great number of their converts. But those days of misfortune were days of triumph for the Faith: in the school of adversity man often learns wisdom. The Hurons in great numbers besought the boon of baptism. They acknowledged in the trials of adversity the chastisement due to their long and culpable resistance to grace. In their truly Christian resignation they displayed a courage and an energy of character which will stand higher even than their warlike exploits as their strongest title to glory.

When the missionaries were at last able to enter the Iroquois cantons they found the memory of the servant of God still fresh in the minds of the tribe, and they more than once experienced in a sensible manner the effect of his powerful protection.

Father James de Lamberville, one of the apostles of the Iroquois, himself obtained one of these signal favors in behalf of a sick Iroquois. His relatives, strongly attached to their superstitions and renowned for their fanaticism, had employed every possible practice of the medicine-men to obtain his recovery, but the disease kept making alarming progress. The missionary, who had been informed by some of his converts of the man's danger, made ineffectual efforts to reach him. In this extremity he invoked Father Jogues to have the obstacles removed. His prayer was not in vain. He had scarcely ended his invocation when the doors so obstinately closed against him seemed to open of themselves. The patient cheerfully welcomed him, and showed every docility to his instructions. Grace had triumphed: the suitable disposition of the dying man soon rendered him fit for baptism. On recovering his health the new convert showed no relaxation, but continued faithful to his death (Relation, 1677).

The example and power of the servant of God bore happy fruit even in France. Mother Catharine of St. Augustine, the illustrious Hospital Nun of Quebec, whose wonderful life was written by Father Ragueneau, was indebted to Father Jogues for her vocation to Canada. She became a novice in the convent at Bayeux at the age of fifteen, but had already an ardent desire to devote her life to the distant missions of America, and this desire was shared by her sister, who was a professed Ursuline nun.

But their parents, especially their father, Mr. de Long-pré, opposed it so positively that the elder sister finally abandoned the project entirely. Not so Catharine. Her father, to strengthen his refusal, addressed a petition to the judicial body, the "Parlement," and on her side Catharine addressed Heaven in her behalf. She triumphed. The Relation of the Canada Missions which described the labors, the sufferings, and death of Father Jogues had just reached France. It fell into the hands of Mr. de Longpré, who read it with the liveliest interest. The next night he felt himself very strongly moved to yield to his daughter's wishes, so that on awakening he felt his heart entirely changed. At that very moment, and in the same manner, his wife, who was then at a considerable distance, experienced the same change. It was a warning of Heaven; they did not wish to incur the reproach of resisting the will of God, and gave their daughter the consent which she awaited.

A cure, which seems miraculous, occurred some years afterwards in a community at Poitiers. A pious object which had been used by Father Jogues was preserved there. One of the nuns, named Mary Prévosterie, owed her life to it. The opening of a large abscess was followed by a malignant fever of the worst type. The pain became acute, and in a short time intolerable. Recollecting then the relic of Father Jogues, she implored the Superior to lay it on her wound. At the first instant the pain increased considerably, then it suddenly ceased, and the sick nun was completely cured. The next year, at the same time and under the same circumstances, the disease reappeared. The nun remembered the benefit that she had received, but reproached herself with not having been sufficiently grateful to her benefactor. She had recourse to him again, promising to make known, as well as she could, the favor if she recovered. Her prayer was again heard, and she obtained an immediate restoration. An authentic act was immediately drawn up, with the approbation of the Bishop, and was preserved in the Archives of the Jesuits at Paris.*

---

*Creuxius, " Historia Canadensis," p. 499; Cassani, " Glorias del segundo siglo de la Compañia de Jesus."

RENÉ GOUPIL AND HIS HEROIC DEATH.

Translated from the Autograph of Father Jogues.

"René Goupil was a native of Angers, who, in the bloom of life, earnestly asked admission into our novitiate at Paris, where he remained some months with great edification. His bodily ailments having deprived him of the happiness of consecrating himself in the holy state of religion as he had wished, he crossed over to New France, as soon as he grew better, to serve the Society there, as he had not had the happiness of giving himself to it in the *Old*. And to do nothing of his own will, though perfect master of his actions, he submitted himself entirely to the direction of the Superior of the Mission, who employed him for two whole years in the meanest employments of the house, which he discharged with great humility and charity. They also gave him the care of tending the sick and wounded in the hospital, a post he filled with great ability, for he was well skilled in surgery, and with equal love and charity always beholding our Lord in the person of his patients. So sweet an odor of his goodness and other virtues did he leave in that place, that his memory is still in benediction there.

"As we descended from the Hurons in July, 1642, we asked the Rev. Father Vimont to let us take him, as the Hurons greatly needed a surgeon, and he consented. It were impossible to express the joy of this good young man when the Superior told him to prepare for the voyage. He knew, withal, the great dangers on the river;

he knew how furious the Iroquois were against the
French: yet all this could not deter him from embarking for Three Rivers, at the slightest sign of His will,
to whom he had voluntarily resigned all that concerned
him.

"We left there (Three Rivers) on the first of August,
the morrow of the Feast of our Holy Father. On the
second, we met the enemy, who, divided into two bands,
awaited us, with all the advantage which a large number
of picked men, fighting on land, can have over a smaller
one of all kinds on the water in bark canoes.

"Almost all the Hurons had fled into the woods, and,
having left us, we were taken. Here his virtue was
strikingly displayed; for as soon as he was taken, he
said, 'Father! blessed be God, He has permitted it; He
has wished it; His holy will be done! I love it, I wish it,
I cherish it, I embrace it with all my heart.' While the
enemy pursued the fugitives, I confessed him and gave
him absolution, not knowing what was to befall us after
our capture. The enemy, having returned from the chase,
fell on us with their teeth, like furious dogs, tore out our
nails and crunched our fingers, all which he endured with
great patience and courage.

"His presence of mind in so distressing an accident
was shown specially in his aiding me, in spite of the pain
of his wounds, in instructing, as far as he could, the
Huron prisoners who were not yet Christians. As I was
instructing them separately, and as they came to me, he
reminded me that a poor old man named Ondouterraon
might well be one of those to be killed on the spot, it
being then the custom always to sacrifice some one to
the heat of their rage. I instructed this old man carefully while the enemy were busied with the division of
the booty of twelve canoes, a part of which were laden
with necessaries for our Huron Fathers. The spoil being divided, they killed the poor old man almost at the
very moment when I had given him a new birth. Dur-

ing our march to the enemy's country we had the additional consolation of being together; and here I witnessed many virtues.

"On the way he was always absorbed in God. His words and conversation were all in perfect submissiveness to the orders of Divine Providence and a voluntary acceptance of the death which God sent him. He offered himself to Him as a holocaust, to be reduced to ashes in the fires of the Iroquois, which that good Father should enkindle. In all, and by all, he sought means to please Him. One day—it was soon after our capture—he told me, while still on the way, 'Father! God has always given me a great desire to consecrate myself to His holy service by the vows of religion in His holy Society; till now, my sins have rendered me unworthy of this grace; yet I hope that our Lord will accept the offering I wish to make Him now, and to take, in the best manner that I can, the vows of the Society, in the presence of my God and before you.' Having permitted him, he pronounced them with great devotion.

"Wounded as he was, he dressed the wounds of others, not only of the prisoners, but even of such of the enemy as had received any wound in the combat. He also bled a sick Iroquois, and did all with as much charity as if he were doing it to his dearest friends.

"His humility and the obedience he paid to his captors confounded me. The Iroquois, who had us both in their canoe, told me to take a paddle and use it. Proud even in death, I would not. Some time after, they told him to do it, and he immediately began to paddle; but when he perceived that the Indians wished to compel me to do so after his example, he begged my pardon. At times, on the way, I suggested to him thoughts of flight, as the liberty given us afforded him abundant opportunity. For my own part, I could not forsake a Frenchman and twenty-four or five Huron prisoners. He would never do it, resigning himself entirely to the will of our Lord, who inspired him with no such thought.

"On the Lake (Champlain) we met two hundred Iroquois, who came to Richelieu when they began to build the fort; they covered us with stripes, drenched us in blood, and made us experience the rage of men possessed by the devil. All these outrages and cruelties he endured with great patience and charity for those who ill-treated him.

"On entering the first town where we were so cruelly treated, he showed extraordinary patience and mildness. Having fallen under the hail of blows of clubs and iron rods poured on us, and unable to rise, he was carried, as it were, half-dead on the scaffold, where we were already, in the middle of the town, but in so pitiable a state that he would have moved cruelty itself to compassion: he was all livid with bruises, and in his face we could distinguish nothing but the white of his eyes; yet he was the more beautiful in the eyes of angels as he was more disfigured; and like Him of whom it is said, 'We have seen Him as a leper,' etc.; 'There was in Him neither comeliness nor beauty' (Isaias liii. 24).

"Scarcely had he, or even we, recovered breath, when they came and gave him three blows on the shoulders with a heavy club, as they had done to us. After cutting off a thumb from me as the most important, they turned to him and cut off his right thumb at the first joint. During this cruel operation he constantly repeated, 'Jesus, Mary, Joseph.' During the six days that we were exposed to all those who chose to maltreat us, he displayed extraordinary mildness; his breast was all burned by the live coals and ashes which the boys threw on his body when he was tied down on the ground at night. Nature gave me more dexterity than him in escaping some of these pains.

"After our life was granted us, just after we had been warned to prepare to be burned, he fell sick in great want of everything, especially of food, for he was not accustomed to theirs. Here truly it may be said, '*Non cibus utilis ægro.*'* I could not relieve him, being also sick, and not having one finger sound or whole.

"But I must hasten to his death, which wants nothing to be that of a martyr.

"After we had been six weeks in the country, as confusion arose in the councils of the Iroquois, some of whom were for sending us back, we lost all hope, which in me had never been sanguine, of seeing Three Rivers that year. We consoled one another then at this disposal of Providence, and prepared for all He should ordain in our regard. He did not see the danger we were in so clearly: I saw it better. This made me often tell him to hold himself in readiness. Accordingly, one day when in our mental pain we had gone out of the town to pray more becomingly and undisturbed by noise, two young men came after us and told us to return home. I had some presentiment of what was to happen, and told him, 'My dear brother, let us recommend ourselves to our Lord and to our good mother the Blessed Virgin: these men have some evil design, as I think.' We had a little before offered ourselves to our Lord with much devotion, beseeching Him to accept our lives and blood, and unite them to His life and blood for the salvation of these poor tribes. We were returning then towards the town, reciting our beads, of which we had already said four decades. Having stopped near the gate of the town to see what they would say, one of these two Iroquois drew an axe which he had hidden under his blanket, and dealt René a blow on the head as he stood before him; he fell stiff on his face on the ground, uttering the holy name of Jesus, for we had often reminded each other to close our voice and life with that holy name. I turned at the blow,

---

* " Food is not useful to the sick."

and seeing the reeking hatchet, fell on my knees to receive the blow that was to unite me to my loved companion; but as they delayed I rose, ran to him, as he lay
expiring near me. They gave him two more blows on
the head and extinguished life, but not before I had
given him absolution, which, since our captivity, I had
given him regularly after his confession every other day.

"It was the [29th] day of September, the Feast of St.
Michael, that this angel in innocence and martyr of
Christ gave his life for Him who had given him His.
They commanded me to return to my cabin, where I
awaited during the rest of the day and the next the same
treatment. It was the belief of all that I would not wait
long, as they had begun it; and in fact for several days
they came to kill me, but our Lord prevented it by ways
which would take long to explain. Early the next morning I did not fail to start out to inquire where they had
thrown that blessed body, for I wished to inter it, cost
what it might. Some Iroquois who had a wish to save
me said, 'Thou hast no sense; thou seest that they seek
thee everywhere to kill thee, and thou goest out still—
thou wilt go to seek a body already half putrified, which
has been dragged far from here. Seest thou not those
young men going out who will kill thee when thou art
past the palisade?' This did not stop me, and our Lord
gave me courage enough to be willing to die in that office
of charity. I go, I seek, and by the help of a captured
Algonquin become a real Iroquois, I find it. After he had
been killed the children had stripped him, and tying a
cord around his neck dragged him to a torrent which
runs at the foot of the town. The dogs had already
gnawed a part of his thighs. At this spectacle I could
not withhold my tears. I took the body, and, aided by
the Algonquin, I sank it in the water and covered it with
large stones to hide it, intending to return the next day
with a spade, when there was no one near, and dig a
grave and inter it. I thought the body well hidden, but

perhaps some one saw us, especially of the youth, and took it up.

"The next day, as they sought to kill me, my aunt sent me to her field to escape, as I think; this compelled me to defer it till the next day. It rained all night, so that the torrent was extremely swelled; I borrowed a hoe in another cabin, the better to conceal my design, but on approaching the place could not find the blessed deposit; I entered the water, already quite cold, I go and come, I sound with my feet to see whether the water had not raised and carried off the body, but I saw nothing. How many tears I shed, which fell in the torrent, while I sang as I could the psalms which the Church chants for the dead! After all I found nothing, and a woman known to me who passed by, seeing me in trouble, told me, when I asked her whether she did not know what had been done with it, that it had been dragged to the river, which is a quarter of a league from there, and with which I was not acquainted. This was false, the young men had taken it up and dragged it to a neighboring wood, where during the fall and winter it was the food of the dog, the crow, and the fox. When I was told in the spring that he had been dragged there, I went several times without finding anything; at last, the fourth time, I found his head and some half-gnawed bones, which I interred, intending to carry them off, if taken back to Three Rivers, as was then talked of. Repeatedly did I kiss them as the bones of a martyr of Jesus Christ.

"I give him this title, not only because he was killed by the enemies of God and His Church, in the exercise of an ardent love for his neighbor, putting himself in evident perils for the love of God, but particularly because he was killed for prayer, and expressly for the Holy Cross. He was in a cabin where he prayed daily, which scarcely pleased a superstitious old man there. One day seeing a little child, three or four years old, in the cabin, from an excess of devotion and a love of the cross, and in a simplicity which we, who are more prudent according to the flesh, would not have had, he took off his cap, and putting it on the child's head made the sign of the cross on his body. The old man seeing it ordered a young man in his cabin, who was starting on a war-party, to kill him; and he obeyed the order, as we have seen.

"The mother of the child herself, in a voyage which I made with her, told me that he had been killed for that sign of the cross; and the old man who had given the order to kill him invited me one day to his cabin to dinner, but when I made the sign of the cross before beginning, he said, 'There is what we hate; that is what we killed thy comrade for, and will kill thee too. Our neighbors, the Europeans, do not make it.' Sometimes, too, as I prayed on my knees in hunting time, they told me that they hated that way of doing, and had killed the other Frenchman for it, and would kill me too when I got back to the village.

"I beg pardon of your Reverence for the precipitation with which I write this, and my want of respect in so doing. Excuse me, if you please; I feared to miss this opportunity of discharging a debt I should long since have discharged."

APPENDIX.

A.

GEOGRAPHY OF THE HURON COUNTRY. PAGE 30.

THE Huron country, which was eighteen to twenty miles wide by twenty-five to thirty-seven miles long, lay between latitude 40° and 45° N. and longitude 82° 30' and 83° W. To complete the geography, we ought to give the position of the chief towns, but they have left no trace. With their bark cabins and wooden palisades, the Indians made no permanent foundations. The ravages of fire or time sufficed to sweep away all but the faintest vestiges. The only ruins to be found are those of the two forts erected by the missionaries—one at St. Mary, the other on Isle St. Joseph.

Only one ancient map lays down the Huron villages. This is a little plan in the corner of a large map in a work by Father Ducreux (Creuxius, " Historia Canadensis," 1660). This work—which Father Charlevoix seems not to have known or to have disregarded when he adopted the maps of Bellin, which are very defective on this point —did not escape the learned American historian Dr. Jared Sparks of Cambridge. He was the first to call attention to its importance. Though without a scale, and showing that the engraver misread several names, it is of great aid in identifying the relative position of the important villages. By its help and the information scattered through the " Relations de la Nouvelle France," and explorations made on the spot, we have endeavored to fix the position of some of these towns.

1. Ihonatiria, or St. Joseph (called also Ihoriatiria, Relation 1640, and Jonatari in Charlevoix) had replaced Otonacha, Champlain's landing-place. The old name, too, had variations—Toanchen in Sagard; Toanche, Toachim, and Teandeouiata in Father de Brébeuf. The Recollects called it St. Nicholas and the port St. Joseph. It was on a point running out into Lake Huron, about seven and a half miles from St. Mary, ten from Ossossané, and about seventeen from Teanaustayae. From it a large island was visible on the lake. These data seem to indicate the west entrance of what is now called Penetanguishene Bay.

2. Ossossané, which Champlain calls Caragouha, and Brother Sagard Tequeunonkiae, also bore the name of St. Gabriel (Sagard). Ducreux's map places this town on the west side of the Huron peninsula, and there is a little isolated promontory there which corresponds to all the historical references.

3. Teanaustayae, Teanosteae (Register of Three Rivers), received the name of St. Joseph in 1638, when the village of Ihonatiria dispersed. This is the place where Father Daniel perished in 1648, with seven hundred Hurons. Ducreux's map and historical references seem to indicate as its site a point now called Irish Settlement, in the north of Medonte district. Traces of a large Indian town, and especially fragments of coarse pottery, are found here.

4. Cahiagué (Champlain) or Contarea (Father de Brébeuf) was called St. John the Baptist. This village contained two hundred and sixty cabins, which would represent nearly two thousand souls. It was near the large Lake Ouentaron, now Simcoe, and another smaller lake. It was the frontier Huron town on the east. Champlain set out from it to attack the Iroquois in their own country. Its position must have been north of Lake Simcoe, near the town of Orillia.

5. St. Louis was of recent origin in 1648; no Indian

name is given for it in the Relations. It was only two miles and a half from St. Mary, and near the mouth of the little river which empties into a neighboring bay, now called Hog Bay. It was in this village that Father de Bré-beuf and Father Gabriel Lalemant were captured by the Iroquois in 1649, but they were put to death in the village of St. Ignatius, about two and a half miles distant.

6. There were two villages called St. Ignatius—the one just mentioned, about five miles from St. Mary; the other, known in Indian as Taenhatentaron, was near the Iroquois frontier, between Teanaustayae and Cahiagué. We are inclined to think that its site was on Lot 20, Concession 10, of the present district of Medonte. Many Indian remains have been found there, pipes of various kinds, collars of all varieties, fragments of vessels, and more than two hundred iron hatchets of French make. We visited near it one of the great Huron graves, such as Father de Brébeuf describes in detail in the Relations. It is a great circular pit about five yards in diameter, in which great numbers of bones are still to be seen. When it was discovered in 1844, kettles, pipes, collars, fragments of peltry,—the usual articles used in these solemn burials,—were found there. This town was abandoned from fear of the Iroquois and removed nearer St. Mary, in 1648, as we have said. It is the one shown on Ducreux's map, on what is now called Sturgeon Bay.

7. St. Mary was not an Indian town, but a residence for the missionaries and the French. There is no doubt as to its site. Ducreux's map and the details given in the Relations, point clearly enough to the right bank of a little river, now called the Wye, east of the present village of Penetanguishene. What is more, the ruins still exist. The fort erected by the missionaries more than two hundred years ago (1639) is still traceable, and we drew a plan of it. The stone walls are still more than three feet above ground. The curtains on the east and northeast and the four bastions were of stone ; the

other two curtains were doubtless formed of stout palisades. The square base connected with the south bastion probably supported a tower from which the approaches could easily be seen.

The traces and dimensions of the ditch surrounding the fort, and which could receive the water of the river, and canoes, are still clearly visible. Three little basins, which may have been shelters or landing-places, are also to be seen. On the south an inclosure, in form of a redan, defended by a ditch and parapet of earth, in all probability was used by travelling Hurons to pitch their cabins. By digging the ground within the fort, we found at a depth of some two feet traces of the fire kindled by the missionaries in 1649, when they were compelled to fly with their converts before the Iroquois invasion. This fort contained the chapel and house for the missionaries and the French, as well as the storehouses for provisions; but outside there was a cemetery for Christian Indians, and a small field for cultivation. South of the fort, in the redan rose a large cabin for pilgrims and a hospice for the sick. " This hospital," adds Father Jerome Lalemant, " is so separated from our dwelling, that not only men and boys, but also women can be admitted."

8. Isle St. Joseph (in Huron, Ahoendoe, now Charity Island) lies northeast of the Huron peninsula. After destroying St. Mary on the Wye, the missionaries threw up a regular fort on the southwest side of the island, and gave it the name of St. Mary. The ruins still remain in the midst of the woods.

B.

STEPHEN TOTIRI. PAGE 69.

Stephen Totiri is one of the glories of the Huron Church. His family resided in the town of St. Joseph (Teanaustayae), of which he was the model. He was one

of those taken with Father Jogues; but having eluded
the vigilance of the Iroquois, he escaped, and returned
to his own country to proclaim the Faith. He was poor,
because all he owned had fallen into the hands of the
enemy; but this mattered little, and he made an offering
of it to God. The first news which Stephen heard on
his return was that his mother, Christine Sarihia, whom
he loved deeply, had died. He asked whether she
breathed her last as a good Christian, and on learning
that she had died in the most pious sentiments, he
clasped his hands, and raising his eyes to heaven,
said, "My God, who can mourn? She is happy, she can
never more offend Thee. Provided I and mine die in the
Faith, I cannot regret this life for them or for me. Brethren, let us say no more of what I have lost, but let us
think of the great blessings which await us in heaven.
Your tears and mine will be turned into joy, and the
heathens will know by our faces that we have faith and
the hope of heaven in our hearts. Let us go into the
chapel and praise God."

Stephen was a Christian in 1641 when the missionaries
wished to establish a residence in his village. He had
offered half his cabin for a chapel, and the first Mass was
said there on the 19th of March, the Feast of St. Joseph.
The sacrifice which he had made was an honor in his
eyes, and drew upon him many graces from heaven. He
received especially grace to profess his faith: it was reasonable, resting on solid instruction. When the missionaries were absent, he and his wife instructed the
catechumens of both sexes in Christian doctrine, and discharged this duty remarkably well. This chapel from
time to time drew upon him insults and threats. The
heathen party wished to force him from it in order to
destroy it. "I will leave it," he told them, "but only
when the missionaries who instruct us themselves leave
the town, and then it will be to follow them wherever
they go. I am more attached to them than I am to my

country and kindred, for they bring us the words of eternal happiness. My soul does not depend on my body: a moment can separate them; but you will never deprive me of the Faith.

In 1643 the calumnies and hatred of the heathens in the town assumed a more threatening character, because they saw their most important men side with the missionaries and embrace the "Prayer." The Christians held a meeting to concert steps to meet the storm. Stephen, as one of the leading chiefs, presided. Each one gave his advice; but the unanimous opinion counselled patience and resignation. At last Stephen Totiri summed up the discussion, and put the result in a few words, which showed his faith : " Brethren, since you regard me as chief, this is the thought which God suggests to me: Let us fear nothing but sin."

The missionaries saw in 1644 that they could not, on account of their scanty number, continue the mission which they had begun among the Neutral Nation.* Stephen wished to do something by visiting the tribe with his brother Paul: they showed wonderful zeal, and met with great success. Their rosaries, worn around their necks, according to the custom of the more fervent Christians, attracted attention, excited curiosity, and enabled them to explain our doctrine and praise the " Prayer."

Human respect had no hold on this energetic man: in 1646 an unfortunate Iroquois prisoner went through all the horrors of the stake in his village. The idea that he was going to die a heathen roused Stephen's zeal. Unable to preserve his body from torture, he wished at least to try and save his soul, and he undertook to instruct him. He

---

* The Neutral Nation owed this name among the French to its attitude in the war between the Iroquois and Hurons. It took no part in that fierce struggle between the two nations, leaving free passage to both parties through its territory, but not permitting any fighting there.

alone had no firebrand or murderous implement in his hand. "Fear not," he said, approaching the victim; "I wish only your good. You are about to die, it is true; if you will invoke with me my God, the Master of Life, Him who created us and wishes to make us happy, your soul will be able to enjoy happiness in another world. Those who refuse to honor Him go with the demons to suffer eternally." These words, uttered gently and with conviction, fell like a soothing balm on the sufferings of the wretched man. "I have heard something like this from Hurons whom we have burned," said the Iroquois; "they were comforted by it even in the flames, awaiting the great happiness of heaven. Is it true that it is really so?" Stephen instructed him in the fundamental truths of religion, and found a heart well disposed for the divine seed. The Iroquois earnestly solicited baptism, and Stephen, braving the indignation of the heathens, who in their rage wished to prolong their victim's sufferings, even after death, poured the saving water on his brow, and heard him pronouncing, till his last sigh, words of consolation, hope, and love.

On another occasion his love for the Faith and the holy energy of his zeal excited admiration. Some boys, only too apt to imitate the impiety of their parents, had pelted with stones the cross which had just been erected with great ceremony in the cemetery. They had even smeared filth over it.

On hearing of this profanation Stephen's heart was roused. He resolved that reparation must be made, and he called a meeting of the chiefs for the purpose. When evening came he went to the top of his cabin, and in a voice of thunder raised the cry customary when an enemy is seen or some great danger menaces a town. The warriors all gathered, fully armed. "Tremble, brethren," he cried, "the enemy is in our town. The cemetery of the Christians has been profaned. God will take vengeance. Stop your children, or you share their crime, and the punishment will fall on all. The bodies of the dead are sacred things, and the heathens themselves respect them. No one would touch a paddle hung up at a grave. You may overturn my cabin, strike me, kill me rather; but when the things of God are assailed, I wish, as long as I have a breath of life, to proclaim how enormous a crime it is, and I will tell you what a terrible thing it is to make God your enemy."

These words produced their effect: the parents checked the insolence and impiety of their children.

C.

TERESA OIOUHATON. PAGE 69.

Teresa Oiouhaton was the daughter of a fervent Christian, Joseph Chiouatenhoua, who was the first to receive baptism in the town of the Conception. He became a genuine apostle and the pillar of the Mission, which he supported with all the ardor of the most disinterested zeal. The Iroquois massacred him in his field, in a raid which they made into the Huron territory in 1640. His brother, Teondechoren, who knew his desire to send his daughter to the Ursulines at Quebec, undertook to take her there some time after her father's death. While at the convent she noticed that the nuns every year retired apart for eight days and spent the time in silence. She wished to do the same ; having noticed a grove in a retired part of the convent grounds, she made a little cabin of branches there, where she spent whole days without uttering a word. The curiosity of the other Indian girls at last revealed the mystery of her absence, and made known her retreat by destroying its charm.

When her countrymen came to Quebec they always visited her and her schoolmates: it was her pleasure to act as interpreter when they went to the nuns to have them repeat their catechism and prayers. Two of these Hurons, who remained the whole winter in the town were

a special object of her care. One of them a few days before his baptism wished to amuse himself at her expense,
and pretended to feel doubt and uncertainty. Said he,
"I cannot bring myself to believe all that the black-
gown teaches me; and besides, it is too strict a doctrine:
I must give up everything I like." More indignant than
grieved, Teresa forgot her youth and reproached him
sharply. "What has turned your head?" she cried.
"What are you thinking about? Don't you see that you
may die at any moment? If you died this night you
would go to the demons in hell: think of all this, and return quickly." The Indian pretended to persist in his
hesitation and indifference. Teresa began to cry. Feeling
that she had exhausted her own arguments, she ran to
the nun who had charge of the neophytes. "He is lost,"
she told her with sobs; "he will not believe in God any
more, or obey Him. If I could have torn down the grat-
ing I would have beaten him."

The good religious endeavored in vain to persuade her
that it was only a trick and pretence. It required all the
influence of Father de Brébeuf, who was then at Quebec,
to quiet the fears of this good soul and comfort her.

Teresa could read, write, and speak French. Her
country-people were amazed at her learning, and flat-
tered to see her so virtuous. "These good Indians,"
says Ven. Mother Mary of the Incarnation, "resemble
religious, they are so fervent" (Letter 25). Her uncle
came for her in 1642 ; he proposed to give her in marriage, and he hoped that she would do wonders in the
Huron country, she was so pious and accomplished. The
young girl wished to remain with her teachers, to whom
she was strongly attached; but she yielded to the lesson
which Father Jogues gave her on the obedience due to
parents. She set out; and "by means of our friends,"
wrote the venerable Superior whom we have just cited,
"we provided her with all she required for her marriage"
(Letter 35).

Teresa was captured by the Mohawks at the same time as Father Jogues. She was bound to one of her cousins, aged, like herself, fifteen, and hurried off with the other prisoners. She was not as badly treated as the men, and fell to the lot of a young warrior, who married her. As long as her uncle, Joseph Teondechoren, remained near her he encouraged her by his example and his pious words. After his escape from the hands of the enemy he went to Quebec to tell the Ursulines of his niece's disposition. "She is not ashamed of her baptism," said he. "She prays to God publicly, and goes to confession to Father Jogues every time he visits her village. I often exhorted her to persevere in good and not lose courage. She obeyed me in everything, and I am most grateful to you, Mothers, for the pious education you have given her. This does not prevent her from grieving to be compelled to live in the midst of our cruel enemies. She has suffered much from the cold and inclemency of winter; she has even been very sick, but God has restored her to health. I told her, 'Be patient; this life is short; your troubles will end, and you will be happy in heaven if you persevere.' She has no beads, and to say her rosary she uses her fingers, or little pebbles which she lays on the ground at each *Hail Mary*. She often spoke to me about you. 'Alas!' said she, 'if the nuns saw me in this state among these wicked Iroquois, who know not God, they would take pity on me.'"

We have seen that the Governor and the Ursulines offered a ransom for her deliverance, which Father Jogues presented to the Mohawks. Her marriage was an obstacle to her liberation, or rather a pretext for deferring it; and the treachery of those Indians, which made peace impossible for several years, deprived her friends of all hope of obtaining her liberty. She accordingly remained among the heathens, but she preserved amidst them her faith and her virtue.

Father Le Moyne found her at Onondaga in 1654, when

he went there to confirm a new treaty of peace between the Iroquois and the French. She ran to meet him. He was the only missionary whom she had seen after Father Jogues. In order to profit better by his presence she invited him to the house she occupied outside the village. "My God," cried the Father in his journal, "what a sweet consolation to find so much faith in savage hearts living in captivity, with no help but heaven! God makes apostles everywhere. This excellent woman had with her a captive girl fifteen or sixteen years old, belonging to the Neutral Nation, whom she loved as if she were her own child. She had instructed her so well in the mysteries of the Faith, and had inspired her with such sentiments of piety in the prayers which they recited together in this holy solitude, that I was utterly surprised. 'Why did you not baptize her, sister?' said I, 'since she believes as you do, is a Christian in her life, and wishes to live and die a Christian?' 'Alas! brother,' replied this humble captive, "I did not know that it was lawful for me to baptize, except in danger of death. But baptize her now yourself, since you deem her worthy, and give her my name.' It was the first adult baptism performed in Onondaga, and we are indebted for it to the piety of a Huron woman. The joy I experienced banished all the hardships I had undergone" (Relation, 1654).

The consolation which Teresa had enjoyed in seeing a black-gown once more, and approaching the Sacraments, was complete, when she was so happy as to see the missionaries establish themselves permanently in the Iroquois cantons in 1657. She probably owed the preservation of her life to their presence. Her husband was a hard and cruel man. One day he ordered her to go a day's journey and bring in some game that he had killed. It was beyond her strength, but to disobey was to provoke her death. She hastened to the missionary to prepare for the sacrifice. Fortified by the grace of the Sacraments and the thoughts of faith, she returned to her tyrant and said calmly, "You know that I am not able to do what you order me; but here I am: kill me if you like." This courage and coolness disarmed the savage, and he abandoned his unreasonable order.

Teresa Oïouhaton persevered to the end in the same sentiments, and preserved in her noble heart the sacred seed implanted there in her younger days: from this fruitful source her soul drew its strength, and the only consolation which sweetens all the miseries of this life.

D.

Joseph Theondechoren.   Page 69.

Joseph Theondechoren was the elder brother of Joseph Chiouatenhoua, the first Huron who became a Christian in the town of the Conception. After the death of the latter in 1640, Teondechoren reviewed in his mind the advice which he had received from him. He reflected on what he had heard him say of God, of His justice and His goodness, and he felt completely changed. Three days after the funeral, he solicited baptism. He was put to the test; for the missionaries, knowing that he was addicted to gambling, superstition, and impurity, feared a relapse, and that his resolution might be the result of a momentary impulse, rather than of a solid and durable conviction. His conversion was, however, sincere, and his perseverance dispelled all doubts. He was baptized September 8, 1640. His wife soon followed his example, and received the same grace at Easter 1641, taking the name of Catharine. After his conversion Joseph related how for twenty years he had served as an instrument to the devil. His hands and lips were not at first fire-proof to take live coals and heated pebbles, but after a dream he obtained this power. He was able even to plunge his arm into a kettle of boiling water without suffering any injury. It required courage to renounce all his superstitious practices, and his constancy was admirable in the assaults which he had to sustain from the enemy of salvation and his tools. He did more—he became a real apostle, and his words were of fire.

As the missionaries resided in his cabin, he endeavored to imitate them in everything and to conform to their mode of life. He rose at the same hour, gave the same time to prayer, and shared their labors. His heathen friends could not understand his mode of acting, and especially the blameless life he led. They said to him, "But what have the black-gowns done to you to change you so?" "They have plucked out," said he, "all that was evil in my soul. Believe in the ' Prayer ' yourselves, as you should, and you will experience it better than I can tell you" (Relation, 1642).

When he was told of some calumnies uttered against him, he said, "Wait till the day of judgment, and you will see how it is. Your wickedness does me good, for I offer it to our Lord in satisfaction for my sins." *

So good a Christian was worthy to form part of Father Jogues' convoy. When he was leaving his country to go down to Quebec he addressed these words to all the Christians present : "Brethren, I am about to go ; we shall never perhaps have the consolation of seeing each other again here below. I wish to speak to you as though I were at the point of death. Whatever misfortune may befall us, let us remember that we are Christians, that our hopes are in heaven, and that earth possesses nothing capable of satisfying a soul that has given itself to God. For all eternity we shall have time to enjoy this truth. It is enough now that faith shows it to us. Let us never lose the grace that we received in holy baptism. This is our treasure. If the devil or all hell endeavors to deprive us of it, let us have greater ardor for our salvation than he has for our destruction. Let

---

* Letter of Father Chaumonot.

us watch night and day over ourselves, and have recourse to prayer as often as we feel our heart attacked. Let us esteem the gift of Faith, and love a God who has first loved us; let all the efforts of our hatred be turned against sin."

When he ceased he made all present kneel down, and in the name of all he pronounced a protestation of fidelity in God's service (Relation, 1644).

Joseph was taken prisoner, with his two brothers, his son, and his niece, and like the other captives endured with admirable courage torments and insults at the hands of his executioners. He saw his son and one of his brothers killed by the Iroquois. To support him in his captivity he had recourse to prayer and the sacrament of penance. He loved often to commune with God. "I spoke to Him in my heart," he added, "as though we had been two conversing together, and so I never wearied."

His devotion to the Blessed Virgin was very great: he said his rosary every day, counting on his fingers. He often recited it with Father Jogues, even in the streets of the Mohawk town, unperceived by the heathens. "How I love that prayer!" he said afterwards. "I never am tired of saying it, and invoking the Mother of my God." To this devotion he ascribed his deliverance from the hands of his enemies. Joseph went twice to the Dutch with his masters. One of these Protestants having seen him make the sign of the cross, rebuked him for it, and ridiculed the practice. Joseph listened, but, inaccessible to human respect and firm in his faith, did not lay aside the custom, but maintained it without ostentation and without any cowardice.

In the spring of 1643 the Iroquois took him with them, as well as his brother and another prisoner, on an expedition to the St. Lawrence. The three Hurons succeeded in escaping by night, and reached Three Rivers, where they were so happy as to find Father de Brébeuf, and then returned to their own country. There Joseph had more than one opportunity to show what the firmness and resignation of a true Christian can effect.

On reaching his country he could not contain his joy and his gratitude, and he said to the missionaries, " Truly the God whom you preach and in whom I believe is alone omnipotent and all good. He has conducted me and protected me for a year amid a thousand perils, and if He had wished that my body should suffer, it has only been that my soul should feel that there are joys even in suffering, and that there are no terrors for one who hopes in God."

His words to the idolaters prove that the Holy Ghost makes even the tongues of children eloquent. "You feel joy to see me delivered from the cruelties of the Iroquois," he said to those who congratulated him; "while it saddens me to find you still under the bondage of the demons, and for my part I do not consider myself as entirely free while I am in this world, where sin can plunge me into a captivity even more unhappy than the one I have suffered. The tortures I endured were horrible; what then must eternal fire be?

"I am told that several rejoiced when they heard that I had been taken prisoner, and that they made it a pretext for reviling the God whom I adore; that they pretended that He was under their power; that the misery into which He had permitted me to fall would prevent others from following my example, and from serving a master who had no power or will to render us forever happy, since He did not begin in this life. Brethren, I do not know God's designs in my regard. In my most cruel sufferings I did not dare to ask of Him either life or death, believing that I was a child who did not know what is for my good, and that He, my Father and my sovereign Master, had more wisdom to guide me, and that He would never fail to love me, so long as I did not fail to trust in Him.

"Here I am, delivered contrary to all my hopes. I do

not know whether you have caused it by your horrid blasphemies.

"I believe that God wished to justify Himself in my person, and show you that He had not forsaken me, and that His power and love will never fail those who belong to Him.

"I do not know for what death He reserves me, but whatever misfortune may befall me, do not accuse Him: it is enough that He has confounded you once before you die. Your impiety cannot compel Him always to work miracles. If you recognize neither His goodness nor His power in this life, He will justify Himself forever at the day of judgment. Then those who have blasphemed against Him will be strangely disabused when they see the eternal rewards which He prepared for us, even when He seeemed to forsake us, and that for the impious there is no longer anything but endless torments and despair."

After his return to his own country Theondechoren formed one of a convoy of a hundred warriors who went down to Quebec. They were attacked on the way by the Iroquois, and sustained two serious reverses, in which they lost several men, with nearly all their baggage and goods.

Joseph, wounded in the shoulder, succeeded in escaping to the woods; but he remained alone for two or three days, losing blood freely, and with no one to assist him. With failing strength, and believing that he was going to die, he addressed this prayer to God. As he repeated it subsequently to the missionaries, he said, "My God, I continue to acknowledge that Thou art everywhere, my God—on these rocks where I see myself forsaken, as in the midst of my captivity, and my whole heart is consoled by the single thought that wherever I am Thou dost witness my sufferings. I escaped from the enemy in order to die near my Fathers who have begotten me in the Faith. But, my God, if Thou reservest this pleasure for me in heaven, blessed be Thou forever! I die as willingly on these rocks as in the Huron country, for wherever I die it is Thou alone who disposest of my life."

Meanwhile some of his companions found him, and though still pagans, they were so touched by his words that they took pity on him and carried him with them.

These were not the only trials which Joseph had to undergo, and among the keenest must be enumerated the jealousy of his second wife. Her constant reproaches culminated in anger, often shown in public. In the midst of a banquet which Theondechoren was one day giving to his friends, she misinterpreted a very innocent action on his part. Blinded by passion, she took her children, in presence of all his guests, and dragging them to the door, said, "Come, let us seek another home. You have no father; do you not see that he disowns you, since he does not recognize me as his wife?" She rushed from the cabin into the depth of the wood. Good Joseph remained unshaken before the storm; but his mildness and constancy triumphed at last over her angry and jealous disposition.

Let us cite for this good Christian the testimony of Father Charles Garnier, who often lived under his roof: "This good young man shames me, seeing how he advances in the service of God, for he has no heart or thought or words, except for God. Sometimes the devil suggests to him some evil thought, but he at once takes a firebrand and applies it to his arm or hand, saying, 'Can you suffer the fire of hell?' He once said to me, 'Brother, let me propose to you a doubt that I have. Sometimes after being long at prayer it seems to me that God, as it were, takes possession of my heart, and that I have none but for Him; but I believe that I sometimes commit a fault, when, finding myself in this state, I leave prayer to go and work, or sometimes even to go and rest.' He fears no man where God's glory is concerned " (Letter of 1646).

When the Hurons were driven from their country by

the Iroquois in 1649, Theondechoren retired with the missionaries to Ahoendae, or St. Joseph's Island, and the next year he followed them with a good number of his tribe to seek safety under the fort of Quebec, where he continued to edify the French and Indians by his admirable piety. More than four months before his death he spoke frequently of the uncertainty of life, as if he had had a presentiment of his fate, and he urged all to be ever ready, for "we shall be surprised," said he. While going to Tadoussac he perished in a storm, June 26, 1652.

E.

CHARLES TSONDATSAA. PAGE 69.

Charles Tsondatsaa was the son of a chief of the village of Ossossané. With a feeling heart and upright mind, he had never been opposed to the missionaries, nor hostile to the Faith. He even opened his house to the Jesuit Fathers when they were driven out on all sides, and before he became a Christian he permitted his children to be baptized. Yet he continued to act as a medicine-man, and was regarded as a very expert one; but he unhesitatingly sacrificed all the implements of his evil craft when he resolved to take his place among the catechumens.

He had already been soliciting baptism for a year when Father de Brébeuf was obliged to go down to Quebec. Out of affection and devotedness for him, Charles undertook to guide him. The only reward he sought was his admission into the Church of God. During the voyage his conduct was very edifying: no one was more assiduous or more fervent in prayer than he; none more eager to listen to the missionary's instructions. His excellent disposition made him notable as soon as he reached Quebec, and the Governor wished to see and converse with him. This increased his esteem for the neophyte, and he asked that his baptism should be no longer deferred; he even offered to be his godfather, and gave him his own name. For the cause of religion, he invested the ceremony with unusual pomp. It took place at Sillery, in presence of all the Indians of that Mission.

Father de Brébeuf acted as interpreter, and put the usual questions to elicit from the catechumen a public testimony of his faith. The replies of Tsondatsaa, made aloud and with ardent conviction, showed the deep sincerity of his heart. After the ceremony the Governor embraced the neophyte, and made him a present of an arquebuse, telling him, "I rejoice to see you a Christian. Keep faithfully the word you have given to God. Baptism will give you arms against your invisible enemies; take this arquebuse to repel the visible enemies who wish to exterminate your nation. You will exhort your countrymen to follow your example; assure them of my protection."

The chief of the Sillery Indians then addressed him, saying, "Brother, all the Indians whom you see here are Christians. By embracing the Faith you become really our brother. We have only one Father, who is in heaven, and one mother, Holy Church. Your friends are our friends, and your enemies our enemies. Since Onontio has given you a firearm, here is something to use with it;" and he presented him a bag of powder. Charles' emotion was so great that he could only stammer his thanks, and renew his profession of faith, but in all proclaiming his joy and happiness. On returning to his own country, Charles showed clearly that the Huron church counted another valiant champion in him. He at once invited the sachems and chiefs to a solemn banquet to announce his conversion, and thus addressed them : "You see a man who, since he left you, has become a Christian, and so firm a one, that he has resolved to die a thousand deaths rather than renounce his religion. My goods, my life, my courage, are yours—provided you require nothing of me that displeases God. I do not know much, but I offer to teach all who have any desire to imitate me." He never deviated from this line of conduct. When he spoke of what he had seen at Quebec he knew not when to stop. Three things especially had charmed him: the respect and obedience of the French for their Governor; the piety and devotedness of the nuns; the devotion and charity of the new Christians at Sillery.

The trials through which he passed gave new lustre to his virtue, for he was often exposed to the sarcasms and persecutions of his kindred and neighbors. Immediately after his baptism sickness and death struck down those dearest to him. His heathen relatives ascribed these misfortunes to his change, and wished to draw from it arguments against his faith; but they failed.

Charles Tsondatsaa was, as we have seen, one of the party who accompanied Father Jogues, and like him fell into the hands of the Iroquois. He had the good fortune to escape from their hands; but he had lost all he possessed. When he returned to his country he said to his tribesmen : " I had never come back so rich from any voyage. God has deprived me of all in a moment, to teach me that earthly goods are nothing, and that it is only in heaven that our real hopes are. Faith alone procures true joy. When, after escaping from death, I found myself at Three Rivers among the Algonquins, Montagnais, and French, whose language I knew not, they consoled me, although they spoke an unknown tongue. One wept with compassion on seeing me; another raised his hand to point up to heaven. I understood without hearing a word; I felt an invisible hand confirming my mind, and making me find happiness in all my losses."

Charles was always the model and pillar of the young Huron church. One day, when he was returning very weary from a long journey, he found his cabin in disorder. The cause of the grief was the serious illness of his little niece, five years old. "You are grieving in advance over her death," said he; "and what saddens me most is that she has not been baptized." He ran out at once, and hastened to the chief Christians to find one who knew the mode of administering the Sacrament. At last he met good Joseph Theondechoren, and brought him to the cabin. The child received baptism. Charles then addressed all present : "Now let us be comforted; her soul is safe: she will soar away to heaven, and will pray to God for us. For my part, I deem myself happy that I have four children already in heaven; I invoke them with consolation." Thus on all occasions this ex-cellent convert sought to diffuse around him the faith that filled his heart and the hope that sustained his soul. His. old friends made many efforts to draw Charles back into his old bad habits, but could not gain anything. He always replied that he feared fire less then he feared sin. They resolved to test it, and under the form of an act of charity carried their temptation to cruelty. At the close of a laborious day they invited him to take a vapor-bath—a very common remedy among these people. A cabin is prepared, and covered with bark and several thick skins to prevent all evaporation. A small opening is left at the bottom to push in stones, heated red-hot. On these water is dropped, which rises in vapor and fills the confined space.* Unsuspicious of their perfidious de-sign, Charles entered the cabin, and they began to heat it. The heat soon became excessive, and a real torture. Cnarles called out that the heat was sufficient for the vapor-bath, and that if it was increased he would stifle.

The author of this infernal stratagem then told Charles that to satisfy a dream he had had the night before, he must pronounce three words in favor of his tutelar de-

---

* These vapor-baths under the same form were found among several ancient nations. Herodotus mentions the Scythians and Strabo the Lacedemonians and the Lusitanians. They also prevailed among the Celts.

mon, in order to avert a danger which threatened him.
"Do me this friendly service," he added, "and I will set
you free." Seeing that they wished to extort from him
by force what they could not obtain by persuasion,
Charles bravely answered, "Comrade, hell-fire is hotter
than this. To avoid one, I should be a fool to rush into
the other. You may kill me if you like, but you will
never get me to utter an impious word. I have no
tongue to commit a sin." He was urged not to persist
in his refusal, and not to be cruel to a friend. "And
after all," they said to him, "the compulsion used to you
will be a good excuse to the black-gowns. You know,
too, that there are remedies for all sins, and if you pre-
fer, we swear inviolable secrecy; they shall never know
a word about it." "Friends," replied the Christian hero,
"I do not fear men, my countrymen, or the French, or
the Iroquois ; but I fear God, whose eye sees the depth
of our conscience. Hope of pardon is good to excite to
repentance, but not to incite one to offend." Meanwhile
the heat was steadily rising. "Friends," cried Charles,
"I lack air, not courage; I cannot breathe, but know
that I will not yield." His feeble voice showed his weakness, and his approaching end. The main author of this
cruel trick, seeing himself baffled, became furious, and
vomited a thousand blasphemies against the Faith and
the Christians ; but his accomplices, unwilling to push
the trial any further, at last blamed his obstinacy, and
forced him to give up his infernal work.

When they opened the cabin Charles was almost
dead. He recovered, however, and his only vengeance
was a kind look he gave his torturer, saying, "You killed
me, but you could not make me sin" (Relation, 1644).

Charles survived this fiery trial for a long time, and
continued to edify the Christians, and the very pagans.
He had the consolation of seeing more than one of his
persecutors embrace, like himself, the law of the Gospel.

F.

EUSTACE AHASISTARI. PAGE 69.

On account of his antecedents and his character, Ahasistari was regarded by the whole nation as their head chief. "He was in fact," says Father Charles Garnier, "the greatest warrior in the land." He deserves to be known. "The life of this man," wrote Father Jerome Lalemant, "is only one succession of battles, and from boyhood war was his only thought, and it was through it that God made him a Christian. He belonged to the village of Teanaustayae, or St. Joseph. Before bending his neck to the yoke of faith, he had long been interiorly urged by the Lord. He admired it, without yet fully understanding it. He often, indeed, though in secret, invoked the God of the Christians. A blind attachment to the absurd native superstitions, always held him back. He seemed so inveterately attached to them, that even after his conversion the missionaries for some time entertained doubts as to his sincerity. They kept him on trial for three years before they yielded to his earnest entreaty to be baptized. Yet his zeal for the Faith and his desire to receive the sacrament of regeneration were seen to be constantly on the increase. During the winter of 1641 there was a renewal of fervor in his soul. It might be thought that he had a presentiment of what was soon to befall him. To give a higher idea of the Faith, the missionaries had introduced the custom of admitting some Indians to baptism at each one of the principal holidays of the year. They all gathered in the chapel at St. Mary, to give the ceremony all possible solemnity.

On the approach of Easter, Ahasistari felt interiorly moved to take a new step to obtain his desire. He went to St. Mary to plead his cause in person with the Superior of the Mission. "I have the Faith in the bottom of my heart," he said, with admirable frankness and a holy ardor, "and my conduct last winter proves it. In a few days I start on the war-path. If I die in battle, where will my soul go without baptism? If you could see into my heart as clearly as the Master of Life does, I should be a Christian now, and the fear of hell-fire would not haunt me the moment I face death. I cannot baptize myself; I can only tell you sincerely my desire. After that, if my soul burns in hell, it is your fault; but whatever you do, I shall always pray to God, since I know Him, and He will perhaps show me mercy, for you teach me that He is better than you." "But how did the first thoughts of the Faith come to you?" asked the missionary. "Even before you were in the country," said the Huron, "I had escaped a thousand dangers, in which my comrades fell before my eyes. I saw clearly that it was not to myself that I was indebted for being rescued from these dangers. It came into my mind that there was some more powerful genius, unknown to me, who came to my aid. I was convinced that our belief was mere folly, but I knew nothing better. As soon as I heard of the God whom you preach, and what Jesus Christ did on earth, I recognized the one who has preserved me, and I resolved to honor Him all my life. When I go to war I commend myself to Him night and morning. To Him I owe all my victories. In Him I believe, and I ask baptism from you, that after my death He may show me mercy."

This open and energetic declaration affected the missionaries to tears. It was impossible to fetter such ardent desire with new delays. On Holy Saturday, the Chapel of St. Mary was arrayed in all its pomp. The Christians attended in great numbers. Ahasistari and several of his countrymen received the character of children of the Church. He took the name of Eustace. The next year, when our new-made Christian **heard** of the perilous mission confided to Father Jogues, he was one of the first to offer to bear him company, ready to defend him in case of attack, or die with him. His prayers were heard.

G. Page 152.

We here insert in full the curious description of Manhattan Island and the Dutch colony which Father Jogues himself wrote in 1646. We follow the autograph, which Mr. John Gilmary Shea reproduced in *fac-simile* in 1862, with a translation and very valuable notes, of which we have availed ourselves.

Novum Belgium.

"New Holland, which the Dutch call in Latin *Novum Belgium*—in their own language, *Nieuw Netherland*, that is to say, New Low Countries—is situated between Virginia and New England. The mouth of the river, which some people call Nassau, or the Great North River, to distinguish it from another which they call the South River, and from some maps that I have recently seen I think Maurice River, is at 40 deg. 30 min. The channel is deep, fit for the largest ships, which ascend to Manhatte's Island, which is seven leagues in circuit, and on which there is a fort to serve as the commencement of a town to be built here, and to be called New Amsterdam.

"The fort, which is at the point of the island, about five or six leagues from the mouth, is called Fort Amsterdam; it has four regular bastions, mounted with several pieces of artillery. All these bastions and the curtains were, in 1643, but mounds, most of which had crumbled away, so that they entered the fort on all sides. There were no ditches. For the garrison of the said fort, and another which they had built still further up against the incursions of the savages, their enemies, there were sixty soldiers. They were beginning to face the gates and bastions with stone. Within the fort there was a pretty large stone church, the house of the Governor, whom they call Director-General, quite neatly built of brick, the storehouses and barracks.

"On the Island of Manhatte, and in its environs, there may well be four or five hundred men of different sects and nations; the Director-General told me that there were men of eighteen different languages; they are scattered here and there on the river, above and below, as the beauty and convenience of the spot invited each to settle: some, mechanics, however, who ply their trade, are ranged under the fort; all the others were exposed to the incursions of the natives; who, in the year 1643, while I was there, actually killed some twoscore Hollanders, and burned many houses and barns full of wheat.

"The river, which is very straight, and runs due north and south, is at least a league broad before the fort. Ships lie at anchor in a bay which forms the other side of the island, and can be defended from the fort.

"Shortly before I arrived there three large ships of 300 tons each had come to load wheat; two found cargoes; the third could not be loaded, because the savages had burned a part of their grain. These ships came from the West Indies, where the West India Company usually keeps up seventeen ships of war.

"No religion is publicly exercised but the Calvinist, and orders are to admit none but Calvinists, but this is not observed; for there are in the colony besides the Calvinists, Catholics, English Puritans, Lutherans, Anabaptists, here called Mnistes, etc., etc. When any one comes to settle in the country they lend him horses, cows, etc.; they give him provisions, all which he returns as soon as he is at ease; and as to the land, after ten years he pays to the West India Company the tenth of the produce which he reaps.

"This country is bounded on the New England side by a river which they call the Fresche River, which

serves as a boundary between them and the English.
The English, however, come very near to them, choosing
to hold lands under the Hollanders, who ask nothing,
rather than depend on English lords, who exact rents,
and would fain be absolute. On the other side, south-
ward, towards Virginia, its limits are the river which
they call the South River, on which there is also a Dutch
settlement, but the Swedes have one at its mouth extremely well supplied with cannons and men. It is
believed that these Swedes are maintained by some Amsterdam merchants, who are not satisfied that the West
India Company should alone enjoy all the commerce of
these parts. It is near this river that a gold mine is
reported to have been found.

"See in the work of the Sieur de Laet of Antwerp, the
table and chapter on New Belgium, as he sometimes
calls it, or the map 'Noya Anglia, Novum Belgium, et
Virginia.'

"It is about forty years since the Hollanders came to
these parts. The fort was begun in the year 1615; they
began to settle about twenty years ago, and there is
already some little commerce with Virginia and New
England.

"The first comers found lands fit for use, formerly
cleared by the savages, who had fields here. Those
who came later have cleared the woods, which are most-
ly oak. The soil is good. Deer-hunting is abundant in
the fall. There are some houses built of stone; lime
they make of oyster-shells, great heaps of which are
found here, made formerly by the savages, who subsist
in part by that fishery.

"The climate is very mild. Lying at 40⅔ deg., there
are many European fruits, as apples, pears, cherries. I
reached there in October, and found even then a considerable quantity of peaches.

"Ascending the river to the 43d deg., you meet the
second Dutch settlement, which the tide reaches but

does not pass. Ships of a hundred and a hundred and twenty tons can come up to it.

"There are two things in this settlement (which is called Renselaerswick, as if to say, settlement of Renselaers, who is a rich Amsterdam merchant)—1st, a miserable little fort called Fort Orange, built of logs, with four or five pieces of Breteuil cannon, and as many swivels. This has been reserved, and is maintained by the West India Company. This fort was formerly on an island in the river; it is now on the mainland, towards the Hiroquois, a little above the said island. 2d, a colony sent here by this Renselaers, who is the patron. This colony is composed of about a hundred persons, who reside in some twenty-five or thirty houses built along the river, as each found most convenient. In the principal house lives the patron's agent; the minister has his apart, in which service is performed. There is also a kind of bailiff here, whom they call the Seneschal, who administers justice. Their houses are merely of boards and thatched, with no mason work except the chimneys. The forest furnishing many large pines, they make boards by means of their mills, which they have here for the purpose.

"They found some pieces of ground all ready, which the savages had formerly cleared, and in which they sow wheat and oats for beer, and for their horses, of which they have great numbers. There is little land fit for tillage, being hemmed in by hills, which are poor soil. This obliges them to separate, and they already occupy two or three leagues of country.

"Trade is free to all; this gives the Indians all things cheap, each of the Hollanders outbidding his neighbor, and being satisfied provided he can gain some little profit.

"This settlement is not more than twenty leagues from the Agniehronons, who can be reached by land or water, as the river on which the Iroquois lie falls into that which passes by the Dutch; but there are many low rapids and a fall of a short half league, where the canoe must be carried.

"There are many nations between the two Dutch settlements, which are about thirty German leagues apart, that is, about fifty or sixty French leagues. The Loups, whom the Iroquois call Agotsagenens, are the nearest to Renselaerswick and Fort Orange. War breaking out some years ago between the Iroquois and the Loups, the Dutch joined the latter against the former; but four men having been taken and burned, they made peace. Since then some nations near the sea have killed some Hollanders of the most distant settlement; the Hollanders killed one hundred and fifty Indians, men, women, and children. They having then, at intervals, killed forty Hollanders, burned many houses, and committed ravages, estimated at the time that I was there at 200,000 liv. (two hundred thousand livres), they raised troops in New England. Accordingly, in the beginning of winter, the grass being trampled down and some snow on the ground, they gave them chase with six hundred men, keeping two hundred always on the move and constantly relieving one another; so that the Indians, shut up in a large island, and unable to flee easily, on account of their women and children, were cut to pieces to the number of sixteen hundred, including women and children. This obliged the rest of the Indians to make peace, which still continues. This occurred in 1643 and 1644."

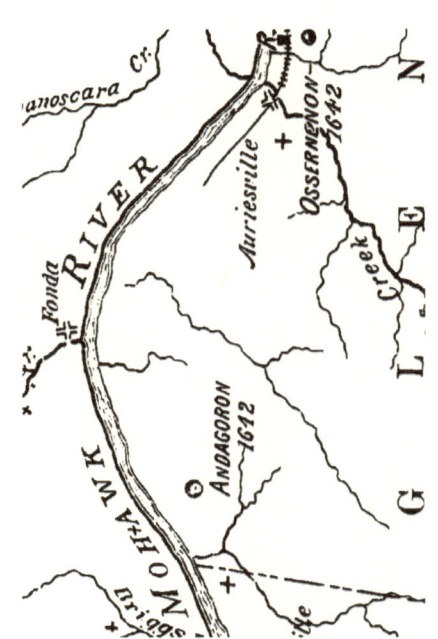

NOTE.

The Identification of Mohawk Sites—The Pilgrim Shrine—Recent Petitions for the Introduction of the Cause of Beatification.

In the year 1884 was first published the result of the very thorough investigations by General John S. Clark of Auburn, N. Y., of the sites of the villages formerly occupied by the Mohawk Nation. He has long been recognized as the leading authority in this line of research, and in the present case his labors were crowned with the most gratifying success. Others who had been working at the data independently, without the local explorations and topographical attainments of General Clark, had come to only negative results, which, however, confirmed in every particular the identification now happily and finally made. The following brief statement of the evidence has been reviewed by General Clark, and agrees in all points with the verification made by Dr. J. G. Shea and the writer in "The Pilgrim of Our Lady of Martyrs."

1. The three Mohawk villages, Ossernenon, Andagaron, and Tionnontoguen, from 1642 to their destruction by fire at the hands of the French in 1666, were certainly on the south bank of the Mohawk, and west of the Schoharie River (as is clear from the contemporary maps in Vanderdonck, the Relations, the Expedition of De Tracy, Jolliet's Map, etc., and from the letters of Fathers Jogues and Poncet). Louis Jolliet, who with Father

Marquette explored the Mississippi River, and who was one of the best and most accurate hydrographers of his time, as his many maps show, left one on which Osser-nenon is shown in the angle between the Mohawk and Schoharie rivers, where Auriesville railway-station now is.

2. Father Jogues, in his account of the captivity and journey of himself and René Goupil to the villages in 1642, says: "We arrived at a small river distant about a quarter of a league from the first Iroquois village" (Relation 1647, p. 22). A quarter of a French league was considerably less than three quarters of a mile; the same distance is given in the MS. of 1652, taken from the lips of Father Jogues himself by his Superior, Father Buteux). In the account as given by Bressani, who had been a captive in the same place, the words are: "On the Eve of the Assumption of the Blessed Virgin, about three o'clock, we reached a river which flows by their first village; . . . both banks were filled with Iroquois, who received us with clubs, sticks, and stones. They then led us to their village on the top of the hill." The MS. of 1652 says: "On the other side of this river were many Iroquois who were waiting for the prisoners." This locates the village south of the Mohawk, on a hill a quarter of a league distant from the river.

3. In his account of the death of René, Father Jogues says: "They told me that the body had been dragged to a river a quarter of a league distant, with which I was not acquainted." This can only apply to the Scho-harie, as the Mohawk was in plain view of the village, and Father Jogues must certainly have been thoroughly well acquainted with it at this time; whereas the Scho-harie was separated from the village by the hills and woods between. The village then must have been on a hill at a point between the Mohawk and Schoharie rivers, about a quarter of a league distant from each. At this exact point, on the hill near Auriesville Station,

is found abundant evidence of an Indian village. These two accounts alone taken together appear to be conclusive and unanswerable. (For an instance of the impossibility of otherwise according the data, see the explanation formerly given of the two rivers by Dr. Shea, "Catholic Missions," note, p. 218. At this time (1854) it was commonly supposed that the villages were on the north bank of the Mohawk.)

4. In addition, several allusions to the topography are made by Father Jogues in the different accounts he gave of his captivity. From the river to the foot of the hill the bank was steep (MS. 1652; the word used is the old French *escors*, now written *écore*, or, more commonly, *accore*, and still employed in naval engineering. It signifies, not cliff-like, but simply a strongly inclined ascent. The name is still given in Canada to a part of the banks of the mouth of the Ottawa, near St. Vincent de Paul, opposite Montreal Island. It exactly describes the condition of the ascent from the river beach to the plateau at the foot of the hill at Auriesville Station. Up this Father Jogues and the other captives were forced with a rush, pursued by sticks and stones; he said pathetically to Father Buteux, "We climbed up with great difficulty").

Near the village was a ravine. In the same MS. of 1642 is given the further detail in regard to the precise spot of the ravine where he found the body of René, that it was at the union of a small water-course with a rivulet. The ravine, as now existing, could not be more exactly described than by this and the other details given of it in the different accounts.

In all the accounts the hill of prayer, overlooking the village, is mentioned; the MS. of 1652 describes it as it still is—"a small hill, distant from the village a musket-shot."

5. Besides all this, the first village was at a known distance from Andagaron, the second castle; and this

again a given distance from Tionnontoguen, the third. Both of these are found at the precise points thus indicated.

To sum up, a few only of these details thus verified would render strongly probable the identification of the sites; the meeting of all in one spot places it beyond reasonable doubt; while the fact that no other spot of the carefully explored Mohawk Valley verifies any number of them taken together, as General Clark from personal study of every site known by map, account, or tradition declares positively, puts the matter beyond all possible doubt, or, in other words, gives the conclusion absolute certainty.

On the plateau the outline of the Indian town is still visible, and remains of Indian occupation have been constantly found there. The field in which are found the chief remains of the Indian village has recently been bought by the Fathers of the Society of Jesus. They are now (1885) taking steps toward the erection of a chapel on the site; this will restore the shrine of *Notre Dame de Foy*, which existed in the flourishing mission church among the Mohawks until broken up by the threatened war between the French and English in 1684. It will also serve as an historical commemoration of the blood shed in this spot by René Goupil and Father Jogues, and the many other French and Indian Christians here massacred, and of the edifying Christian church which later on sprung from their blood, renewing the holiness of the primitive age of Christianity in the good Catherine Tegakwita and her companions.

All these circumstances, and the finding during the necessary researches of the necessary documents for taking up the Cause of Beatification, led to the presentation of the whole matter before the Third Plenary Council of Baltimore in December, 1884. This resulted in a Conciliar petition to the Holy Father, Leo XIII., for the formal introduction before the Sacred Congregation of Rites at Rome of the Cause of Beatification of the three servants of God, René Goupil and Father Isaac Jogues, both of the Society of Jesus, as Martyrs, and Catherine Tegakwita as Virgin.* Since that time other important petitions of the same nature have also been sent to Rome, especially from various members of the venerable Canadian hierarchy, and from more than a score of different Indian nations, each in their own language. There are reasonable grounds for hoping that Providence will at length, by the authoritative voice of the head of His Church on earth, confirm those titles, and that religious veneration and confidence which all who have studied these holy lives have already in heart bestowed on these true servants of God.

---

* Rev. Father Martin, who is still living at an advanced age in Paris, France, has taken an active interest in these recent labors. He had already completed a life of Catharine Tegakwita some years since, which still remains unpublished. To this and to the original documents the author of a new life in English, nearly ready for publication, has had access. The details relating to the history of the Mission of the Martyrs, and of the pilgrim shrine founded there and now restored, are given in "The Pilgrim of Our Lady of Martyrs," brought out by the Superior of the work, the Rev. Joseph Loyzance of St. Joseph's Church, Troy, N. Y.

www.ingramcontent.com/pod-product-compliance
Lightning Source LLC
Chambersburg PA
CBHW020353030726
47496CB00007B/2116